The Aikenhead Honours
Three gentlemen spies:
bound by duty, undone by women!

Introducing three of England's
most eligible bachelors:
Dominic, Leo and Jack
code-named Ace, King, Knave

Together they are

The Aikenhead Honours
A government-sponsored spying ring,
they risk their lives, and hearts,
to keep Regency England safe!

Follow these three brothers on a dazzling
journey through Europe and beyond as they
serve their country and meet their brides, in
often very surprising circumstances!

Meet the 'Ace', Dominic Aikenhead,
Duke of Calder, in
HIS CAVALRY LADY

Meet the 'King' and renowned rake
Lord Leo Aikenhead, in
HIS RELUCTANT MISTRESS

Meet the 'Knave' and incorrigible playboy
Lord Jack Aikenhead, in
HIS FORBIDDEN LIAISON

Joanna Maitland was born and educated in Scotland, though she has spent most of her adult life in England or abroad. She has been a systems analyst, an accountant, a civil servant, and director of a charity. Now that her two children have left home, she and her husband have moved from Hampshire to the Welsh Marches, where she is revelling in the more rugged country and the wealth of medieval locations. When she is not writing, or climbing through ruined castles, she devotes her time to trying to tame her house and garden, both of which are determined to resist any suggestion of order. Readers are invited to visit Joanna's website at www.joannamaitland.com

Recent novels by the same author:

A POOR RELATION
A PENNILESS PROSPECT
MARRYING THE MAJOR
RAKE'S REWARD
MY LADY ANGEL
AN UNCOMMON ABIGAIL
  (in *A Regency Invitation* anthology)
BRIDE OF THE SOLWAY
HIS CAVALRY LADY*

*The Aikenhead Honours

HIS RELUCTANT MISTRESS

Joanna Maitland

MILLS & BOON®
Pure reading pleasure™

First published in Great Britain 2009
Harlequin Mills & Boon Limited,
Eton House, 18-24 Paradise Road, Richmond, Surrey TW9 1SR

© Joanna Maitland 2009

ISBN: 978 0 263 86782 4

Set in Times Roman 10½ on 12¼ pt.
04-0609-79286

Printed and bound in Spain
by Litografia Rosés S.A., Barcelona

HIS RELUCTANT
MISTRESS

Chapter One

The butler's discreet cough interrupted what was promising to be a most rewarding encounter.

Lord Leo Aikenhead raised his head from the naked breast of the damsel sitting in his lap and swore fluently. She might be only a member of the muslin company, albeit a highly paid one, but even she did not deserve to have her charms exposed to the gaze of a disapproving servant. Unhurriedly, he began to restore a semblance of decency to her clothing, all the while keeping his back between his light o' love and the butler. Gibson knew better than to gawp. He would wait by the door until Leo was good and ready to attend to him.

'Have to excuse me, m'dear,' Leo said at last, allowing a touch of regret to enter his voice as he retied the final silken ribbon of her bodice. 'Much as I should like to continue our…um…conversation, I fear that pressing business calls.' He put his hands to the girl's trim waist and set her on her feet.

When she began to protest coquettishly, Leo looked up into her lovely face, spoiled now by the mulish curve to her mouth. 'Go and find William,' he said easily. 'You know he's been ogling you since the day he arrived. He'll be more than happy to take over where I left off.'

She made no move to obey.

'Go along now, do,' he said, rather more sharply, giving her a friendly slap on the bottom. 'He's a better bet than I am, you know. Much more of a stayer. And richer, to boot.'

With a sudden giggle, the girl ran from the saloon.

Leo quickly checked the state of his own dress before turning to the butler, who stood impassively by the door, staring straight ahead. 'You may cast off your puritan blindness now, Gibson. The young woman has gone. For the moment, at least.'

'As you say, my lord.' The butler's tone was clipped.

Leo rose and walked slowly across to the fireplace. In the huge gilt-framed mirror hanging above it, he saw that, although his coat was surprisingly uncreased, his cravat looked as if he had been rolling around in bed. *Pretty near the truth, too.* He began to straighten it. In the glass, he could see that Gibson's patience was under strain, for he was almost hopping from one foot to the other. Just what he deserved for that unwelcome interruption. Leo deliberately spent another thirty seconds carefully rearranging his cravat. Then he said into the mirror, 'Well, Gibson?'

The butler did not make any apologies. He merely said crisply, 'Your lordship's brother has arrived. He asks to see you urgently. He is waiting in the small saloon.'

This time, Leo's curses were even more choice, but he managed to swallow most of them. Leo's elder brother, Dominic, Duke of Calder, had been sent to Russia on government business some weeks before. That left only Lord Jack, the youngest of the Aiken-heads. He was an engaging lad, and both Dominic and Leo were very fond of him, but his scrapes were becoming increasingly expensive. Dominic and Leo, both older than Jack by more than ten years, had indulged their brother for too long, as both would now admit. Jack would soon be twenty-five, an age when he ought to be preparing to become master of his own estate. But he was still far from ready.

It seemed that life, to Jack, was one long, rollicking spree in which responsibility played no part. His problem would be gambling again, no doubt. Whereas Leo's tastes ran to women—and lots of them—Jack had a fas-cination for the gaming tables. Sadly, and predictably, he tended to lose much more than he won. Well, if he needed yet another tow out of River Tick, it was perhaps time to refuse. Let the boy struggle a bit and get the feeling of what it would be like to drown before anyone threw him a lifeline. It really was time he began to grow up.

Leo started for the door. Gibson reached to open it for him, but Leo stopped him, slapping a hand flat on the panel. 'How does Lord Jack seem on this occasion, Gibson?'

Gibson stared unblinkingly past his master's shoulder. 'Not…er…not precisely *à point*, my lord. As if he had undertaken his journey in some haste.'

'Hmm. Has he not brought his valet?'

'No, my lord. And no valise either.'

Leo grunted and flung open the door. If Jack had fled from London to The Larches without even taking the time to pack a valise, he was undoubtedly in deep, deep trouble.

His anger mounting, Leo strode down the corridor and into the blue saloon. 'So you decided to come and join my little orgy after all, brat?' Behind him, Gibson closed the door without a sound. 'Good of you to favour us with your company. Planning to remain long?'

Jack jumped up guiltily from the wing chair by the fireplace. There was the beginning of a flush on his neck. He was wearing evening clothes, with silk knee-breeches and hose, and dancing shoes. Totally inappropriate dress for driving well over a hundred miles. Leo let his gaze travel disapprovingly over his brother's dishevelled and grubby cravat, his creased coat, then on down to Jack's feet and, finally, back up to his face. Jack's mouth had opened, as if he were straining to speak. The flush had reached his cheekbones.

'Valet abandoned you at last, has he?' Leo said sardonically. 'Can't say I blame him. But we can't present you to the ladybirds looking as if you've been dragged through a hedge, y'know.'

Jack's jaw slackened and his mouth opened even wider.

Suddenly, Leo had had enough of playing games. 'Oh, sit down, for heaven's sake, and stop looking like the village idiot at the May fair. You've come hot-foot to The Larches, without so much as a spare cravat. So you're in trouble again. I take it you *were* planning to tell me what you've done this time?'

Without waiting for a response, Leo crossed to the small piecrust table by the window, poured two large brandies and thrust one of them into Jack's hand. Jack tossed it down in a single swallow and held out his empty glass for a refill. Leo said nothing. He set the empty glass aside and replaced it with his own full one.

Jack barely seemed to notice the switch. Shaking his head, Leo took his seat in the wing chair opposite Jack's and waited for the story to tumble out.

Jack sighed out a long breath, took a large swig of his drink, and then sat forward in his chair with his elbows on his knees, nursing the brandy balloon in his cupped hands as if it were his most treasured possession. He stared at the floor. 'I'm in real trouble this time, Leo. I don't think even you can help me out of it.'

'Perhaps you'd best let me be the judge of that. Well?'

'I…I played cards at one of the halls, after Lady Morrissey's ball. With Falstead and Hallingdon and…and a host of other fellows. I was on a winning streak.'

Leo raised his eyebrows, but Jack's gaze was still fixed on the floor.

'I won nearly six thousand pounds, Leo.' Jack looked up then. His eyes were shining. Then, as if a veil had descended, the light of triumph died. 'But I…I lost it again. All of it. And more.'

Leo waited. Jack seemed to have shrunk in his skin. This was going to be very bad.

At length the silence was too much. Leo's patience snapped. 'How much?' he snarled.

'Thirty-two thousand.' Jack's voice was barely audible.

'Damn you, brat! D'you intend to ruin us all? Even Dominic couldn't lay hands on that much. And I certainly can't. It's more than three times my income.'

'I'm sorry, Leo.'

Leo flung himself out of his chair, forcing himself to unclench his fists and to master the urge to plant his brother a facer. Jack deserved it, of course, but it would not do. Leo sucked in a deep breath and went to pour himself a brandy. He needed it now almost as much as Jack did.

'Who holds your vowels? And how long has he given you to pay?'

'Er…that's the problem. It's—'

Leo exploded. 'Dammit, Jack, it is *not* the problem. *You* are the problem. You and your insatiable lust for gaming. You know you can't afford it, yet you will persist. You are a fool. And a damned expensive one, too.'

'I am sorry, Leo,' Jack said again. He had not moved even an inch in his seat.

'So who is this problem friend of yours?'

'No one you know. One of the secretaries at the Prussian Embassy. He's been summoned back to Berlin. To prepare for the Congress of Vienna, I understand. He's leaving in two days' time. That's why I had to get here in such an almighty rush. I didn't even have time to—'

'And this secretary fellow expects to be paid before he leaves, I collect?' Leo interrupted in icy tones.

Jack tried to reply, but failed. He nodded wretchedly into his brandy.

'In other words, I have two days to come up with a fortune, or risk having the Aikenhead name dishonoured across Europe.' It was not a question.

'I'm s—'

'Confound it, Jack, if you say you're sorry just one more time, I'll wring your miserable neck. Sorry? You don't begin to know the half of it.'

Jack straightened in his chair. 'I was going to say that

I'm s-sensible of the wrong I've done the family, Leo. I will give you my word that I'll never gamble again, if it will help.'

Astonished, Leo stared at his brother. Jack returned his gaze unflinchingly.

'By Jove, he means it,' Leo whispered.

'I do,' Jack said, with dignity. 'And I will keep my word. Though it's precious little consolation in the cir-cumstances, I know.'

Leo fetched the decanter and added a generous measure to Jack's glass. 'You give me your solemn word never again to gamble more than you can afford to lose?'

'I won't gamble at all in future, Leo. Not even for chicken stakes.'

'Don't say that. I'm not asking for a promise that would be well-nigh impossible to keep. Especially given the fellows you run with.'

Jack dropped his gaze.

'If you give me your word that you will not play beyond your own means, I will find a way of dealing with this little…er…inconvenience.'

Jack drew in an audibly shaky breath and looked up at Leo with glowing eyes. 'I give you my word, Leo. You may rely on it. And I will find a way to repay you, I promise.'

Leo laughed mirthlessly. 'I shall pretend I did not hear that last promise, brat. You know, and I know, that you could no more find thirty-two thousand pounds than you could swim to America. Now—' he laid a friendly hand on Jack's shoulder '—I suggest you go and get some sleep. I don't want you appearing in front of my guests, male or female, until you are presentable

again. At the moment…' Leo looked his brother up and
down and shuddered. He reached out to pull the bell.

Gibson appeared so quickly that he must have been
hovering outside the door.

'Conduct Lord Jack to a bedchamber, Gibson. And
direct my man to provide whatever he may need by way
of clothing. Lord Jack is extremely fatigued after his
journey and will not be joining us again this evening.
He will take a light supper in his room.'

Jack rose and straightened his back. He yawned
theatrically.

Leo felt his lips twitch. It was very difficult to remain
furious with Jack for long, even when he thoroughly
deserved it.

'If your lordship would follow me?' Gibson said,
opening the door for Jack.

'Leo, I—'

'Goodnight, Jack,' Leo said harshly. Then, more
gently, 'Sleep well, brat.'

As the door closed behind them, Leo's mask of
control shattered. He knew that, if there had been a
mirror in this room, it would have shown him the face
of a stricken man. *Thirty-two thousand pounds!* What
on earth had possessed the boy?

Leo began to pace, but the room was too small. He
needed space, and air. He made his way along the
corridor and out on to the terrace. Low laughter from
the shadows announced that the terrace had become a
place of dalliance. He tried his library. It, too, was
occupied. For the first time in the ten years since
Dominic had given The Larches to him, Leo regretted
having invited his boon companions and their ladybirds
to make free of his hospitality. It seemed that nowhere

in the whole house could provide the seclusion he craved.

He returned to the hallway just as Gibson emerged from the back stairs. Leo raised an eyebrow.

'Lord Jack is in the Chinese bedchamber, my lord.'

Leo snorted with laughter. The Chinese bedchamber had been a flight of fancy of a previous tenant and Gibson, it seemed, had been indulging in a spot of retribution on his own account.

'I am going riding.'

Gibson's eyebrows shot up towards his hairline.

'Have Jezebel saddled and brought round in ten minutes. And tell the kitchen that dinner is to be delayed by one hour.'

'Very good, my lord. If any of your lordship's guests should ask…?'

'Tell them I have gone out. I am sure they will be able to find some means of diverting themselves until I return.'

Dinner was almost over when Leo made his announcement. 'Afraid that some unexpected business requires me to return to London. I'll be leaving at first light.'

His guests reacted with dismay. 'But we've been here less than a week,' one said, slurring his words a little.

Leo smiled round the table. 'And you are all most welcome to continue to enjoy my hospitality until I return.'

The ladybird on Leo's immediate right laid a caressing hand on his sleeve. 'But it wouldn't be the same without *you*, dear Leo. Who shall take charge of our frolics?' She fluttered her long, dark eyelashes at him and gave his flesh a tiny squeeze.

Leo lifted her hand and set it gently on the polished wood table. 'Have no fear. M'brother, Jack, shall act as host in my absence. He is fixed here until I return.'

'Jack?' The protest came from one of the older men at the far end of the table. 'No offence, Leo, but I can give Jack the best part of fifteen years. As can others.' Some of the other gentlemen nodded. 'We didn't come to The Larches to gamble with your madcap little brother. If you're off tomorrow, then so am I.' There were murmurs of agreement around the table.

Leo was not sorry. He would not show his friends the door, but he was heartily glad they had decided to leave.

'Quite understand, of course, if you feel you wish to leave. And I cannot, at this moment, say how soon I might return. Apologies for that.'

'Not your fault, old fellow. Business is business. Besides, the night is still young.' The man got to his feet rather unsteadily. 'Since this is to be the last night of one of Leo Aikenhead's famous orgies, I give you a toast, gentlemen. To our next meeting at The Larches. To beautiful women and flowing wine.'

Chairs scraped across the polished wooden floor. The men raised their glasses to the ladies. 'The Larches. To beautiful women! And flowing wine!'

By the time Leo returned, ten days later, it was impossible to tell that the house had ever been full of scandalous goings-on. Apart from Jack and the servants, the house was empty. Every bawdy ballad and erotic picture had been banished. The Larches could have been the home of the most upright of clerical gentlemen.

Jack was sitting soberly in the library, reading a magazine, when Leo walked in. 'You're back. Thank God!' Jack sprang to his feet. Then he stood still. He did not ask the question that was clearly on the tip of his tongue.

'I have brought your man, and some clothes,' Leo said, looking Jack up and down. 'My coat may be well cut, but on you it looks decidedly disreputable.' Since Jack was of a much slighter build than Leo, it was hardly surprising that Leo's clothes did not fit him. 'I suggest you go and change. We can have a quiet dinner, and an early night.'

'But aren't you going to tell me what—?'

'We have work to do tomorrow, Jack. The Foreign Secretary has ordered the Aikenhead Honours to Vienna. While Ace is in Russia, I am to take charge. I have already written to Ten. He is to make his own way to Vienna and join us as soon as he can.' The Ace in the Aikenhead Honours was Dominic, the eldest Aikenhead brother. Leo's codename was King and Jack's was Knave. Ben Dexter, the fourth member of their spying band, codenamed Ten, was Jack's closest friend. Unlike Jack, Ben did not gamble. His father had been killed in a duel following a quarrel over cards.

'So we're leaving immediately?' Jack asked, puzzled.

'Yes. As soon as may be. Castlereagh has already left for Paris.'

'Oh. I see. But what about—? I mean—I can't leave England if—'

'Forget about it, brat. Your little Prussian friend took

ship for Holland over a week ago, with all his winnings
tucked safely in his pocket.'

Jack's jaw dropped and his eyes widened.

'And now, if you don't mind,' Leo said pointedly, 'I
should be grateful for the return of my coat.'

'Again.'

Obediently, Sophie took a breath, braced her
stomach muscles, and began again, humming the top
three notes and then opening her throat to allow the
volume to increase as she sang down the scale. Her head
was buzzing from the humming. Very satisfying. Her
voice was placed precisely as it should be.

'Hmm. Good enough. Now, a semi-tone higher, if
you please.' Verdicchio touched a key on the pianoforte.

Sophie sang the scale. But she had to repeat it three
times before her voice coach was satisfied. Then, gradually, he took her up another half-octave until she had
reached the top of her range. The sound was good, and
right in the centre of the notes. Sophia Pietre was famous
as the Venetian Nightingale, the singer who was never
shrill, and never sang flat. It had taken her years to perfect
that round, gleaming tone. It had brought her wealth, and
a certain notoriety. But she remembered, very well, what
it had been to be poor, totally dependent on Verdicchio,
and never sure whether she would be thrown out on the
street for failing one of his interminable tests.

'Sophie! Pay attention!' He slapped his hand down
on the keys, producing a loud, discordant sound.

'I apologise, Maestro. I will do better.' She swallowed. 'What would you have me sing now?'

He took her through a number of simple ballads, of

the kind she sang to entertain the guests at private parties. They showed off the range and colour of her voice, without overpowering the audience as operatic arias sometimes did. After the songs, Verdicchio insisted she rehearse two of the arias from the operatic role she was currently performing. Sophie did not need to practise them, but she humoured him, omitting only the highest notes, as he always advised her to do during practice. 'Your top Cs, my dear Sophie,' he used to say, 'are diamonds of the first water. Not to be squandered. Only to be shared with those who are prepared to pay the price for them.'

He was nodding now. 'Good, good. Excellent even. Your phrasing has improved here.' He pointed to a passage in the score. 'It makes the words clearer and the effect more emotional. You will have the ladies swooning in their boxes tonight.'

Sophie smiled. 'Let us hope so. For we have only two more performances and no promises yet of any further roles. We live a very expensive life now, Maestro.' She gestured round their rehearsal room which, at Verdicchio's insistence, had been furnished with every possible luxury, just like the rest of their Venice apartment. 'If I am not offered another role soon, we shall be hard pressed to pay the bills.'

'You do have another role, my child.'

Sophie's stomach clenched. How long had he known? Why had he said nothing until now?

'You are to sing for a most august audience.' He looked up from the pianoforte and smiled into her face. It was a sly, knowing smile. She distrusted it totally. 'You are to sing at— But, no. Let it be a surprise. We leave Venice on Friday.'

Sophie opened her mouth to protest, but Verdicchio was no longer looking at her. He had turned back to the pianoforte and was idly playing a composition of his own, closely modelled on a Mozart sonata.

She bit her lip. After so many years, he still had her in his power. He controlled not only her career, but also every penny she earned, for he was determined that she should never be able to break free. He was succeeding. For now. The little cache of money she had saved was not yet enough to allow her to flee from him. But it was growing, week by week, and month by month. In another year, perhaps, she would have enough.

'That was beautiful, Maestro,' she said dutifully, as he played the final extravagant arpeggio and turned to receive her approval. She hoped he would not notice that she was avoiding his eye. 'And our new home? I can wait until Friday to learn where we are going, if that is your wish. Though it would perhaps be profitable to allow me to mention our destination to some of my gentlemen admirers. They might wish to follow us, or even to provide a parting gift. Some of them, as you know—' she lifted her left hand so that the diamonds at her wrist caught the light '—have been exceedingly generous.'

Verdicchio frowned up at her. 'You may be right,' he admitted at last. 'The Baron especially. He seems to have more diamonds than an Indian nabob. It would do no harm at all, for our finances, if he strung a few more round your lovely neck.'

Sophie smiled to acknowledge his great wisdom, and waited.

'Very well, my dear. You will not like it, I know, but

the contract is signed. You are to sing before the crowned heads of Europe. At the Congress of Vienna.'

'Vienna? No! Impossible! You know I cannot go there. Half the German aristocracy will be there. What if someone were to recognise me? I should be disgraced.'

'You are a singer. So you are disgraced already. And no one will recognise you, in any case. As far as the world knows, you are Sophia Pietre, an Italian singer trained here in Venice, by a noted Venetian master.' He smirked. 'Why should anyone suspect otherwise? After all, you are a grown woman now.'

A grown woman, but in thrall to a monster since I was thirteen years old, Sophie thought. But she said only, 'How then am I to account for my ability to speak German?'

'You learned it here in Venice, in order to be able to sing the German arias of Signor Mozart, among others. And to converse in their native tongue with the German gentlemen who visit the opera. After all, you speak English almost as well as you speak German, and there are no English operas to perform.'

For once, he was absolutely right. She spoke four languages fluently: Italian, German, English and French. Her ability to speak German like a native probably would not betray the secret of her past. Probably.

But the thought of going to Vienna and meeting Emperors, Kings, and Princes, one of them the ruler of her own country, was more terrifying than the prospect of a whole life ruled by Verdicchio. For, if any of her countrymen should divine who she really was, even the most glorious voice in the world would not save her from ruin.

Chapter Two

Leo rose in his saddle and looked around him, savouring the warm late October sunshine and the glorious countryside around Vienna. It was very satisfying to have some solitude at last. The city was full to overflowing with incomers, many of whom were spending fortunes to impress the local populace and the visiting monarchs. Leo and Jack did not. They could not afford to live in anything like the style appropriate to their rank, for paying off Jack's gambling debt had made money very tight. They had been forced to take cramped rooms above an inn, the Gasthof Brunner, a long way from the centre of the city.

There were picnics and dinners and balls and all sorts of extravagant entertainments every day, even on Sundays. Leo and Jack had had to divide their forces in order to attend as many as they possibly could, in hopes of picking up useful intelligence. In fairness, they had had some minor successes, and their contacts in the British delegation were pleased with the results so far. But Vienna society was a sore trial. So many petty aristocrats, some of them with their pockets even more to let than Leo's, yet very quick to sneer at any man without a title.

As it happened, he and Jack did have titles. But they were also spies. So they had to be extremely careful not to be caught and expelled from the city. It had happened already to others. A suspected spy was simply summoned to the office of Baron Hager, the chief of police, to be informed that his passport was not *quite* in order. He was then invited to leave Vienna. Forthwith.

Very neat indeed. The Austrians were doing their very best to ensure that the Congress proceeded without embarrassment. Not that the Austrian Emperor Francis, or the other monarchs, were taking any obvious part in it. While their chief ministers met and plotted in deepest secrecy, the monarchs and their courtiers danced. Alexander, Tsar of all the Russias, was the most prominent of them all. The man seemed to need no sleep and to be able to dance all night, provided only that there were enough beautiful ladies to partner him. The Tsar was never seen to dance with an ugly woman, no matter how elevated her station.

Leo shifted in his saddle and stroked his gloved hand down his mount's glossy neck. At least Jack had managed to locate a livery stable with excellent horses for hire. Leo's bay gelding, Hector, was a very fine animal indeed, and Leo had soon established a rapport with him, using his few words of basic German.

'I fancy I see an inn yonder, old fellow,' Leo said thoughtfully. 'A good gallop across this turf and we will both be able to rest and refresh ourselves.' Hector's ears twitched. He understood the tone of voice, if not the words. Leo stroked him again. 'Good fellow. *Nun*,' he said, touching his heel to the horse's flank, *'los!'*

Hector responded by lengthening his stride into an effortless canter and then a gallop. Leo bent low over his neck, relishing the breath of the warm wind on his face and the power of the fine beast under him. *'Sehr gut, Hector. Sehr gut.'* Responding, the horse laid his ears back and flew faster.

Hector was blowing hard by the time they reached the inn. It was a typical country *Gasthof*, with a steeply pitched roof against the winter snows, and flower-hung wooden balconies on the upper floors. The heavy door stood open into the yard where stable lads were bustling about, unhitching the horses from a fine carriage. It bore no crest, but its gleaming burgundy-purple paint-work, elegantly picked out with gold, suggested that its owner was a man of means.

Leo dismounted and passed Hector's reins to the ostler. 'Walk him until he cools and then see he has a good rub down. I shall be returning to the city in an hour or so.' The ostler frowned in response. He did not move.

Leo swore inwardly. His German was not yet up to this. He explained again, in French. The ostler still looked bewildered.

'Darf ich Ihnen behilflich sein?' said a man's voice from behind him. Then, switching to slightly accented French, 'May I be of service to you, sir?'

Leo turned to find himself looking down at a much older man dressed in a coat of purple cloth over a purple velvet waistcoat embroidered with gold. Was this the owner of the carriage? Did he match his dress to the colours of his conveyance? He certainly looked extraordinary for, in addition to his splendid clothes, he had eyebrows as extravagant as a Prussian officer's mustachios.

Leo hoped his smile did not betray his amusement at the thought. 'Why, thank you, sir,' he replied. 'Most kind. I need to ensure the care of my horse.'

'Pray allow me.' The purple-clad gentleman translated Leo's instructions to the nodding ostler. Hector was led away.

'Thank you, sir.' Leo bowed. 'May I have the honour of knowing the name of my interpreter?'

The older man smiled up at Leo. 'The Baron Ludwig von Beck,' he said proudly, clicking his heels and bowing from the neck.

Leo returned the bow, in a rather more nonchalant, English fashion. 'Lord Leo Aikenhead. Most grateful to you, Baron. My German is, sadly, not good. And I doubt that the man speaks English any more than French.'

'Alas, no. He does not even speak German. Or not German that anyone from my country would recognise.' He chuckled at his own wit.

'You are not an Austrian then, Baron von Beck?'

'No, indeed.' There was more than a touch of hauteur in his voice. 'I am a Prussian.'

'I see. You are attending his Prussian Majesty at the Congress?'

'No. I am simply returning from Italy. I have been there for some months, seeing the antiquities and buying art for my collection. And you, Lord Leo?'

Leo's story had been very well rehearsed since his arrival in Vienna. 'My brother and I have taken the opportunity of Bonaparte's defeat to travel in Europe,' he said smoothly. 'We were planning to go to Italy, but all the world is in Vienna for the moment. Decided to indulge our curiosity and join them. For a few weeks, at least. Promises to be quite amusing, do you not think?' Leo's lazy drawl made it sound as if the brothers were a pair of rich wastrels with nothing to do but follow their latest whim. Unflattering, but necessary. While Vienna society believed them to be harmless gawpers, there was a good chance that people would forget to guard their tongues in their company.

'No doubt. But you must not miss the sights of Italy, sir. You will find it most rewarding. For example, I have spent the last few months in Venice. A beautiful city, sir, beautiful. Have you visited it?'

'Alas, no. Due to the recent...er...difficulties, it has not been possible. But we do hope to journey there. In a few months. Perhaps, Baron, you would do me the honour of taking a glass of wine with me?' Leo gestured towards the inn behind them.

Baron von Beck shook his head. 'Thank you, Lord Leo, but I am afraid I must decline. I am expected shortly in Vienna.'

Leo did not press the invitation. The Baron was scrupulously polite, but there was something about his manner that jarred. Perhaps that stiff-necked pride? Whatever the cause, Leo had no desire to know him better.

The two men took their leave of each other and Leo entered the inn. There, to his relief, he discovered that the innkeeper had more than a smattering of English, plus adequate French, so it was easy for Leo to order a light meal and a bottle of wine. His host showed him into a private parlour where a bright fire was burning in the grate, in spite of the warm weather outside.

Throwing his hat on the settle, Leo sank gratefully into a cushioned chair by the fire and stretched out his legs towards the flames with a sigh of pleasure. A moment later, a pretty blonde servant appeared with his wine. She was wearing a plain gown with a very low-cut neckline that displayed her ample charms.

Leo mumbled his thanks in his best German. She was attractive enough, and he had enjoyed the view, but he had never yet had to resort to the servant classes to find his mistresses. He did not mean to start here in Austria, even though he was beginning to feel the lack of a woman in his bed. Still, there was yet time. Once he was more familiar with the ways of society here, he would be able to choose safely. He was not so desperate that he would put his mission at risk for a quick fumble in a dark corner.

The girl straightened and curtsied, saying something in a broad accent that Leo found totally unintelligible. It seemed that no response was expected, he was glad to note, for she turned and left the room.

Leo felt a sudden draught hitting the back of his neck. She must have failed to close the door properly. No point in calling her back. He rose to shut it himself.

Over the general hubbub of a busy posting inn, he heard raised, angry voices. A man's and a woman's. And the woman's voice, though speaking in what might be German, contained an unmistakable thread of fear.

Leo flung the door wide and strode out into the corridor. Baron von Beck was gripping the arm of a beautiful young lady shrouded in a long, dark cloak, and trying to drag her towards the inn yard. Her hood had fallen back, exposing lustrous black hair, coiled at the back of her head. She was trying, vainly, to push him off with small, gloved hands. Her frightened protests were being drowned by the Baron's angry words. And all the inn servants seemed to have mysteriously melted away.

Leo did not stop to wonder what might be going on. He simply seized Beck roughly by the shoulder. 'You go too far, Baron,' he snarled in French. 'I suggest you let the lady go.' When Beck made no move to obey, Leo tightened his grip and forced the man back against the opposite wall, holding him there with his superior strength. He would not free Beck until he was sure that the man's cowardly attack would not be repeated. Behind them, the lady pulled her cloak more closely around her body, automatically putting up a hand to rub her injured arm.

The two men stared at each other in open hostility for what seemed a long time. For a moment, Leo fancied they were about to come to blows. He stiffened in readiness, but the martial glint soon faded from the Baron's eyes, to be replaced by injured pride as he recognised that he was outclassed. Leo was relieved. The last thing he wanted was an unseemly brawl at a public inn, especially with a gentle lady as audience. He allowed the Baron to shake himself free.

'You are very quick to judge, sir,' Beck said haughtily, pulling himself up to his full height. 'And on this occasion, your judgement is wrong. Quite wrong.'

'Nothing justifies such brutal treatment of a lady,' Leo growled, dismissing the man. He was no longer a threat. Leo turned back to give his full attention to the lady. 'Perhaps you would like to sit by the fire to recover your composure, *madame*?' he said, still in French. The lady looked darkly exotic. He imagined she was more likely to speak French than English.

She swallowed hard and put a gloved hand to her lips. Then she looked up at Leo with glowing dark eyes and nodded slightly.

Ignoring the Baron's spluttering outrage, Leo ushered the lady into his private parlour and closed the door firmly. She stood for a moment, gazing round the empty room as if she did not know quite where she was. She looked ruffled, Leo decided, like a bird caught by the wind from an unexpected quarter. 'Will you not be seated, *madame*?' Leo pulled forward his own chair and was glad to see the lady smile at last. She was recovering some of her composure. Good.

With exquisite grace, the lady took Leo's seat by the fire and accepted the glass of wine he offered her. 'Thank you, sir. You have been most kind. Believe me, I am truly grateful to you for rescuing me.' Her French was almost perfect, Leo decided. Almost good enough to pass for a native. Almost, but not quite.

She was looking around the room again, and this time there was the faintest hint of a blush on her cheeks. She was becoming concerned to find herself alone, closeted with a man she did not know. Any virtuous lady would feel so.

Leo hastened to reassure her. 'May I fetch your maid to you, *madame*?'

Her blush was subsiding, Leo was pleased to see. None the less, he kept his distance. She had been assaulted once already, and by a nobleman, too. He would not put her in fear of another such attack.

'I…I am travelling with my uncle, sir. He is above stairs, at present. As is my maid.'

'If you will give me your uncle's name, *madame*, I will instruct the landlord to fetch him at once.' Leo smiled across at her in what he hoped was a reassuring manner. She reminded him of a frightened doe, backed into a trap, her huge brown eyes wondering what dangers she must face next. Leo was a hunter, to be sure, and a connoisseur of beautiful women, but he liked them to come to him willingly, and without fear. He knew, instinctively, that this lady needed to be gentled. It would be a fortunate man who earned the right to unpin those tresses and spread them across his pillow.

Leo felt his pulse start to quicken at the thought of this lovely lady in his arms, in his bed. Definitely too long since he had paid off his last mistress. His body was starting to become as demanding as the Baron von Beck.

'I would not have you disturb my uncle, sir. Indeed, if that gentleman has gone, I should prefer to return to my own chamber.'

Leo shook his head as she made to rise. The poor lady had escaped from the clutches of one man. Now she was doing her best to escape from the second, even though his intentions were purely honourable. Leo bit down on a smile at that. His body's intentions were anything but honourable. Given the slightest encouragement, he would rip off her dark cloak in order to feast his eyes on the lush beauty that he sensed lay hidden beneath. But that would be a wicked way to respond to a virtuous lady. Especially this lady.

He needed to put even more space between them. He took a couple of steps towards the door and was pleased to see that she began to settle back into her chair. 'Better that you remain here, *madame*, and compose yourself,' he said gently. 'You will allow me to summon your maid?'

This time, she nodded.

He put a hand to the door latch, waiting. His eyes remained fixed on her perfect oval face. He would not soon forget the image she made. There was a quality of serenity about her which touched him deeply.

'Thank you, sir. Pray ask for Teresa, the maid of Madame Pietre.'

Ah! So she was Italian. Somehow, that pleased him. 'At once, *madame*. I shall bid you farewell now, if you permit.' He bowed and made to leave the room.

'A moment, sir.'

Leo turned back. A tiny frown marred her white brow.

'Will you not tell me your name? I would know to whom I am indebted.'

Leo smiled across at her. She was demonstrating a fine lady's impeccable manners, now that the door was partly open. 'Lord Leo Aikenhead, at your service, *madame*,' he said, bowing as he would to a duchess. It seemed fitting.

'You are an Englishman?' She sounded more than a little surprised.

'Yes, *madame*.'

'An Englishman who speaks perfect French,' she said, changing in an instant to near flawless English. 'You will forgive me, Lord Leo, if I say that I am surprised to encounter such a man.'

'And you will forgive me, I hope, Madame Pietre, if I express surprise that an Italian lady should speak my native language so well. After all, we have been at war with most of Europe for decades.'

'That has not prevented some of your compatriots from making their way to Venice, sir. One learns to speak many languages there.'

Madame Pietre, from Venice. A pearl of a woman from the pearl of the Adriatic. The words came into his mind unbidden, but he knew instantly that he would always remember her in that way. She should wear a collar of priceless pearls around that swanlike throat, glowing against her skin.

Leo's hand gripped the latch fiercely. His body was urging him to go to her, to lift her gloved hands to his lips, to discover, from the distance of a breath, whether her complexion was as delicate as it appeared, and her lips as luscious. His body was tempting him to treat this gentle lady as if she were a mere strumpet. He forced himself, instead, to bow in farewell. He was not a black-guard like Beck. He would not allow her extraordinary beauty to undermine his sense of honour.

'If you will permit me, *madame*, I shall take my leave of you now. Your maid will attend on you in a moment.' He forced himself to step out into the corridor and fasten the door behind him, leaving the lovely Italian alone with his wine and his fire. For a second, he leant back against the door and closed his eyes, breathing deeply. Was that her subtle scent in his nostrils? It was so faint that he could not be sure if his senses were playing tricks on him. Yet he could almost have sworn that, for a fraction of a second, he had smelled the scent of a wildflower meadow in spring.

He berated himself for a numbskull. Even if his senses were right, it was of no import. She was Madame Pietre. Probably a married lady. And a lady Leo was unlikely ever to encounter again. No doubt she was bound for her home in Italy, while he was fixed in Vienna, probably for months. Just as well, in the cir-cumstances, he decided. He could not afford to be diverted into wooing a virtuous lady from her husband's bed. He had done it often enough, of course, when the lady was ready to be wooed, but it took both time and money, neither of which he had at present. He must take a mistress here in Vienna—his overeager reaction to the beautiful Venetian had amply demonstrated his needs in that direction—but he would content himself with one of the many courtesans in the city. In that regard, Madame Pietre was far above his touch.

Sophie held her breath until the door had closed firmly behind him. Then she raised her glass of wine with a slightly shaky hand and took a long swallow to ease her parched throat and racing pulse.

What on earth was the matter with her? Why was she reacting so to a man who was simply offering help to a lady in distress? Beck she could easily deal with. She had been a little frightened, to be sure, but only because she imagined she was going to have to cry out for assistance. That would have created a distasteful scene in a public inn and sullied her reputation even further. Her life was already difficult enough, for her would-be lovers assumed, as did all the polite world, that to be a professional singer was to be a whore. High class, perhaps, but still a whore.

Sophie had accepted jewels from the Baron von Beck, at Verdicchio's insistence. As a result, the Baron believed he had rights over her person, even though she had twice rejected his advances. She had thought to be rid of him by leaving Italy. Was he following her to Vienna? She did not know, but their meeting had proved what she already suspected: the Baron was both dangerous and vindictive. He was now prepared to take her

by force if he could. And if he could not, he was like to
seek other ways of having revenge upon her.

Sophie shuddered and pulled her chair a little closer
to the comforting warmth of the fire. If Beck were to
be in Vienna while Sophie was performing there, it
would be dangerous to go out alone or to have private
meetings with gentlemen, even gentlemen like Lord
Leo Aikenhead, whose motives had been of the very
highest. His kindness had warmed her more than the
fire.

The contrast between the two men was stark. Beck,
as ever, had been immaculately and expensively
dressed, but nothing he wore could give him the effortless presence of Lord Leo Aikenhead. It was not merely
that Lord Leo was taller and of a more athletic build.
Beck's meanness of spirit was written in his features.
Lord Leo, by contrast, had the open, easy air of a man
who was respected by everyone. He would not need to
assert his rank in order to be obeyed.

What was his rank? Sophie was not absolutely sure,
but she fancied he was possibly a younger son. She had
encountered quite a few such men over the years, all of
them eager to know her better, and none of them plump
in the pocket. There was no reason to suppose that Lord
Leo was any different. Still, she could always make
discreet enquiries of the embassy staff, and if—

Good grief! She was losing her wits!

She shook her head in an attempt to clear her unruly
thoughts. Truly, she could not afford to allow Lord
Leo's attractive person to cloud her judgement. He was
only a man. And she had long ago learned to be wary
of all men, even men who rescued ladies in distress.
Besides, she might never lay eyes on him again. He

might not be going to Vienna. Even if he were, why should he attend performances by the Venetian Nightingale? He had the air of a man who took his pleasures outdoors, with horse and dog and gun, not a man who frequented salons and musical soirées.

She would do well to forget him. It was much more important to concentrate on saving enough to pay for her escape from Verdicchio. A little siren voice whispered that, if she had accepted the suit of one of her many admirers, she would have had money aplenty, and a protector against Verdicchio, besides, but she knew she could not do such a thing. Just the thought of being touched by them made her feel soiled. She had refused, thus far, to sell her body. She would not sell it now, when her freedom was almost within her grasp.

One day, perhaps, she would bestow it. But as a gift, a gift of love. And thus far, she had met no man worthy of that gift.

No, not even Lord Leo Aikenhead.

Chapter Three

'**W**e do have to go, Leo. Everyone will be there. Even the Russian Emperor is expected to attend.' Jack's lips twitched into a hint of a cynical smile.

Leo grunted. 'If so, this singer must be beautiful as well as talented. His Russian Majesty is reputed to be something of a connoisseur of women.'

Jack pursed his lips. 'I wonder, though. They call her the Venetian Nightingale. Sounds more like a ravishing voice but plain brown feathers, wouldn't you say?'

'Possibly. Shan't know till we see her. What's her name?'

'No idea. The invitation just called her the Venetian Nightingale.'

'Hmm. We'd best be on our way if we're to catch any of this nightingale's trilling, since the venue is half a day's march from here.' He shook his head in mock disgust. 'Damned inconvenient to be lodged this far from the centre.'

Jack shrugged off the implied rebuke and crossed to the window to look down into the square below. 'No sign of the carriage. What the devil is keeping the man? I ordered it for fifteen minutes since.'

'Probably not his fault, Jack. With tens of thousands of visitors in Vienna, it's sometimes impossible to move in the streets. And with a carriage…' Leo shrugged and settled himself into the corner of the striped damask sofa, as if he suddenly had all the time in the world. 'Pity we don't have an attractive woman in the Honours,' he said after a few moments. 'Dominic always said we needed a Queen to stand alongside Ace, King, Knave and Ten. Now imagine if we had a Queen to pique the Russian Emperor's interest. A little pillow talk might provide just the information we need at present. Don't know nearly enough yet about what his intentions are.'

Jack turned back from the window. His face was full of animation. 'What about this Venetian soprano, Leo? If she has the kind of beauty to attract the Emperor, maybe we could…er…enlist her services in our cause? She's an opera singer, after all, so she's more or less a courtesan. If she's prepared to sell her body to him, perhaps she could sell his secrets to us at the same time.'

Leo ran his fingers over his chin and frowned thoughtfully at the empty fireplace. 'Might work, I suppose, though we'd have to touch the embassy for the cash to pay her. Let's look her over first.'

'Don't take too long about it, Leo. We might miss our chance. The Emperor is said to change his women as often as he changes his coats. You'd have to make sure you greased her palm before the Emperor started greasing—'

'Point taken, Jack,' Leo interrupted sharply, shaking

his head as he rose to his feet. 'A word of brotherly advice,' he added, frowning. 'I've a deal more experience with the fair sex than you do, you'll admit. And I've found that it pays to treat them all as if they were true ladies. Even members of the muslin company. This nightingale of yours may earn her living on her back, but she has probably had no choice in the matter. If you took that silver spoon out of your own mouth once in a while, you'd have more understanding of how the less fortunate are situated.'

Jack coloured and hung his head a little.

Leo shook his head at his own outburst. Their lack of real progress here in Vienna was beginning to make him as surly as a bear. 'Confound it, I'm beginning to sound as prosy as Dominic.' He gave a snort of embarrassed laughter.

Jack grinned, his normal good humour quickly reasserting itself. 'I'd rather take your advice than his when it comes to women, though. Not a good picker, our noble brother. Whereas you seem to stay on good terms with all the females you encounter, even your past mistresses.'

'Not the same as picking a wife, brat, which I haven't done and don't intend to start upon. As for Dominic, I admit he made a mull of his first marriage, but this time may be different.'

'This time?' When Leo would not respond, Jack added, 'Is *that* why he was so eager to be off to Russia?'

Leo pursed his lips. It was not his secret to share, though it sounded as if his slip of the tongue had simply confirmed what Jack already suspected. Sometimes brother Jack was too sharp for his own good.

Jack's eyes widened. 'So I was right. But surely Dom

can't marry a girl who's served in the Russian cavalry? She's probably warmed the beds of half the Russian army.'

'You know, Jack,' Leo said grimly, taking a step forward and gripping his brother's shoulder tightly, 'I doubt that. Very much. And if you have hopes of seeing your next birthday, I strongly suggest you forget any and all slights on that particular lady's honour. Unless you fancy being on the receiving end of Dominic's fists, or looking down the barrel of his pistol.'

Jack blanched visibly, then reddened. He looked incredibly young, Leo decided.

'I'm sorry, Leo. I didn't think. I—'

'That's your problem, Jack. You speak and you act without thinking of the consequences. Good God, man, you're twenty-four years old. High time you learned some responsibility, don't you think?'

Jack pulled himself very erect and looked his brother straight in the eye. 'I gave you my word about the gambling, Leo. Do you doubt me?'

'No, not on that,' Leo said hastily, and in a gentler tone. 'But on other things, you— It would be wise to be a little more careful, that's all.'

'And to grow up, I suppose.'

'No need to get testy with me, brat. You know I have your interests at heart. As has Dominic. It's just that—' At the sight of Jack's ever redder face, he stopped abruptly. He truly was turning into a miserable old greybeard. 'Where the devil is that carriage?' He strode across to the window and began to drum his fingers on the pane. 'Damn the man. We're going to be late.'

Sophie gazed round at the applauding audience, but she did not smile. She needed to maintain her concen-

tration for this last aria. She had sung well, but this
would be the *pièce de résistance*. The Russian Emperor,
sitting in the front row, had been clapping enthusiastically so far. If she could truly impress him, she might
secure an invitation to St Petersburg. That would be a
godsend. The Russian capital was very rich, and a long
way from the countries she so desperately wished to
avoid.

Verdicchio looked round from his place at the pianoforte, waiting for her signal. The cellist and violinist
were also waiting. She took a long, slow breath and let
her eyes travel around the salon. She gave Verdicchio
the signal and raised her chin, allowing the low, passionate notes of the cello introduction to flood her being
with the essence of the music. After a few bars, the
violin joined in, answering the cello like a bird flutter-
ing over and under denser, darker branches. And then
the pianoforte, soft and sonorous—

The noise of the door opening at the rear of the
salon, and of raised voices, shattered Sophie's concen-
tration. How dare they? With a gasp of rage, she
whipped round to reach for the glass of water on the
table behind her, leaving the audience to gaze at her
back. The music stuttered to an untidy stop.

After a few moments of breathing exercises,
Sophie was once more in control. The commotion in
the salon had subsided into silence. Slowly, majesti-
cally, she turned back to the sea of waiting, expectant
faces. She refused to focus on any of them. Not even
the Russian Emperor. Adopting her haughtiest
posture, she gazed out over their heads and allowed
herself to think only of the tragic heroine whose role
she was about to interpret.

At her nod, the cello began to sing. And as the harmonies of the introduction rose and swelled, Sophie opened her throat and began her aria on a single, perfect pianissimo.

The brothers' tardy arrival was the height of bad manners, Leo knew. Jack had been so sure they could slip in unnoticed at the back of the grand salon. He could not have been more wrong; their timing was as bad as it could possibly be. It seemed that the Venetian Nightingale had been just about to sing, though she had turned away so rapidly that Leo had not caught even a glimpse of her face. But her ramrod-straight back and stiffly held neck told the whole audience that she was absolutely furious about the interruption to her performance.

Leo held his breath, waiting for her to turn back to face the room. Beside him, in the back row of spindle-legged gilt chairs, Jack began to whisper something. 'Stubble it!' Leo muttered. Confound the boy, would he never learn?

The Nightingale had mastered her temper, it appeared. Very slowly, and holding herself with the pride of a queen, she turned, automatically arranging the flowing folds of her bronze-green silk skirts, while she gazed out over the heads of all of them. Diamonds glinted at her throat and on her wrists. The diamond drops in her ears sparked fire against the heavy black hair coiled against her neck.

Madame Pietre! His damsel in distress from the country inn!

She nodded to her accompanists like a duchess to a servant. Leo could not take his eyes from her. She was glorious. She was burning with anger. And she was nothing at all like the virtuous matron Leo had believed her to be.

Mad, confusing ideas tumbled through his brain. Perhaps she could indeed be persuaded to act the spy on behalf of the Honours? Perhaps that luscious body— which was every bit as delectable as Leo had imagined when he had first seen her wrapped in that plain cloak— had already graced the beds of half the crowned heads of Europe? Leo's pulse began to race at the thought of this extraordinary woman in some lucky man's bed. The rest of his body was responding, too. It was urging him to possess her, whatever the cost. He discovered, in that moment, that he cared not a fig for emperors and kings, or for whatever valuable information the Venetian Nightingale might discover by sharing their pillows. It was Leo's pillow she had to share!

And then the Nightingale began to sing. Lord Leo Aikenhead, who had never cared above half for music, was instantly transported to a land of dreams, and ravishing beauty and of profound, heart-rending tragedy.

Sophie made a deep curtsy to the Emperor Alexander, as etiquette required.

He immediately took her gloved hand to raise her to her feet. 'No, *madame*,' he said in his immaculate French, 'it is I who should bow to you. Such an exquisite voice. And such emotion. I swear that half your listeners were near to tears. I have never heard such a touching rendition of the tragic heroine.'

'Your Imperial Majesty is more than generous.' Her admirers in Venice had been gentlemen or aristocrats; never monarchs. Sophie smiled shyly up at the

Emperor. He was much taller than she was, with light brown, slightly receding hair, fine side-whiskers, and a ruddy, cheerful face. The many stars and orders on his dress uniform caught the light every time he moved. Yet, in spite of that daunting splendour, he gave the impression of geniality. And he was showing knowledgeable appreciation of an artistic performance.

He shook his head, returning her smile. 'No, indeed. Your singing, *madame*, has been the musical highlight of my visit to Vienna. May I hope to have the pleasure of hearing you sing again, on another occasion?'

'I am engaged for a number of performances in Vienna, your Majesty. Perhaps your Majesty—'

'Ah, yes. Yes, indeed. As you say, *madame*. But may I hope that there is still some free time, in your busy schedule of engagements, for performances to a more select audience?'

Sophie swallowed. Did he really mean what she suspected? He would certainly not be the first to try to turn a recital into a more carnal assignation. But he was the Emperor of All the Russias. A mere opera singer could not openly question his motives. 'Maestro Verdicchio has arranged all my engagements, your Majesty,' she said, a little uncertainly. 'If your Majesty wishes, I could—'

He pursed his lips a little, as if trying to hide a smile, and reached for her hand once more, raising it for a gallant kiss. 'I shall look forward to hearing more of that radiant voice. For the moment, *madame*, I must bid you *adieu*.' With an elegant bow, he strode away to join his host on the far side of the huge salon.

The other guests, in deference to the presence of the Emperor, had stood at a discreet distance. Sophie now found herself alone. Little groups of aristocratic women were gossiping quietly, some of them nodding in Sophie's direction. She could very well imagine what they were saying. *It seems that his Russian Majesty has decided to bed the Venetian Nightingale, just as he dallies with every other beautiful woman he encounters.*

Sophie felt a tiny shudder run down her spine. How did one refuse an Emperor who had too much finesse to proposition a lady directly? If Alexander of Russia asked Verdicchio to organise a private recital for him, it would be a gross insult for her to decline.

'Madame Pietre? May I compliment you on your magnificent performance?' The low voice came from just behind Sophie's shoulder. Something about it was familiar, as if—

For a second time, her hand was taken and raised to a man's lips. He stood before her. Lord Leo Aikenhead. Her champion. And the man who had been troubling her dreams for more than a week. She could feel the colour rising on her neck. This man had thought her a lady, but now he knew what she was. Would she see contempt in his eyes? She did not dare to look.

'You must be thirsty after singing for so long, *madame*. A glass of champagne, perhaps?' With the ease of an old friend, he tucked her hand under his arm. 'I saw that you were besieged by half the men in the audience, and then by the Emperor, but not one of them had the wit to offer you more than fine words. I am hoping that my more practical offering will encourage you to keep me company for a little.' He drew her towards the side of the room where a waiter stood with a huge salver of champagne flutes.

She had misjudged him. He was still treating her as if she were a lady. Sophie allowed herself a tentative smile and relaxed a fraction.

'Much better,' he said gently. 'If you will forgive my remarking on it, *madame*, you were as tense as a spring. I could feel it, even in your fingertips.' As if to emphasise his words, he placed his free hand over her fingers for a second or two. It seemed to be intended as a friendly, reassuring gesture from a gentleman to the lady he was escorting.

But for Sophie there was nothing in the least reassuring about it. The shock ran up her arm like a stab of pain, so sharp that she almost gasped aloud. She should not have dared to relax, not even for a moment. Not with this man.

It seemed he had not noticed her body's reaction this time. He had turned aside to take a champagne flute from the tray.

'Try this, *madame*.' He put the glass into her unresisting fingers. Then he caught up another for himself and touched it to Sophie's. 'To the Venetian Nightingale. Whose spellbinding performance has been a revelation to me.'

Sophie forced herself to nod in acknowledgement of his words. He was watching her carefully as he drank, his deep blue eyes scrutinising her face intently. What could he see there? Disconcerted, she took a large swallow of her champagne. Too large. The bubbles caught in her throat. She choked.

'Water for *madame*!' Lord Leo snapped to the waiter. 'At once!'

The servant rushed to obey. Lord Leo set down both champagne flutes and led Sophie to an alcove at the side of the salon. She sank gratefully on to the red-velvet bench seat, her coughing now more or less under control. But when she tried to speak, no words came out.

Lord Leo looked round impatiently for the servant and almost snatched the glass from his hands. 'There's barely enough water there to wet the inside of the glass,' he said testily. 'Go and fetch more. Quickly now.'

Sophie drank it in long gulps. It soothed her bruised throat. 'Thank you, sir,' she said, in something akin to her normal voice. Had she done any damage? Verdicchio would swiftly disown her if she could no longer earn enough to keep them both in the luxury he felt to be his due.

'You permit, *madame*?' Lord Leo indicated the vacant space beside her.

Sophie nodded. 'That is the second time you have rescued me, Lord Leo.'

'I think not, *madame*. On this occasion, I fear that I was the cause of your difficulty. Ah, here is what you need.' He indicated to the servant that he should place a small table at Sophie's hand and put the decanter of water within easy reach.

Sophie busied herself with refilling her glass, slowly, so that she had time to think. What did he want of her? At their first meeting, she had doubted that Lord Leo Aikenhead was a connoisseur of music. He had said nothing so far to change her mind. Mischievously, she murmured, without turning back to him, 'That last aria was one I seldom perform in gatherings such as this. The heroine's plight is so very tragic. Audiences seem to prefer the lighter pieces, as a rule. Is that your taste also, Lord Leo?'

His response was initially a little hesitant, but he soon recovered his normal confidence. 'I must tell you, *madame*, that your final aria was more touching than any I have ever heard,' he finished.

'You are too kind,' Sophie responded automatically. Was his compliment sincere? Rashly, and against her better judgement, she risked a glance up into his face to find those fierce blue eyes fixed on her with an intensity that was almost frightening. She found herself recoiling a little. The elemental force of him was too powerful to withstand. He was dangerous, and yet she was drawn to him. Too close and he would burn her up.

She must keep her distance from this man.

She set down her glass with a sharp click. 'If you will excuse me now, sir, I think that Maestro Verdicchio wishes to speak to me.'

'Stay.' It was a low, almost animal growl.

He did not touch her or move to close the proper distance between them, but Sophie felt as if he had seized her and dragged her tight against his body. She could almost feel the heat of him prickling her skin. And yet they still sat half a yard apart!

'Sir?' She was hoarse all over again.

'Madame Pietre, I must tell you how ardently I admire you. Your voice, your beauty.' He allowed his gaze to roam slowly over Sophie's face and figure. 'You are exquisite. Incomparable.' He sighed rather theatrically. Then he nodded dismissively in the direction of Verdicchio, who was talking too loudly to one of the Emperor's entourage at the far end of the room. 'I understand that you already have a protector. But I beg you to consider my earnest desire to know you more nearly.'

Sophie was incapable of speech. Hot anger was starting to boil in her breast. But she remained motionless, except for a single raised eyebrow.

He seemed to take it as an invitation to continue with his proposition. 'I am fixed in Vienna for some time, *madame*. I would deem it an honour to be allowed to enjoy your company, and to serve you while I am here. Vienna has become something of a city of pleasure, has it not?'

There was now so much relaxed confidence in his face that she itched to slap him. It was clear in his eyes. They had become dark and limpid, full of desire. Not the slightest hint of wariness, or of doubt. He knew he was a personable man, and he expected Sophie to accept him as her new protector.

She swallowed and hardened her feelings against him. He was just like all the others. Worse, even. He had been prepared to consider her a lady, and to treat her as one, until the moment he learned that she was a mere opera singer. One song, one recital, and the last vestige of his respect for her had vanished. All he could think of was how to persuade this fallen woman into his bed.

Well, aristocrat or no, he was wrong, and Sophie Pietre was going to make him smart for his insolence. 'Pleasure, Lord Leo, comes only at a price,' she murmured silkily, looking up at him through her lashes.

'Of course, *madame*. I had expected nothing less.' He edged a little closer to Sophie. She could truly feel the heat of him now.

She retrieved her glass of water and took a tiny sip, holding his gaze all the while. 'I am relieved to hear we are of one mind on this, Lord Leo. But you would not expect me to accept such a nebulous offer, I am sure.

Even from you.' She narrowed her eyes. 'Did you have something more specific to propose, perhaps?'

This time he really did look uncomfortable, but he was equal to her challenge. He raised his chin a little, and named the price he was prepared to pay. 'In addition,' he continued smoothly, 'I would of course provide you with all the luxuries such a beautiful lady could desire.'

She had expected him to suggest at least as much as the Baron von Beck. But this was not even a quarter of the Baron's offer. In that instant, Sophie almost felt sorry for Lord Leo. He had made things so easy for her.

But then she looked into his eyes once more, and saw there the desire for possession that had inflamed so many of her suitors, not one of whom had cared for more than her body and an opportunity to slake his lust. She hardened her heart. Lord Leo was no different from all the rest. Just meaner, when it came to money.

She rose swiftly to her feet and gazed down at him, lifting a stern hand to prevent him from moving from his seat. She wanted him to remain there, below her, gazing up like a suppliant. She wanted this arrogant aristocrat to learn how it felt to be humiliated. 'I thank you for your offer, Lord Leo. I do not stoop to call it insulting. That would demean both of us. Suffice it to say that, having heard the paltry value you set upon my company, I prefer to remain as I am. I was indebted to you before, I freely admit. But now, sir, I fancy that we are even. Goodnight to you.' She dipped him a tiny, impudent curtsy and walked serenely away before he had time to utter a word.

Chapter Four

Leo marched straight out into the garden. The moment he was alone, he let fly with a volley of oaths that would not have disgraced the meanest soldier in the British army. He desperately wanted to hit something, or someone. Preferably Jack. If he had not had to mortgage The Larches and most of his annual income to pay off Jack's debts, Leo would have been able to offer the Venetian Nightingale whatever she desired. As it was, he had insulted her by offering her a pittance. And, in revenge, she had made him feel like a worm, to be trodden into the mud under the heel of her shoe.

That did not lessen his unquenchable passion for her, though. If anything, it made his desire even stronger. He could not understand it. He had had many mistresses over the years, all of them quick-witted and a delight to the eye, but he had always remained in control of the relationship. Never before had his body reacted as if he were a green boy, lusting after his first woman.

What was it about Madame Pietre? He closed his

eyes and pictured her. She had a dark, luscious beauty that made him want to put his lips to her skin as he would to a ripe, sun-warmed peach before biting into its sweet flesh. She was only an opera singer, yet there was a kind of nobility in the way she carried her head and in the way she spoke. She was intriguing, exotic, mysterious. And under that polite exterior, a passionate Latin woman lay concealed. He was sure that, as a lover, she would surpass any woman he had ever known. He had to have her!

He began to pace the rose-covered walk where his wandering steps had led him. There must be a way to reach her. Perhaps he could borrow money from—

'Leo! I've been looking for you everywhere.'

Jack! It would be Jack. Just when Leo was ready to plant him a facer!

'I can't imagine what you're doing out here on your own,' Jack continued equably, apparently oblivious to Leo's black frown. 'I thought you'd be in the salon, toadeating the Emperor's retainers.'

Leo did not dare to speak, lest he ring a peal over Jack's head. The boy had apologised, more than once, for the straits they were in. It would be dishonourable to blame Jack for Leo's unaccountable passion for the Venetian singer.

'Ben has arrived at last. I thought you'd want to know at once.'

Leo took a long breath and sighed it out, forcing his mind back to their mission. Action would drive out his demons. 'Where is he?'

'At the embassy. They told him where to find us. His messenger arrived here not five minutes ago.'

'Excellent. We can certainly use his help, though we

shall be even more cramped with three of us, plus the servants, in those poor rooms.'

'He can share mine. And he has brought two servants, so he must be more flush in the pocket than we are.' Jack grinned sheepishly. 'His grandfather must have franked him for the trip. Otherwise he'd have been walking all the way.'

Leo smiled back. Poor Ben was kept on a very tight leash, even though he was heir to his grandfather's title. Perhaps he had dropped a hint or two about the importance of his journey to Vienna? Old Viscount Hoarwithy might have been willing to fund a discreet mission on behalf of the British government. Leo sincerely hoped that was the case. If Ben had arrived in Vienna without any blunt, the Aikenhead Honours really would be in the suds.

'I suggest you go back to the embassy and look after Ben. Buy him a decent supper. I'll join you both later. There is one more person I need to see.'

Jack grinned, delighted to be let off the leash. He wasn't yet very practised at extracting information in social gatherings, so he should really stay to learn, but that was the last thing Leo wanted. He was desperate for one more sight of his lovely Nightingale. And, if he was going to be following her like a stallion after a mare in heat, he certainly didn't want his sharp-tongued younger brother to know of it.

Verdicchio smiled smugly. 'Major Zass, the Russian Emperor's aide-de-camp, has asked that I arrange a private recital for his Imperial Majesty. I have accepted, of course. The fee is very generous.'

Sophie said nothing. The generosity of the fee depended on which services it was intended to cover.

'What is the matter with you, girl? This is the Emperor of All the Russias! After this, you will be the toast of Vienna.'

Sophie nodded obediently. Verdicchio was right, in some ways. She probably would become the toast of the city. Unfortunately, the toast might have nothing to do with her talent as a singer.

'Then you do accept? Sophie?'

'Of course. I will perform at a private recital for his Russian Majesty. That is to say, I will *sing* for him. I take it you will be accompanying me?'

'Er…the final arrangements are yet to be made. I imagine that I will be invited to act as your accompanist.'

Without an accompanist, she would refuse to perform at all. She had absolutely no desire to find herself alone with the Emperor.

'Come, let me introduce you to Major Zass.'

Sophie shook her head. 'There is no need. I know I can trust you to agree all the details on my behalf, Maestro.' She touched his arm lightly.

He smiled again, his momentary flash of temper transformed by her flattering words.

'If you will excuse me now, Maestro,' she said, returning his smile, 'I shall be in the retiring room. One of those clumsy young bucks stood on the hem of my gown, and I need to have it pinned up.' She did not wait for his reply. She simply walked quickly out into the anteroom and towards the stairs.

There were knots of men talking quietly in corners and in groups around the centre of the room. They might have been plotting—many certainly looked like conspirators—but they were probably only gossiping. Vienna was alive with gossip, especially now that it was so full of foreign royalty. She determined to ignore them all and lifted her skirts to make her way through them.

A single name, spoken almost in a whisper, rang in her ears like a death-knell.

She caught her breath. She could not have heard aright. Surely, it was impossible? But she had to be sure. She continued serenely across the room to the foot of the staircase, then turned suddenly, as if she had forgotten something, and made her way back to stand behind a pillar, a yard or so away from the two men in Prussian uniform whose voices had caught her attention.

'Yes. Killed in a duel. Must have been at least six months ago.'

'Von Carstein? You are sure?'

'Absolutely. Heard it myself from one of the seconds.'

'And so who inherits the title?'

The first man laughed. 'Why, no one. Nothing to inherit but a pile of debts. If the old man hadn't been killed in that duel, he'd probably have blown his brains out. He had too much pride to face the world as a penniless wreck.'

The second man grunted. 'I agree. We are well rid of him. He was a disgrace to our class.'

'Aye. I heard it said that he sold his daughter to pay his gambling debts.'

'Truly? He was a blackguard, but surely even he had too much sense of his own rank to do such a heinous thing?'

'It was only a rumour, my friend. Nearly fifteen years ago. Didn't believe it myself. He had no son, of course. Only the one daughter. She probably died. No doubt some malcontent concocted the rumour to blacken the Baron's name.' He chuckled. 'Not that it needed much blackening. He managed that very well for himself.'

'Mmm. Perhaps it would have been different if he had sired a son.'

'Aye, a man needs a son. A nobleman, especially. Daughters are useless. And a burden besides.'

Sophie could not bear it. Her legs had turned to water beneath her, and she had to lean against the pillar for support. She must get away from these men, from their hateful words. She staggered a few steps towards the shadows.

'Madame Pietre? You are unwell. Allow me to help you to a chair.'

Lord Leo! Dear God, why did it have to be Lord Leo, the man she had insulted? Sophie nodded dumbly, wishing him away. She did not dare to raise her eyes to his face. Let him continue to think she was merely a weak woman, fainting from the heat. If he looked into her eyes, he would read how her soul had been seared by that casual dissection of the truth about her family.

Lord Leo took her weight on his arm and gently led her across the floor to the relative seclusion under the staircase, where a number of chairs had been placed. He guided her into one of them and stood alongside, waiting for some kind of response from her.

Sophie's whole body tensed. What could she say? She knew she must still look quite horror-struck. Desperate, she clasped her hands in her lap, focused her gaze upon them, and began to practise the breathing exercises she always used to calm her nerves before walking out on stage.

The familiar routine was balm to her shattered senses. In moments, she was almost back in control.

'I am afraid we are all suffering from the heat here, *madame*. It is no surprise that you were overcome.'

Sophie nodded slightly, still not looking up. She would not tell a direct lie. Not to this man. She had already done quite enough to humiliate him. So why was it that he, of all people, was now prepared to treat her with kindness? In rejecting him, her pride had spoken, and loudly. Her purpose, to make him suffer as she had been made to suffer, had been achieved. Why then did she not feel triumphant? Was it because her conscience was troubling her? After all, he had only assumed, as all society did, that Sophia Pietre was for sale.

Her actions had been vindictive and dishonourable. However low Lord Leo's opinion of her, it was deserved. And it was nowhere near as bad as Sophie's opinion of herself.

Guilt-ridden and now thoroughly embarrassed, she could not think of a single thing to say to him. She berated herself for a coward. Either she must speak to him, or she must leave.

He should not have followed her. Considering how she had delighted in mortifying him, he certainly should not be looking to her comfort. But that stricken look on her face had hit him like a blow. She was suffering, and not from the heat. Why? What had been done to her? He was sure that she would never say, particularly not to him.

She was refusing to look at him. If she did not speak to him soon, he must leave. Just as he straightened to walk away from her, he noticed that her hand was shaking. She truly was suffering!

'Madame Pietre, you need more than rest here to restore you. Will you allow me to summon your uncle? He should escort you home.'

She shook her head vehemently and murmured something incoherent.

Whatever the trouble that beset her, she would not share it with Verdicchio. Leo found he was glad. Verdicchio was a sly weasel, a manipulator of souls. If he was the Venetian Nightingale's lover, it was probably because he had some hold over her. Gazing down at the lustrous ebony hair coiled against her delicate neck, Leo failed, yet again, to bring himself to think ill of her.

He felt an overpowering urge to protect her, in spite of what she was.

'If you will not ask your uncle to escort you home, *madame*, perhaps you will allow me to do so?' The words were out before the thought was fully formed.

Her head jerked up. She stared at him wide-eyed. Her lips opened a fraction, as if in astonishment.

Committed by his own words, and feeling suddenly glad of it, Leo gazed steadily into her face. He was determined to help her and, for some reason, it was vital that she should understand that.

'Lord Leo,' she said very softly, 'you—' She shook her head a little. 'I do not know what to say.'

He took that as agreement. Giving her no time to say another word, he swiftly arranged for her carriage to be brought round. Unlike the Aikenhead brothers, the Venetian Nightingale could afford to keep her own carriage in Vienna, he discovered.

Seeing that her colour was beginning to return, he

offered her his arm. 'Perhaps you would like to walk a little until your carriage arrives, *madame*? Some cooler air will make you feel stronger, I am sure.'

He had made it impossible for her to decline, but she was clearly reluctant to take his arm, perhaps even to touch him. He cursed inwardly. Was it any wonder that he disgusted her? He was, after all, the man who had offered a pittance for the favours of the most glorious woman in Vienna. And offered it, besides, as if he were bestowing an enormous honour upon her. He had insulted her, and, in return, she had humiliated him. Which of them was the worse?

They walked, in silence, through apparently endless corridors hung with paintings. Leo tried to converse with her about them, but she simply shook her head, or closed her eyes or gazed at her feet. After only a few minutes, she withdrew her hand from his arm so that they were walking side by side, but separated by a small, daunting distance. Her meaning was very plain. She wanted none of him. His insult had been too great.

'I expect that your carriage will be waiting by now, *madame*.' He was trying to sound as normal as he could, but she was still refusing to look at him. She gave a tiny nod and allowed him to escort her to the entrance, where a footman waited with her wrap and Leo's hat and cane.

Leo took the wrap himself and placed it carefully round her shoulders. He could not prevent his fingers from touching her bare skin. To be honest, he did not want to try. It might be the last time he was given the chance to do so. But the response horrified him. Her whole body shuddered as if she found him repellent.

He closed his eyes on that clear rejection. She

wanted him to leave her. Now. But his body would not comply. He had never before known desire to possess him like this, but here, now, he had no time to worry at the cause. Leaving her was something that he could not do.

She was betraying far too much of what she felt. He would be able to read her, which would make her vulnerable to him, but her responses were beyond her conscious control. It had never happened before. Never. But with Lord Leo Aikenhead she was unable to maintain the icy-calm demeanour she usually adopted with so-called gentlemen. Perhaps it was because Lord Leo was a true gentleman? He had certainly been more generous than Sophie deserved.

At the door to her carriage, she turned and offered him her hand. 'Lord Leo, you have been more than kind to a poor drooping female. I shall take your advice and return to my lodgings to rest. Pray believe that I am in your debt.'

'Madame Pietre, forgive my presumption, but you cannot drive home alone. What if you were to be subject to another swoon? Since neither your uncle nor your maid is here to escort you, I hope you will allow me to perform that humble duty.' He was smiling down into her eyes as he spoke. And his gaze was full of concern, and kindness.

It would be the height of ill manners to refuse his offer. Manners were part of a lady, as much as breathing. And in her heart, Sophie remained a noble lady. In such circumstances, she found it impossible to be rude to the one man who had come to her aid. 'You are too good, Lord Leo. Thank you.'

He handed her up, ensuring she was comfortably settled on the seat with a rug across her knees. Then he sprang up himself, gallantly taking the forward seat so that he did not crowd her. Many another man would have insisted on sitting beside her, so that their bodies touched whenever the carriage swayed.

He gave the coachman the office. The carriage started forward, very slowly.

Sophie looked across at him in surprise.

'I took the liberty, *madame*, of instructing your coachman to drive slowly. I imagined that a faster pace would be uncomfortable for you. Do you object?'

Sophie responded with a tiny shake of her head. His concern was all for her comfort. And if it meant that she would remain in Lord Leo's company for rather longer than otherwise, was that such a hardship? He was a most personable gentleman—even if he did want to make Sophie his mistress—and now that their respective positions were clear, he would probably be good company. Provided he did not touch her again.

She wriggled back into her seat and fussed with the rug, trying to think of some innocuous topic of conversation. But her mind kept repeating 'Touch me, Leo. Touch me, again.' Her body had turned traitor.

'This is a splendid carriage, *madame*. The purple and gold are most elegant. I admit that, the first time I saw it, I rather assumed that it belonged to—' He stopped suddenly. 'That is to say,' he continued, in almost the same nonchalant tone as before, 'that I thought it belonged to a gentleman. I must say that it is much more suited to a lady.'

Ah, yes. Lord Leo had clearly assumed it belonged to the Baron von Beck, probably because their colours matched. The very idea made Sophie want to laugh. Laughing at the Baron would be one of the best ways of mastering her fear.

She looked across at Lord Leo. She could say nothing, for he had been careful not to name the Baron, lest the memory embarrass her. But perhaps Sophie's ardent look could show him how much she appreciated his tact and discretion?

He must have seen something in her face, for he smiled, though a little tentatively. Then, with another demonstration of his impeccable manners, he began to talk about the sights of Vienna and the various entertainments he had attended.

Sophie responded as best she could. Unlike Lord Leo, she and Verdicchio had been in the city for little more than a week. As a mere singer, she was not normally invited to the grandest events, which were reserved for the visiting monarchs, their retainers, and the exalted foreigners who filled the city. Sophie and Verdicchio could go only to the larger events that the common people might attend, on purchase of tickets. The message was clear. Sophia Pietre was not to be counted amongst the notables of society.

It had been so for many years, but it still hurt.

They arrived at the door to her apartment long before she expected it. His conversation had been so soothing that she had lost track of time. The truth was that she had enjoyed it, once she had overcome her initial embarrassment at the violence of her physical reactions to him.

If only he had not made that horrid proposal. If only she had not rebuffed him so rudely!

'Lord Leo, I must thank you again for your kindness.

My coachman will take you back to the reception, of course. Or anywhere else you wish to go.'

'Madame Pietre, it was recompense enough to have been able to enjoy your company for these few minutes. It has shown me what I have lost, as a result of my boorish approach to you earlier. I hope I may ask you to forget it.'

She knew she was blushing now. 'If that is your wish, sir, I shall certainly do so. As I hope you will forget the terms of my reply.'

He said nothing, but the glow in his face suggested that he was more than ready to do so, and that some kind of peace had been restored between them.

Sophie waited. She assumed he would alight from the carriage and help her down.

He did not. He reached for her gloved hand and raised it to his lips. And he never took his eyes from hers all the while. The glow was even more intense. Burning.

Sophie knew she should snatch her hand away, but her body seemed to be frozen. She could not move a muscle. Their joining, even in such a very proper way, seemed special. And meant.

At length, Lord Leo gently returned her hand to her lap. Without a word, he sprang from the carriage and turned to help her down. He was attentive, but now no more than properly polite. The moment, the connection between them, had been that kiss through her glove, and the message exchanged when they looked at each other. That message was unmistakable.

He wanted her. And—heaven help her—she wanted him too.

Chapter Five

Leo took the precaution of alighting from the purple carriage two streets away from his lodgings. Jack might not know the owner of the opulent vehicle, but he would ask and ask again until he learned the truth. And then he would demand to know about Leo's dealings with the Venetian Nightingale. Leo could not possibly admit that he had asked her to become his mistress.

Jack, knowing Leo's ways with women, would suspect as much, the moment he learned that the two had been together. As it was, he had been roasting Leo about his unaccustomed celibacy ever since their arrival in Vienna. He had remarked on a couple of very pretty local girls, daughters of the bourgeoisie. 'Their fathers are happy to sell their services, it seems. Provided, of course, that the buyer is a man of status.'

The thought of a man selling his own daughter made Leo's stomach turn. He had known many women, in every sense of the word, but he would never be responsible for turning an innocent child on to the path of prostitution. If he was going to take a mistress, she would be from his own class, and a woman who was already well versed in the ways of dalliance. He was happy to wait until the right woman appeared. Or so he had thought.

Then he had seen Madame Pietre at that recital. All thoughts of pursuing any other woman in Vienna had vanished on the spot. His desire for the singer was all-consuming, in a way that Leo found totally new and more than a little disturbing. He was not used to losing control, not where women were concerned. With the Venetian Nightingale, he had no control left to lose.

He ought to hate her, to have been planning her undoing. She had embarrassed him deeply, after all. She had led him on, forcing him to name his price in the most sordid way. Then she had spurned his offer. With relish. And in favour of Verdicchio, one of the most self-seeking and untrustworthy men in the city.

Threading his way through the busy streets to his lodgings, Leo tried to fathom his own reactions to this extraordinary woman. What strange impulse had made him go to her aid? Why had he not simply stood on the sidelines watching her distress and enjoying the spectacle? He had a reputation for being fair and generous to women and to men, but not for being soft-hearted. Or weak.

He shook his head, confused. He had to admit he felt a strange magnetic attraction to Sophia Pietre. He had allowed that, plus some deeper instinct, to drive him to help her. Perhaps it had been the right course to take? It had certainly led them to some kind of understanding. And then that kiss… So chaste, yet so primitive. As if their naked bodies had touched along their entire length, in a lovers' embrace. As if—

Good grief! He must be touched in his upper works

to imagine such things. What he needed was a woman in his bed, a woman who was *not* the Venetian Nightingale!

Leo strolled into the tavern on the ground floor below their lodgings, knowing that Jack would probably have taken Ben there. Why go further afield when there was both food and wine to be had at the Gasthof Brunner?

His guess was right. Almost as soon as Leo entered, Ben jumped up from his seat in the corner, knocking over his chair as he hurried forward through the crowded room. He gave Leo a friendly slap on the shoulder, grasped his hand and shook it heartily. 'Leo! I'm here at last. Good to see you.'

The young man's good humour was just as infectious as Jack's. They were a matched pair in temperament, if not in looks. In looks they could not have been more unlike. Jack was a younger image of their elder brother, Dominic, with dark hair, deep blue eyes and a lithe, athletic figure. Ben, by contrast, looked much more delicate. He had a shock of fair hair, light blue eyes and finely sculpted, almost feminine features. He was much the same height as Jack, but a lot slighter in build. And, being fair, he still had hardly any trace of beard, in spite of the four-and-twenty years in his dish. Leo smiled inwardly at that thought. Ben's looks had been useful, many and many a time, for he was the only one among the Aikenhead Honours who could even begin to pass for a woman.

In the far corner, Jack had risen quietly and was setting the table and chairs to rights. He had long ago acquired the habit of tidying away his friend's clumsiness.

Ben led Leo back to the table, which was covered with empty dishes. To Leo's surprise, there was also a jug of the local beer. It was almost empty. 'Beer?' He looked enquiringly at his brother.

'Ben was thirsty after his long journey. It seemed the obvious answer. Besides, it's much better than the wine. Hadn't you noticed how thin it is?'

Leo nodded slightly, but said nothing. It would not do for him to start insulting mine host's wine. He did not want the tavern keeper to have any excuse to bar the Aikenheads from his hostelry. The nearest alternative was several streets away.

'Won't you join us, Leo?' Ben lifted the jug, grimaced at the small amount remaining and waved it aloft, without giving Leo a moment to respond.

'Aye, why not?' he said, with a smile, pulling out a chair. They were right about the ale, which was generally excellent throughout Austria. The same could not be said for the wines in Vienna. They were so poor that Prince Metternich had set up a warehouse of imported wines to supply the foreign dignitaries.

A buxom maid set a huge jug of foaming golden ale in the middle of the table with a fresh glass for Leo. She cast him an extremely flirtatious glance from under her thick, blonde lashes, and bent forward to clear away the plates, ensuring as she did so that he had an opportunity to view the goods on offer. He deliberately kept his eyes on his companions. Tavern wenches had never been to his taste.

The girl had barely turned her back on their table when Ben's excited voice broke into Leo's musings. 'What's the news? Do we have a mission? Is there something for *me* to do this time?'

Leo couldn't help but grin. Except when disguised as a woman, Ben had generally been the one who was made to stay behind to defend their hideout and their escape route. He had always longed to be truly in the thick of the action and intrigue. Perhaps now it was time he had his chance.

Leo raised an eyebrow at Jack, who shook his head. For some reason, Jack had not briefed Ben. Possibly because the two young men were instantly absorbed in exclaiming over the sights and pleasures of Vienna? Leo shrugged his shoulders. In Dominic's absence, he was the leader of the Honours. This was a leader's role.

In a confidential undertone, Leo swiftly explained how they attended as many events as possible in order to eavesdrop on the plots and plans of the countries represented here in Vienna. A number of local spies had been recruited, too, some of them servants in foreign embassies, others employed as watchers and followers. Finally, he ran through a list of the notables in the city, among the native Austrians and among the delegations from Russia, Prussia, and the lesser states.

'You've left out one key player,' Jack put in, eagerly. 'The Venetian Nightingale, remember?'

Ben raised his eyebrows.

'She's an Italian opera singer, from Venice,' Jack continued. 'Ravishing voice. And an even more ravishing person.' He put down his beer in order to shape an exaggerated hourglass in the air with both hands. 'It seems the Russian Emperor is enamoured of her. We were hoping— At least, I was hoping that she could be persuaded to work for us. Pillow talk, you know?'

'Keep your voice down, Jack! Remember who may

be listening.' Leo glanced warily over his shoulder. No one was within earshot.

'Sorry, Leo.' Jack, a little abashed, continued in a low tone, 'I assumed that, after you sent me off, you were going to approach her. Did she agree?'

Leo swallowed hard, trying to control the mixture of anger and nausea that rose in his throat at the thought of Sophie Pietre sharing the Emperor's bed. 'What the hell did you think I was going to say to her?' His voice was almost a snarl. '"Madame Pietre, I understand you are about to be bedded by Tsar Alexander. Might I persuade you to ask him a few political questions while he is distracted by your charms?" That the sort of thing you had in mind?'

'Well, I—'

'For heaven's sake, Jack, will you never learn any finesse? If we are going to persuade her to work for us, we must first persuade her to make common cause with us. Why would she agree to work for our country, rather than her own?'

'Money?'

'You assume, I collect, that her services are for sale to the highest bidder?'

'I— Well, yes, I do. She's an opera singer. Opera dancers sell themselves. It seemed reasonable to assume that opera singers did the same.' Jack smiled a little ruefully. 'Am I wrong?'

'Don't believe you are,' Ben put in. He took a large swig of beer and sighed with pleasure, relaxing back into his chair. 'First-class ale.' He set down his half-empty glass. 'I know my experience is not as…er…extensive as yours, Leo, but I did know a couple of opera singers. Last year, in London. Sadly, as soon as the blunt ran out, they rather lost interest. But we parted on pretty good terms. I'm sure that, if I had access to the readies again, they'd be more than willing to keep company with me. Why should this Madame Whatever-her-name-is be any different?'

In truth, there was no reason at all why Sophie should be any different. Yet, in his gut, Leo felt, almost knew, that she was. He took a deep breath and frowned across the table at his companions. How on earth was he going to reply?

Jack's suddenly serious voice intervened. 'Leo, I'm sorry I was so boorish. I'll do better in future, I promise. But I've had an idea.' He lowered his voice even more. 'We have at least two local recruits without enough to do. I'll set them to following the Nightingale. Find out where she goes and whom she sees. If she has an assignation with the Russian Emperor, you'll be the first to know.'

Leo felt his gut begin to churn.

Jack was looking more and more sure of himself. 'We may even be able to bribe one of her servants. That would be the best of all, don't you think?'

What choice did he have? The Honours were here in Vienna to provide Castlereagh with information. Jack was proposing a thoroughly practical solution. Leo managed to nod at his brother, hoping that his reluctance did not show.

Jack sprang up from his chair. 'No time like the present. The sooner I set them on, the sooner we'll discover what we need to know.' He squeezed between the back of Ben's chair and the wall, pausing only to say, 'Leo will show you where we're lodged upstairs. Quarters are rather cramped, I'm afraid, so you'll have to share my bedchamber. The best bed is the one by the window.' He grinned wickedly at Ben. 'Yours is the other one.'

Sophie was revelling in being free of Verdicchio for the day. Once she reached Schönbrunn Palace, she would be able to relax a little. She would sing for the Empress Marie-Louise, of course, since that was why she had been invited, but she hoped that she would be able to enjoy the company of cultured women, too, at least for a little while. She so rarely had an opportunity to forget about the attentions of the many men in Vienna who were hoping to bed her.

The Tsar she could happily forget, for he was a man who took his pleasures easily, using his wealth and power to buy any woman he wanted. Lord Leo? Lord Leo was different. He was a rake, of course. Any woman of sense could tell that. And yet he had qualities Sophie did not associate with rakes. For a start, he had been kind to a woman who had gone out of her way to insult him. And then there was that kiss, burning through her glove…

Just the memory of it set her pulse racing. She glanced down at her gloved hand. The back of it felt as if it were on fire, and even hotter than it had two nights ago, when Lord Leo's lips had touched her. Only her glove, not her skin, and yet that kiss seemed to have been burning its way through during all the hours since he had left her. She was tempted to remove her glove again, to check her heated skin. Would there be a mark now, an impression of his lips? It felt as if there should be.

She shook her head, desperately trying to dismiss

him from her unruly thoughts. She must forget him. He was only another rake. She must not allow his practised charm to beguile her. She must concentrate on her work.

But the carriage was already bowling up the approach to the palace. It was utterly magnificent, much grander than she had imagined. In Vienna itself, the palaces and mansions were squeezed in among ancient rows of houses, but here, in the countryside, there were no such limitations. Schönbrunn was a vast, winged edifice of decorated stone, warmed by the late autumn sun, its myriad windows gleaming and sparkling like polished gemstones. In spite of its size, and the ornate rococo façade, there was something welcoming about it. Schönbrunn looked like a place designed for comfortable, family life. Probably just the home that Bonaparte's wife needed for herself and her infant son.

The carriage drove through the twin obelisks marking the entrance to the parade court. It was making for the central grand staircase leading up to the *piano nobile*, but it soon turned aside for the small ground-floor entrance used by common visitors and servants. Sophie was used to such humiliations, but it still hurt to be treated like a servant. She alighted from the carriage with her head held very high, determined to do her best to behave like the aristocratic lady she truly was. A liveried servant led her through the bare stone hallway, explaining that her Imperial Majesty was engaged at present, but would receive her shortly. Would *madame* like to be shown to a saloon to refresh herself?

Sophie glanced round. The sun was shining through the rear doorway and the palace's beautiful gardens looked most inviting. She had no desire to be made to wait in a room used by the senior servants. 'No, thank you,' she replied. 'I have a mind to take a turn outside while the weather is so fine.'

For some reason, the gardens were almost empty, in spite of the fact that the people of Vienna were allowed to wander there at will. Sophie strolled through the great parterre, admiring the geometric patterns of the late summer flowers. She was tempted by the huge Neptune fountain below the Gloriette, but she dare not go so far from the palace. She wandered instead in the tree-shaded pathways at the edges of the parterre.

She had been outside for about a quarter of an hour when she heard a high-pitched cry. Was it her summons? Shading her eyes against the low autumn sunshine, Sophie scrutinised the alleyways carefully. Nothing.

But then another joyous shout gave her the direction. Over by the back of the palace, partly hidden by the columns supporting the first-floor balcony, she could see two indistinct figures, one of them very small. A child. He must be the young son of Marie-Louise and Napoleon Bonaparte and the centre of all that monster's hopes. Should she approach him? He was hardly more than an infant, perhaps a little over three years old, but he might already have been taught to be as arrogant and imperious as his sire.

The boy came running to meet Sophie as soon as he realised that she was obeying his summons. He was smiling broadly at her, but when they were a few yards apart, he stopped dead and bowed most prettily. Without hesitation, Sophie dropped him a curtsy. It was fitting for the offspring of an Emperor, even one who had lost his throne.

The child came forward with his hand outstretched. *'Madame,'* he said in French, 'welcome to Schönbrunn. May I invite you to view my battle?'

For several minutes, the child concentrated on explaining to Sophie exactly how his soldiers were set out, and why. He was a precocious child, Sophie decided, particularly in military matters. Perhaps that was not surprising, given the brilliance of his sire on the field?

'Now, you must meet Maman Quiou-quiou,' he said, taking Sophie's hand to pull her across to his dozing companion. 'Maman Quiou-quiou,' he said loudly, tugging at the older lady's skirts. 'Maman Quiou-quiou, we have a visitor.'

The elderly lady woke with a start, automatically reaching up to straighten her lace cap. She blinked sleepily a couple of times. Then, as her eyes focused on Sophie, they became sharp and hard. She rose to her feet. 'I am the Comtesse de Montesquiou, governess to the Prince Napoleon, King of Rome. And you, madame?'

Sophie curtsied. 'My name is Sophia Pietre. I have been bidden to Schönbrunn to sing for her Imperial Majesty.'

The countess frowned forbiddingly, and Sophie waited for the inevitable dismissal. But the little prince said, in his piping voice, 'Maman Quiou-quiou, this lady is my new friend. *Madame* and I have been discussing the dispositions of my battle.'

It seemed that a friendship had been sealed.

As the last note of the string accompaniment died away, Sophie sank into a deep curtsy. Marie-Louise had been born an Austrian Archduchess and had become Empress of France on her marriage. She would expect nothing less.

Marie-Louise, clapping enthusiastically, rose from her chair and came across to Sophie. She offered her hand most graciously. 'My dear Madame Pietre,' she said in her clear voice, 'that was absolutely splendid. So affecting. I understand now why they call you a nightingale.' She led the way into the small Rosa room next door and waved Sophie to a seat. Sophie was relieved. She felt uncomfortable towering over an Empress.

'Tell me, *madame*, about that last aria you sang. It was most beautiful, but I do not recall having heard it before.'

'It is from an opera by a Viennese composer, Herr van Beethoven, your Imperial Majesty,' Sophie said carefully. 'His compositions are not often given, I believe, even here in Austria. I think he is seen as…difficult.'

'But tell me about Herr van Beethoven's opera. What is it called?'

'It is called *Fidelio*, your Majesty. And it is the story of—' Sophie swallowed a gasp. Why on earth had she chosen an aria from *that* opera? It was much too close to home for the ex-empress.

'Madame?' The Empress leaned forward, her eyebrows raised.

Sophie had to go on. 'It is the story of…of a faithful wife, your Majesty, who assumes the disguise of a boy, Fidelio, to seek out her husband who has been…er…unjustly imprisoned.' Sophie had only just avoided saying 'beloved husband imprisoned by a tyrant'. That certainly would not do here, since

Bonaparte had been exiled with the agreement of Marie-Louise's own father, the Austrian Emperor, and Marie-Louise herself had done nothing at all to help her husband since his exile to Elba.

'And does she succeed?' There was a degree of childlike eagerness in Marie-Louise's voice.

Looking up, Sophie saw that her hostess's face was full of animation. There was not the least hint of guile or irritation. Perhaps the gossips in Vienna had been right when they said that the Empress was not at all clever? Perhaps she had failed to see the parallel with her own situation?

'Yes, your Majesty, she does succeed. Fidelio finds work at the prison where her husband, and many other brave men, are being held. She helps to free them all. And while she is doing that, the daughter of the governor of the gaol falls in love with her.' Sophie allowed herself to smile, and was pleased to see that it was returned. 'A singularly inconvenient love affair, of course, since the woman dressed as the boy Fidelio dare not spurn the governor's daughter.'

The Empress laughed. 'I can imagine.' She paused for a moment. 'And does it end happily? The couple are together? And free?'

Sophie swallowed. 'Yes, your Majesty. It seems that Herr van Beethoven likes to write happy music. He is a remarkable man.' That was a safe topic, well away from happy, reunited couples. 'I understand that he is totally deaf, and yet the music he writes is full of soaring power, and…and joy.'

The Empress was nodding, with a slightly far-away look in her eyes. 'The couple are reunited,' she said softly. 'And free. Yes, I see.' With a swift movement, she rose and moved across to the window to look out on to the gardens.

Sophie rose immediately, as did everyone else in the room. They stood around a little awkwardly, waiting to see what the Empress would do. At the long window, Marie-Louise stood motionless for a long time, silhouetted against the light. It made a kind of halo through the outermost curls of her fine, fair hair.

Sophie's heart was beating very fast now. If disaster struck, it would be the result of her own stupidity.

The Empress turned back to face them. She was smiling.

Sophie's heartbeat skipped, then raced, then began to slow. She dared to breathe again.

'I can see that I shall have to learn more of Herr van Beethoven's joyous music, Madame Pietre. If the musicians are still in the music room—' she nodded to her lady-in-waiting, who immediately curtsied and left the room '—I should very much like to hear the *Fidelio* aria again. Now that I understand its meaning, I imagine I will enjoy it so much more.'

Sophie gulped. She had given Bonaparte's wife treasonous ideas of freedom, and of happy, reunited couples, while her father, the Austrian Emperor, was bent on ensuring that no reunion would ever take place.

'And after we have listened to your recital, we shall be able to talk about music over a glass of wine. I hope you are not engaged elsewhere today?'

Sophie agreed that she was not.

'Good. We will send to the city for a valise of whatever you may need for tonight. We have so few truly interesting visitors here at Schönbrunn.'

'Your Majesty, I—' Sophie was at a loss.

The Empress had misinterpreted Sophie's hesitation. 'I know that a nightingale's voice is easily tired. Sing to me from *Fidelio*, just once more, and I promise I will be satisfied.'

It was a royal command. Sophie curtsied low and led the way back into the glittering white-and-gold splendour of the Grand Rosa room.

Chapter Six

'The Nightingale has escaped from her cage.' Jack sounded pleased with himself.

'What do you mean, "escaped"?' Leo asked sharply.

Jack's smile widened. 'The first thing her coachman told me, after I'd greased him in the fist, was that he had the day off. His mistress had been driven to Schönbrunn in the Empress Marie-Louise's own coach to sing there. Without Verdicchio. The coachman said the Nightingale looked remarkably content as she left.'

'Did she now?' Leo allowed himself a small smile. 'That could be of use to us. Did your man say when his mistress was expected to return?'

'He said she had no engagements for this evening, if that's what you mean. So it might be late. Why do you ask?'

'Because, if we're going to have any chance of re-cruiting her, we need to meet her again without arousing suspicions. Especially from Verdicchio.'

Jack nodded.

'Any other men we might use to watch her house? Apart from the coachman, I mean?'

'I had one there. But when she left for Schönbrunn, I stood him down.'

'Send him back,' Leo ordered. 'He's to report to you as soon as she returns. And he's to find out what she'll be doing over the next few days. Get him to butter up her other servants. We need to know much more about Madame Pietre.'

Jack hurried out without another word. He was looking very serious about his duties now, Leo was glad to see. Responsibility seemed to suit him after all.

Leo strode over to the window and looked down into the square. Jack had already disappeared. No doubt he and Ben would meet later to discuss progress.

And Leo? What was he to do? There was no point now in trying to find another woman to warm his bed. He had spent much of the previous evening doing precisely that. The noble lady had been beautiful and well versed in the rules of the game, but by the time Leo had delivered her to her door, all desire had vanished. She was the wrong woman. He had bid her goodnight and left.

Now here he was, pacing up and down, wondering how on earth he was to ensnare the beautiful Madame Pietre. He was neglecting his duties. He should be planning their next moves, making sure that the British had the best possible chance of outfoxing the Russians. But every time he stopped for a moment, his mind was filled with the sight, and the scent, of Sophie Pietre. No other woman would do.

The door slammed back on its hinges as Jack dashed in. His face was flushed with exertion. 'She's staying there!' he gasped.

'What do you mean? Where?'

'The Empress's coach has just returned empty. Her maid climbed in, carrying a valise, and then it was off again. Back to Schönbrunn.'

Leo's eyebrows shot up in surprise. 'An opera singer staying with an ex-empress? Are you sure, Jack?'

Jack was breathing almost normally again. 'Absolutely sure, Leo. Spoke to her coachman myself. He said that Marie-Louise was so taken with the Nightingale's singing that she has invited her to remain at Schönbrunn for at least one night. Having heard her sing, can't say that I'm surprised. Are you?'

No, Leo was not surprised. He too longed to command the Nightingale to stay and sing, just for him. Preferably in a room with a bed in it!

He cleared his throat harshly, trying to control his unruly thoughts. 'And what is Verdicchio doing while his golden goose is elsewhere? I'd lay money he's plotting something.'

'I thought the same. I've left Ben on watch. And with all these sudden developments, I thought it best not to stand the paid man down. Who knows? Verdicchio may go skulking around the city at any moment. I hope I did right, Leo.' Jack sounded suddenly a little anxious.

'Absolutely right.' Leo nodded reassuringly. 'We're pretty short of the readies, but we daren't let that influence what we do. If the Nightingale is getting close to Bonaparte's wife, anything might happen.'

At least if she was still at Schönbrunn, she couldn't be in Verdicchio's bed. Or anyone else's.

Or so Leo fervently hoped.

* * *

It was late next day by the time the Schönbrunn carriage brought Sophie back to the outskirts of Vienna. Another glorious, golden autumn afternoon such as few could remember. It seemed that the weather had decided to welcome all the royal visitors and to show them Vienna and the Danube in their fairest garb. The trees still held their leaves, the waters of the Danube sparkled, and the people wore their gay summer clothes, daring winter to approach with its icy fingers.

It had been a most remarkable visit: the opera singer being treated as the honoured guest of an empress. They had talked long into the evening, about literature, and music and places they both knew. Marie-Louise's ladies had remained largely silent, many of them frowning darkly when their mistress's eye was not upon them. But Marie-Louise was eager and excited to talk of things beyond the confines of her extravagant prison.

Today, Sophie had been surprised to be invited to take a light luncheon with the Empress and her son. She had suspected it was largely at the little boy's urging, though Marie-Louise was polite and welcoming. Then, as Sophie was about to take her leave, came the greatest surprise of all. She was invited to come again, and often, to play with the Prince and to entertain the mother.

At first, Sophie had been unable to understand such an invitation. It was not fitting. But then she recognised the shadow of loneliness in Marie-Louise's eyes. She was surrounded by French retainers, all totally devoted to Napoleon Bonaparte, her husband. She seemed to have no one about her in whom she could safely confide. Was that what she hoped for in Sophia

Pietre? It would be very strange if it were so, but strange things happened in royal households.

As the coach drove into the walled city, Sophie wondered what Verdicchio might have been up to while she was at Schönbrunn. 'Was Maestro Verdicchio engaged during my absence yesterday, Teresa?' she asked innocently.

Teresa started. She had been almost asleep, rocked by the gentle movement of the sumptuous imperial carriage. 'He was out, *madame*, but I do not know where. I did hear him say that he was hopeful of a very good engagement for you.'

Oh dear. Sophie swallowed. Verdicchio's idea of a good engagement might be a recital in the theatre or a performance in some man's bed.

'Will you be going out this evening, *madame*? I hung out your red silk gown before I left for Schönbrunn yesterday. Just in case.'

Sophie smiled. 'There are no engagements this evening that I am aware of, Teresa. As soon as we return to the apartment, I will take a bath, I think. In the meantime, you will go to the maestro, if you please, and ask him whether anything is planned. In that way, we shall make the most of the time available, for it is already quite late.'

'Yes, *madame*.' Then, with a little grin, 'Perhaps the maestro will have arranged tickets for another of the grand balls. It is splendid for you to be able to meet the Tsar and the King of Prussia and the King of Denmark and the—'

'Yes, Teresa, but it is also difficult. Remember, I am only an opera singer. Kings and princes do not entertain opera singers. Not in public, that is.'

'Oh. But the coachman said that you had danced with the Tsar.'

'Did he, indeed? Well, the coachman was mistaken. I spoke with the Tsar. Or rather, he spoke with me, to compliment me upon my singing. But that was all. The Tsar of All the Russias does not consort with a mere opera singer.'

But he would if he could, said a small voice in the back of her head. *He would if he could. And if Verdicchio has anything to do with it, he will.*

Jack and Ben were making their report. 'She arrived back from Schönbrunn in the early evening, in the Empress Marie-Louise's carriage, the one with the imperial crest,' Jack said. 'She is not a very clever woman.'

'What do you mean?' Leo snapped.

'The Empress, I mean, not the Nightingale. Marie-Louise does not seem to notice how the Austrian people resent her flaunting her status as the Empress of France. She refuses to revert to being an Austrian Archduchess. Not only does she have Bonaparte's imperial crest upon her carriage, her servants all wear his livery.'

'But more important,' Ben broke in, 'is that we found out about the Nightingale's plans.'

Leo's stomach lurched. 'Go on,' he managed.

'While the Nightingale was at Schönbrunn—and we still have to discover precisely why she was there so long—Verdicchio was closeted with the Tsar Alexander's retainers. As we suspected, the Tsar hopes to bed the Nightingale. He has requested a recital. A private recital, in his rooms in the imperial palace.'

Leo felt as if all the blood in his body had drained

to his feet. He had known this would come. And yet...
'Tell me more. When is it to be?'

'Day after tomorrow, by all accounts,' Ben said.

'Mind you,' Jack put in, 'the prospect of bedding the
Nightingale hasn't stopped the Tsar from visiting his
other mistresses. He was at the Princess Bagration's
palace yesterday.'

'That's not surprising,' Ben said. 'She's a Russian,
after all.'

'But he was at the Duchess of Sagan's in the afternoon. And she is a German,' Jack added triumphantly.

'And also the paramour of the head of the French
delegation here,' Leo added with a frown. 'Very
murky waters. Heaven knows what the Tsar might
find out by that route.' He shook his head, trying to
concentrate on politics rather than on the desires of
his increasingly ungovernable body. 'However,
France is of no immediate importance to us. We must
concentrate on the Tsar. There seems to be no limit
to his appetite for beautiful women. He has power,
and they are attracted by it.'

'He has charm, too,' Ben said. 'Have you seen him
dance? He whirls all the beautiful women of Vienna into
the waltz and makes every single one of them feel as
though she is the most important in the city. It is a great
gift.'

'Aye,' Leo snarled. 'It is a great gift. For a monarch.'

'Or for a rake,' Jack said, with a laugh. 'I seem to
recall that you have it, too, although it has not been
much in evidence since our arrival here. Never known
you go so long without a woman, Leo.'

That was much too near the knuckle. Leo slammed
his closed fist down on the table. 'We are not here to

amuse ourselves, Jack. We are here to discover information that will be useful to the British government.'

Jack had the grace to look a little sheepish.

'I will dance with beautiful ladies when it serves our purposes. Otherwise, I will spend my time—as you two should—seeking information. Now, we need to know more about this assignation between the Nightingale and the Tsar. Find out exactly when it is to be, and who is to go.'

'She'll go on her own, surely?' Jack said.

'No. If it is a recital, she needs someone to play. Now, that could be Verdicchio, or someone else altogether. We need to know. Make sure you have a man outside the Nightingale's apartment at all times, whether she is there or not. We need to watch Verdicchio as well. Report to me as soon as you have any more information. This is too important for any mistakes.'

The two younger men, now looking rather chastened, rose and left the room. As the door closed behind them, Leo sprang to his feet and began to pace, cursing viciously all the while.

She was going to become the Tsar's mistress! Damn her! And damn him, too, with all his power and wealth and charm. He had already bedded half the aristocratic women in Vienna, and the rest were panting to fall into his arms. So why did he have to lust after a mere opera singer? Was it just to prove that he could have her, while others could not?

A shadow of distaste flickered across Sophie's face as she gazed at her reflection in the glass. She looked like a fairground whore decked out in all her tawdry tinker's gewgaws. The only difference was that every one of the gewgaws—every single last bauble Sophie wore—was real. She had managed to find a way of wearing almost every piece of jewellery she owned. Even some of her earrings had been pinned together into a sort of crude hair ornament. It was her insurance for this unwelcome visit to Tsar Alexander. If it did not go well, she might have to flee Vienna with only the clothes she stood up in.

Verdicchio had insisted that she attend this private rendezvous. She, in turn, had insisted that Verdicchio attend as her accompanist and that her own carriage, with her own maid, driven by her own coachman, should wait for her at the imperial palace. She was not prepared to risk being stranded there.

For at least the third time, she checked that her small store of ready money was concealed in the pocket beneath her evening gown along with her little pistol. She might need that on the road if she were forced to flee. She wore her poison ring, too, containing a good dose of the potion she always carried on such occasions. It would not kill a man—she was no murderess—but it would certainly incapacitate him long enough for her to escape. She had used it on two previous occasions, though Verdicchio had never learned of it. The gentlemen in question had been much too embarrassed to admit they had been bested by a mere woman, and an opera singer at that.

'Bring me my black velvet cloak, Teresa. The one with the hood.'

The evening was warm, and the heavy cloak would have been unnecessary, except that Sophie needed it to conceal all the jewels she wore. If Verdicchio saw them, he might be astute enough to work out Sophie's reasoning. So she would remove the cloak only once she was in the presence of the Tsar himself. By then, it would be much too late for Verdicchio to say or do anything.

Sophie squared her shoulders and raised the hood to cover her hair and the excess of jewellery blazing there. She was ready.

Sophie ended the recital with the aria from *Fidelio* that she had sung for Marie-Louise, though it did not sound as good, with only the pianoforte accompaniment. As her final note died away, she sank into a deep curtsy. So far, her plan had worked better than she had dared to hope, but what would happen now?

There was a short pause, a near silence in which the only sounds were the fading echoes of the pianoforte. Then the silence became total.

She waited.

Tsar Alexander began to applaud loudly. He had risen to his feet. He was beaming at her, and the enthusiasm in his face was at least partly due to his appreciation of her music. He was not a total philistine, it seemed.

'*Madame*, I had heard you sing before, but here, in my private quarters, the effect is magical, bewitching. At times you made my heart race. At times, I wanted to weep for the pathos in your beautiful voice. *Madame*, I am at your feet.' He bent down to take both her hands. As she rose, he lifted first one hand, then the other, to his lips, kissing her through her fine kid gloves. She felt nothing. When Leo had kissed her, she had burned. But for this man, no matter how great his power, she felt only disdain. And now she would discover his true intentions.

To her surprise, he crossed to ring the bell. The aide-de-camp appeared almost instantly.

'Bring champagne. *Madame* will be thirsty after singing for so long.' The ADC's gaze moved shiftily from Sophie to Verdicchio and back again. 'And for the maestro also,' the Tsar added, almost without a pause. 'He has played with great virtuosity. He deserves our thanks.'

The ADC returned, barely a minute later, with a tray of champagne and three crystal flutes. He presented the tray to the Tsar, who took two glasses so that he could offer one to Sophie with his own hand.

Sophie allowed herself a small sip of the champagne. Looking up into the Tsar's eyes, she said, with a bland but encouraging smile, 'Your Majesty, the champagne is splendid, of course, but might I have some water also? I find that only water salves my throat after a recital.'

The Tsar waved a hand to his aide-de-camp.

Sophie quickly downed half a tumbler of the iced water he brought and felt much better. 'Thank you,' she said. And this time she meant it.

'Perhaps you would care to sit, *madame*? You have been standing throughout the recital, unlike the maestro and I. I imagine you are a little weary.'

It did not matter that she was not. She inclined her head and moved towards a single gilt chair, near the instrument.

The Tsar was too quick for her. 'Ah, no, *madame*, I cannot allow you to sit there, for the light is too poor, and I would be unable to admire your beauty.' He caught up her hand and led her to the sofa from which he had listened to her recital.

Unable to resist, Sophie took her seat on the sofa. Unfortunately, there would be plenty of room for the Tsar to join her. 'Maestro, would you be good enough to put the water where I may reach it? You know that I shall need to drink yet more.'

Verdicchio set the silver tray on the small gilt table alongside the sofa.

'But you must not forget your champagne, *madame*.' The Tsar caught up Sophie's glass and brought it to her.

She took it, trying not to seem unwilling. She even put it to her lips and took the smallest possible sip.

The Tsar did not sit. Instead, he stretched out his hand to Verdicchio, who had to set down his champagne glass in order to make his bow. Sophie found herself admiring the manoeuvre. The Tsar was clearly practised at this.

'I am most grateful to you, Maestro,' the Tsar said, 'and I shall ask my ADC to arrange a future recital of some of your own compositions.'

Verdicchio was beginning to flush in response to the Tsar's blatant flattery.

'But, for this evening, it is not possible. Thank you again. I bid you *adieu*.'

Verdicchio bowed once more and walked backwards to the door. Sophie prayed that he would keep his promise—the only real concession she had been able to extract from him—that he would leave her carriage in the courtyard and make his own way home. She raised her eyebrows at him. He responded with a tiny nod. Was there a shadow of compassion in his face at the thought of leaving her to the mercy of this man? It could not be. Verdicchio felt compassion for no one.

But he might, perhaps, keep his word.

Chapter Seven

Leo took an even larger swig of his wine and set the glass down on the scrubbed wooden table. The wine in this hostelry had not improved, but he had no real taste for beer. He had no real taste for anything, if truth were to be told. He had lost all patience, and most of his ability to think logically.

And where the devil were Jack and Ben? They should have reported back long before now. The Honours had only this one night to persuade Madame Pietre to help them, for tomorrow night she would have her tryst with the Russian Emperor. It had to be now, much though it disgusted Leo. His duty to his country had to come before his own desires. If Jack or Ben could discover where she was going this evening, Leo might be able to manufacture a chance encounter and have private words with her.

If I do find her, I will not be distracted by her beauty or my own desire for her. I will not! I have known enough women over the years, and I have never lost control with any of them. I refuse to allow Sophie Pietre to change that.

He took another gulp of wine. It almost choked him. The wine was sour, the inn was hot, and it smelt of rank bodies. He could not bear to sit and wait. Throwing some coins on to the table, he flung himself out of his chair and marched out into the blessed freshness of the square.

And now what? He could not leave, for this was the agreed rendezvous with Jack and Ben. Leo was the leader. It was time he started behaving like one.

Frustrated and increasingly angry at his own failings, he began to pace up and down the square, caring not a whit for what any onlookers might think of him. One local threw him a very strange look, but there must have been something forbidding in Leo's face, for the man ducked as if he had received a blow and scurried away.

Leo continued to pace. After some minutes, he realised that he was punching his clenched right fist into the palm of his left. How long had he been doing that? His painful left hand suggested it had been some time. Yet he had been totally unaware of it. For, in spite of all his endeavours, his thoughts continued to be fixed on the ebony-haired Venetian.

The Tsar turned back to Sophie and looked down at her enquiringly.

It suddenly occurred to her that she should not be seated while he stood. He was an anointed monarch, after all, even if a lecherous one. She jumped up guiltily. She had a feeling that she was blushing, too. Unfortunately, the Tsar was quite likely to read all sorts of sexual messages into a lady's blush, especially when that lady had consented to be alone with him in his private apartment.

The situation was getting worse and worse, like a trap closing in on her. Verdicchio was gone. Only the Tsar's servants were within earshot, and they would surely be conveniently deaf. Tsar Alexander himself stood between Sophie and the door.

I will not give in to him.

The words swirled and echoed in her brain. She clung to them as to a talisman. Her virtue, her honour, were her own. If, one day, she yielded them, it would not be at the urging of a man she could not esteem, emperor or no.

'Madame Pietre, I beg of you, please, to resume your seat. We are quite alone now. And we shall not be disturbed.'

No, I'm sure you have made absolutely sure of that.

'I would not have you stand on ceremony when we are alone. I may be an emperor, but I am also a man. And you are a most beautiful and desirable lady. When you sang, my heart was at your feet. Now, when I have but a fading memory of that wonderful voice, I would gladly lay more than my heart at your feet.'

Courage! But be careful of this man. He does not expect to be refused, and you cannot predict how he will react when you do.

'Pray, *madame*,' he said again, advancing towards her, 'resume your seat.' He fixed her with his gaze until she did so, then crossed to the tray where the champagne stood and topped up both their glasses. 'It has been a glorious evening so far, *madame*.' He held out Sophie's flute to her. 'And if you are willing, it can be more glorious yet. Will you allow me to propose a toast?'

Sophie took the proffered glass, forcing her hand to remain steady. This was just another performance. As an accomplished actress, she would make it one of her best. 'A toast, sire?' She was looking up at him through her lashes, trying to sound flirtatious.

'Aye, *madame*. To your beauty. And to our better acquaintance.'

'Leo is going to be furious. Again,' Jack hissed, as he and Ben hurried along the narrow streets leading to the Gasthof Brunner.

'It wasn't your fault,' Ben said. 'The information seemed reliable enough last night. What reason did we have to doubt it?'

'Won't matter a jot. He'll still be furious. And he'll blame me for being irresponsible. For failing to be thorough.' Jack sighed. 'Maybe he's right.'

'What you need is a drink.' Ben grinned suddenly, which made him look extremely young. 'Since we appear to have missed the boat on this one, maybe Leo will allow us a decent supper and some good wine for a change. After all, there's nothing else we can do, is there?'

They rounded the last corner. Jack grabbed Ben's coat and pulled him to a shuddering halt. He pointed to the far side of the square. 'See the way Leo's pacing? He's absolutely seething. I'd wager his anger is directed at you and me.'

Ben paled a little.

'Don't worry,' Jack said ruefully. 'He won't take it out on you. Not when he has me to kick. Come on. Let's get it over with.'

Leo immediately launched into a flood of questions. 'Where the devil have you been? Why have you taken so long? Confound it, how on earth are we to—?'

'Leo! Keep your voice down!' Jack said hurriedly. He was astonished that Leo should take such a risk. Normally he was the careful, calculating one.

In response, Leo lowered his voice. 'What do you have to report?'

'Not here,' Jack said urgently. 'Somewhere less public. There.' He led the way to the shadowy alley alongside their inn. It was dark enough. No one would notice them there, especially if Leo kept his voice down. 'Leo, I'm sorry, but… Oh, blister it, we…we were misled. We thought we had tonight to persuade the Nightingale to work with us. We don't. Her assignation. It's for tonight.'

Jack fully expected to feel the angry lash of Leo's tongue. A few choice curses, at the least. But Leo's reaction was totally out of character. He said not a word. All Jack heard was a sharp intake of breath, hissing between clenched teeth. Then Leo's clenched fist struck out at him.

Leo's blow might have broken Jack's jaw if it had made contact properly. But he instinctively dodged sideways. Leo's fist struck him only a glancing blow. 'Leo!' Jack gasped, staggering backwards.

'For God's sake, Leo!' Ben cried. 'What are you doing?'

In the half-light of the alley, Jack saw a wave of horror pass across his brother's features. What on earth could have provoked such a reaction? Leo was normally a man who never lost control.

'Jack, I…I'm sorry.' Leo's voice was very gruff and not totally steady. 'I don't know what— I'm sorry. It's just so frustrating, and— I shouldn't have taken my anger out on you. I know you're doing your best.' He smiled weakly.

Jack could see that Leo was struggling to come to terms with what he had just done. Jack was struggling with it, too. He had always looked up to his older brothers. They were the leaders, the planners. Jack was just a foot-soldier in their little band, content to allow Dominic and Leo to make the decisions. Now, suddenly, brother Leo had shown he was far from infallible. Jack was truly shaken. Did that mean he would have to rely on himself in future?

Jack straightened his shoulders and gingerly put a hand to his jaw. With luck, Leo had not made a good enough contact to leave a noticeable bruise.

Sophie was feeling, yet again, that nervous desire to giggle. The Tsar of All the Russias was a charming and practised lover, with too much finesse to throw himself upon her, as some men had done. He really was trying to seduce her, even though he clearly assumed that she was a willing partner in this assignation.

The trouble was that she was running out of excuses and ways of delaying the critical moment. She had complained about the heat, she had had him send for more water, she had paced up and down the room, claiming that sitting still for more than a few minutes made her back ache. On every occasion, the Tsar had smiled and complied with her wishes, seemingly most anxious for her comfort.

And now she was sitting on his sofa once again. He was looming over her, greedily gazing at the exposed expanse of breast revealed by her gown. She felt as if he were stripping her naked.

'May I sit, *madame*?'

'Of course, your Majesty.' He took his place elegantly, tugging down the front of his tightly tailored uniform jacket so that it sat without a wrinkle around his chest and waist.

He wishes me to admire his person as well as to yield to his lust.

The Tsar reached across for the champagne glass that Sophie had set down almost untouched. 'You are not a lover of champagne, *madame*?'

Sophie shook her head. 'I fear not, sire. I find the bubbles sometimes irritate my throat. For a singer, you understand, that is dangerous.'

He smiled, rather knowingly, Sophie thought, but he did set her glass down once more. Unfortunately, that freed his hand. He laid his fingers against the side of her jaw and stroked gently down to the jewels around her neck. 'It is a most beautiful throat that produces a glorious sound. I would not, for the world, have it harmed in any way.' His smile widened a fraction.

Sophie's natural reaction was to pull away from those encircling fingers, but she did not dare.

Without moving any other part of his body, or even his fingers, the Tsar raised his thumb and began to caress the line of Sophie's jaw.

This time she shivered. She could not suppress it.

'Beautiful.' His eyes were almost black now. Passion was driving him.

Sophie had no doubt about his intentions. His erection was blatantly outlined by the tight-fitting breeches of his dress uniform.

'Beautiful,' he said again, allowing his hand to slither slowly down her throat towards her breasts.

I must stop him. I am going to be ill.

'A figure such as yours, *madame*,' he murmured, his

eyes now fixed on her bosom, 'deserves to be seen in all its glory.'

His hand crept lower. He leant his head forward, towards her mouth. His own lips were opening. They were wet, and thick, and very red.

'And your mouth, my dear Sophie...' He touched his lips to hers.

It was too much. Sophie's free arm, flailing in the empty space, lighted upon the jug of iced water. She seized it and threw the contents into his lap.

The Tsar gasped and flung himself back from her, too shocked to say a word. His eyes were staring and his mouth hung open.

Sophie made up her mind on the instant. She rose from the sofa with as much dignity as she could muster. She dropped him a small, haughty curtsy. Then she deliberately turned her back on him. She marched to the door, knocking over his champagne glass in the process. It fell to the floor with a satisfying crash.

It was over! She was free. And her honour was still her own.

Leo arrived alone outside Madame Pietre's apartment. He had been unable to remain with Jack and Ben. He, Leo Aikenhead, temporary leader of the Aikenhead Honours, had attempted to floor his own brother because he was incapable of restraining his lust for a Venetian whore. Worse, his obsession was risking his duty to his country and the whole mission.

He had walked alone, all the way from his lodgings to the Nightingale's apartment. He needed the time to come to terms with his own folly. At least, the shock had brought him back to reality. He felt as if someone had tipped a pail of iced water over him. He knew now what he must do, what he *would* do.

He stationed himself in the shadows opposite the entrance to Madame Pietre's rooms. He was here as a spy. Nothing more. He would watch until he saw her leave to meet the Russian Emperor. If he had a chance, he would climb into the carriage with her and attempt to persuade her to help England. But he would not consider her person. Not in any way. She was a pawn in this dangerous diplomatic game. And pawns were, by their nature, disposable.

His rebellious brain tried to remind him that pawns could be queened, that they could become the most powerful piece on the board. But this time, he was able to dismiss it. The salutary effect of that iced water was still with him.

After fifteen minutes of watching no movement at all, Leo began to worry. Could it be that she had already left? There was one way to find out. Jack and Ben had stationed one of their men here, with orders to remain, even if the Nightingale left. Their man would know what was going on.

Leo scanned the square and the various streets around it. There were several men lounging around, some in gossiping couples, some alone. A couple of them were standing smoking, apparently enjoying the evening breeze. Was it one of those? Dammit, Leo did not know. He did not even know who his own spies were. He was clearly losing his grip.

What to do? He could wait here, in hopes that the Nightingale had yet to emerge and that he might have a chance to speak to her. Or he could go to the imperial palace and wait outside the Tsar's apartments. Perhaps the Nightingale's carriage would be there? It certainly was not here.

He was just on the point of leaving for the palace when a voice whispered in his ear, 'Leo.'

'Jack?' Leo was relieved to see that Jack was smiling at him, in just his old way. As far as he could see in the half-light, there was no bruise or swelling on Jack's face. Leo felt himself reddening at the very thought of what he had done.

'Have you spoken to our man?' Jack asked.

Leo decided it was time to eat humble pie. 'Afraid I stupidly forgot to ask you what he looked like. Sorry. Which one is he?'

Jack nodded in the direction of a man leaning lazily against a wall. 'The one in the tobacco-brown frock coat. Perhaps I should have a word with him? He knows me, you see.' He strolled nonchalantly across to the agent.

He soon returned. 'The Nightingale and Verdicchio left together some considerable time ago. Our man does not know where they were going.'

'But we do,' Leo growled.

'More interesting, though, is that Verdicchio returned alone, by chair, some twenty minutes ago.'

Leo tried unsuccessfully to suppress the groan that rose in his throat.

Jack threw him a puzzled sideways glance. 'You're right,' he said. 'We've missed our opportunity to enlist her services.' He paused thoughtfully. 'But there may still be a chance. I'm sure that the Tsar will wish to bed her more than once. Unless she's a complete failure on her back, of course.'

Leo swallowed hard.

'In fact,' Jack continued, 'it could be better this way. If she has established herself as one of the Tsar's mistresses, she will be much more valuable to us. We can talk to her now, after it's all over. Don't you think?'

Leo said nothing while he tried to choke back his jealous anger and disgust. At length he said, 'Let's go to the imperial palace and see what's happening. For all we know, she may have left. The assignation may have come to nothing.'

Jack raised his eyebrows. 'You really think so?'

Leo found himself quite unable to reply.

Sophie tucked her cloak more closely around her shivering body. She had expected to meet the aide-de-camp or some of the Tsar's servants on her way out through the antechambers. But there was no one, apart from an ancient, toothless doorman at the top of the stairs by the entrance to the apartment. The Tsar had certainly prepared most carefully for her visit.

Finally, the double doors closed behind her and she was in the vast courtyard of the palace. Her carriage was still waiting. No doubt her coachman would complain about keeping the horses standing for so long. At that absurd thought, Sophie began to laugh. She, Sophia Pietre, fallen German aristocrat and so-called Venetian whore, had thrown a jug of icy water over the Tsar of All the Russias. It had certainly cooled his ardour. She laughed again, shrilly, at her own sardonic wit. At least she had not shot him, or drugged him. She had intended to. She had even dropped her potion into his glass. But he had been much more intent on her than on his champagne. He had failed to take even a sip of it.

Her coachman seemed to be asleep on the box. And the groom behind, also. Sophie hauled open the carriage door and climbed in, without assistance.

Teresa awoke with a start. '*Madame!* What is the matter?'

'Tell the coachman to whip up the horses. We are leaving Vienna. Now.'

Teresa's eyes widened. Then she stuck her head out of the open door and gave the order. The coach started to move before she had even closed the door.

Sophie sank into her corner and pulled the hood of her cloak more closely round her features. She needed to be in the dark, to hide from everyone.

The coach was moving, but not very swiftly. It still had to negotiate the archways from the courtyard to the square outside. But soon they would be on the open road. To freedom.

The carriage stopped. Sophie sat up straighter. 'Why have we stopped?'

'It must be for the gate, *madame*,' Teresa said soothingly.

There was no scrape of gates being pulled back. Instead, there was a rapping on the carriage door. A rapping as of a gentleman's cane. A moment later, the carriage door slowly began to open.

Chapter Eight

~~~~~~~~~~

'Isn't that her carriage?' Ben's voice carried much too clearly through the night air.

Leo stopped in his tracks and motioned Ben to silence. He looked all around, but could not see the purple carriage anywhere. 'Where? I don't see it.'

Ben pointed to the gate into the passage to the court-yard of the imperial palace.

The gates were closed. Looking more closely, however, Leo could see that a carriage and four was drawn up there, probably waiting for the guard to open the gates. The carriage was in shadow, but it looked to be of the same design as the Nightingale's. It might even be purple. It was impossible to tell.

'I'm sure it's hers,' Ben said confidently. 'I recognise the horses.'

Of course he does. Young men of his stamp think of precious little else.

Jack had joined them, too. 'Yes, that's the one. She's bound to be inside. She wouldn't venture out on foot at this time of night.' His smile was sardonic. 'Looks as if her meeting with the Emperor was just about long enough, doesn't it?'

Leo gritted his teeth. He was trying to think of a suitably cutting reply when he was distracted by the shadow behind the gate. That wasn't a soldier. The hat was wrong. And it was carrying a cane. By God, it looked like—!

The gates swung open. The carriage moved smoothly through and turned away from the palace. When Leo looked back at the gateway, there was no one to be seen, apart from the imperial guards.

'It *was* him,' he snarled in an undervoice. 'I know it was.'

'Leo?'

'By God!' Leo exclaimed. 'She's taken him up! Not content with one wealthy lover, she's taken up another. In the very same night! She deserves to be whipped at the cart's tail!'

Frowning, Jack laid a reassuring hand on Leo's arm. 'What on earth are you talking about, Leo? You're making no sense at all.'

Leo shook him off. 'It makes perfect sense,' he said bitterly. 'You said that opera singers were common whores, Ben.'

'I say! I—'

'Common whores,' Leo repeated, with savage emphasis. 'And the Venetian Nightingale, for all her beauty, is as common as the worst of them.'

'So… What do we do now?' Jack said quietly.

Leo stopped in surprise. Jack was not normally a man who spoke much common sense. Leo took a deep breath. 'I think,' he said slowly, 'that we give up for tonight. Her meeting with the Tsar is clearly over. So there is no great

urgency. Why don't you two go and find yourselves a
decent supper and a bottle or two of Hungarian? You
deserve it, after running yourselves ragged all day.'

Ben grinned. 'Splendid. Thank you, Leo. We—'

'But what about you?' Jack still sounded much more
serious than usual.

'Oh, I ate something earlier,' Leo lied. 'I fancy some
fresh air now. I'll see you later, back at our lodgings.
Don't wait up for me.'

Jack's eyes narrowed assessingly.

Leo had the strong impression that Jack did not
believe a word he said.

'If you say so, Leo,' Jack said quietly. Then he flung
an arm round Ben's shoulder and the two of them
strolled away, chatting in low voices. As they disappeared round the corner, Leo heard a burst of merry
laughter. Knave and Ten had forgotten their dangerous
mission already, it seemed. Leo, the King of the
Honours, found himself envying their carefree youth.
Until duty reasserted its grip.

*We have a mission. We must fulfil it. What on earth
are we going to do now?*

Leo gazed after the purple carriage. It should have
disappeared from view by now, but it seemed to have
stopped. He saw a man's head appear through the
window. No, he had not been mistaken! A curse on the
perfidy of all women!

The head disappeared and the carriage set off once
more. This time, it was moving remarkably slowly,
barely as fast as a man could walk. Very strange. Leo
immediately started after it. He did not dare to run, for
that would make him too conspicuous. But if he
hurried, he might reach it in a few hundred yards.

Maybe he would learn something of use to the Honours' mission?

He focused all his attention on overhauling the carriage. He had had enough of ifs and maybes. Once he reached it—*if* he reached it—then he would decide what to do. And God help that man if he crossed Leo this time!

He had climbed into the carriage without waiting for an invitation.

Sophie stiffened and frowned blackly at him, but he ignored that and calmly took the seat opposite her. 'You forget yourself, Baron,' she spat.

The Baron von Beck smiled languidly and reached out a long-fingered hand to close the carriage door. Lifting his silver-topped cane, he rapped on the roof.

To her fury, Sophie heard the gates open. Her carriage began to move. She began to panic. Would her coachman obey her earlier order to leave Vienna? She could not afford for the Baron to know what she intended.

'Pull the string, Teresa,' she said sharply. 'The Baron is leaving us. Now.'

Teresa reached for the check-string, but the Baron leaned across to grab her wrist. The poor woman cried out in pain. It was no gentle grasp.

'Let her go, Baron.' She refused to let him suspect her fear.

'Certainly,' he replied smoothly. 'Once I have ensured that our little journey together will take place as *I* wish.'

Teresa yelped as his grip tightened yet further. Sophie glared at him. She hated this slimy, vicious man.

But when Teresa moaned again, Sophie had no option but to yield. 'Very well. I will give you ten minutes, Baron. But my maid remains with us. Now, let her go.'

His thin-lipped smile broadened, but his eyes were still hard as flint. 'If I may say so, *madame*,' he said silkily, 'that was a wise decision.' He dropped Teresa's hand as if it had been diseased and stopped the coach himself with another rap of his heavy cane. He pushed down the window glass. 'Drive in the direction of the Prater bridge,' he ordered the coachman. 'Very slowly. *Madame* is in no hurry this evening.' With that, he threw up the glass again.

Sophie pushed herself as far back into her seat as she could, trying to maximise the distance between them. But his knees were almost touching hers. The space between the benches seemed to have shrunk.

He was taking his time. He removed his hat, smoothed it, and laid it reverently on the seat beside him, along with his cane. He was extravagantly dressed, as ever, determined to flaunt his wealth in every stitch of clothing he wore. His lace was priceless. The large pin in his cravat contained a huge, pigeon's-blood ruby and enough diamonds to fill a casket.

The silence lengthened. Sophie refused to be the one to break it, knowing Beck would take it as a sign of weakness. Instead, she schooled her features into an expression of calm superiority, fixed her gaze on the Baron's hat, and waited.

'Ah. This is to be a one-sided discussion. So be it.' He turned his head to fix Teresa with a basilisk stare. The poor woman cowered into her corner. 'You, woman. If you should repeat any word of what you hear now, between your mistress and me, I will have your tongue cut out. Do you understand me?'

Teresa, pale as a ghost, managed a tiny nod.

'Very well. Believe it. For I do not make empty threats.'

'No, Baron, but you make threats against mere servants who are in no position to oppose you. I seem to recall that, when you were opposed by an equal, you were thoroughly bested.' It was a mistake to remind herself that Lord Leo had saved her then, for he was not here to save her this time. Perhaps he would not even wish to do so?

Oh, Leo, I need you now. I needed you earlier, in the palace. Why were you not there?

'We have debts to settle between us, *madame,*' the Baron said flatly.

Sophie knew she had to force all thoughts of Leo from her mind. She would have to fight the Baron by herself, using only her own wits and guile. Her pistol was useless. Beck would overpower her before she could pull it from the pocket under her skirt.

'Debts, as I say,' he continued. He picked up his heavy cane and used the tip to push aside the neck of her cloak, revealing the many jewels she wore. 'Those fine emeralds, for example, *madame.* It is accepted practice, is it not, that when a gentleman bestows fine gems on a lady such as yourself, he is entitled to expect some recompense?'

She would have to answer now. 'You made the gift to Maestro Verdicchio, Baron. Not directly to me. I promised you nothing.' She paused, breathed. His sardonic smile incensed her. 'And nor did the maestro,' she finished daringly. In fact, she had no idea what Verdicchio might have promised Beck.

The Baron made a noise in his throat. He allowed his lecherous gaze to wander over Sophie's body.

Her natural reaction was to grab the edges of her cloak and pull them close. She resisted it. She focused instead on the fact that he had not denied her claims about Verdicchio. She had been right! The Baron had given Verdicchio the jewellery without a specific promise of anything in return.

Sophie straightened and took a very deep breath, allowing the edges of the cloak to spread a little. Let him feast his eyes on what he would never have!

She resolved to take the initiative. 'So, Baron, what do you propose?'

His eyes widened a fraction, but in a second he had his features back under control. 'You are proud, *madame*. And very sure of yourself.'

Sophie raised her chin.

'Very well. You have just had an assignation with Tsar Alexander, I believe.' He waited for her to react, but she did not. 'That is a dangerous proceeding for a woman in your position. It is all very well for princesses and duchesses to share an emperor's bed. But a common opera singer? I think not. The Austrian government would take a very dim view of such a matter, I am sure, were they to learn of it. Had you expected to have many more lucrative engagements—singing engagements, I mean—while you are here in Vienna?'

He was threatening to betray her to the secret police, and to have her expelled. Sophie was hard put not to laugh. Her prospects for lucrative singing engagements—and even for remaining in Vienna—had dissolved in that pool of imperial water.

Sophie smiled broadly, and with great confidence. Quick as lightning, she leant across and pulled the check-string. 'My dear Baron,' she said slowly, letting the words linger on her tongue, 'I think this is the point at which you leave my carriage.'

'That is your response to my proposal?'

'No, Baron. It is this. *Do your worst!*'

When the carriage drew up this time, Beck did alight. Sophie's groom, more wide awake than usual, even opened the door for the man.

She waited, her whole body tense, until she was sure he would not return. Then she dropped her face into her hands with a terrible groan.

'*Madame*! Oh, *madame*!' Teresa cried. 'He threatened to cut out my tongue. What will he do to *you* now? He is a monster.'

Sophie raised her head. 'Yes. He is certainly that.' She cleared her throat. 'Now, leave me in peace, Teresa, while I decide what to do.' She thought for a moment. She was almost certain the Tsar would not create a scandal by summoning the chief of the secret police at this time of night. The information was much more likely to be passed on, discreetly, in the morning. So she had a few hours yet to decide precisely how to escape Verdicchio. And Beck. 'Tell the coachman to drive slowly down to the river. I may need to take a walk among the trees.'

Teresa let down the glass, but she had uttered no more than a few words when the door was pulled open. The poor woman almost tumbled out.

Sophie pulled up her silken skirts and started to fumble for the pocket with her pistol. The Baron would now be even more dangerous than before. She would not yield to him. Never. She would shoot him first.

'No, no, *madame*.' It was a well-remembered voice. But the tone was clipped and cruel.

She looked up from her skirts into the dark, shuttered eyes of Lord Leo Aikenhead. He was stepping calmly into her carriage. He must be following her, too, just like Beck. How dare he?

'Your skirts have been ruffled quite enough already this night, *madame*,' he said viciously. 'Believe me, I have no intention of laying even a finger on them.'

Sophie felt the blood draining from her cheeks at his studied insult. She clutched at the hanging strap. She must not faint. Not before this man.

'Drive on,' Lord Leo yelled up to the box, before casually closing the door. 'You will permit, *madame*?' he said. He took the seat opposite her without waiting for her to speak. 'After all,' he added, 'you have given permission to so many other men this evening. What hurt can there be in one more?'

'You devil!' she spat. 'How dare you follow me and insult me so? You know nothing of me.'

He leaned back and smiled. 'Oh, I know a great deal, *madame*. I know where you have been. And I have no doubt as to what you have been doing. Though I must say that if Beck was one of your clients tonight, he was remarkably quick about it, besides being prepared to tolerate the presence of a witness to his labours.'

Teresa whimpered and shrank into her corner.

'Leave my maid out of this, sir. She has suffered already quite enough.'

'Oh? And how may that be, pray?'

'That is none of your affair.' Sophie was getting angrier by the minute. This was the man she had dreamed of? The man who was going to rescue her? To save her honour? He was worse than all of them. A fiend. The very devil.

She pushed herself back in her place and folded her hands in her lap. *Breathe. You can be calm, Sophie. All you have to do is breathe.*

The silence stretched between them. His eyes were half-closed, but he was watching her, though he was pretending not to. He straightened suddenly. 'This will not do, *madame*. There are things that need to be said between us.' He glanced at Teresa for a split second. 'And *not* before witnesses. I require—' He bit his lip. 'No, I ask you, *madame*, to put your maid down so that we may converse in private.'

'No!' Her cry was very shrill. 'No, I will not,' she repeated slowly and distinctly. She had dealt with one appalling man in this carriage tonight. She could surely deal with another. 'Teresa has had a small accident and cannot make her own way home. She stays.'

His dark brows came together into a fierce, threatening line.

'However,' she continued sweetly, 'since it seems that I shall be rid of you only by permitting you such a private interview, I will take a walk with you. My coachman is on the way to the river, in any case. I was planning to take a cooling stroll in the park, on the Prater island.' She raised her eyebrows haughtily. 'If you wish to speak to me, Lord Leo, you may accompany me. Provided you make this the last time—the very last time—you approach me in such a compromising manner.' She let her smile broaden. She was rather proud of that speech, for she knew it would incense him beyond measure.

She did not have long to wait.

'*Compromising?*' His voice was somewhere between a bellow and a snarl. '*You?* By God, ma'am—'

Sophie raised a hand. 'If you continue to speak to me in that ungentlemanly way, sir, there will be no further speech between us. Ever.'

He looked just a little taken aback. Well, well, well. Attack was clearly the best form of defence when it came to Lord Leo Aikenhead. Sophie resisted the temptation to laugh. Instead, she leaned back, satisfied.

Yes, they would have a private interview. But Lord Leo Aikenhead would not have the mastery of it.

Leo had tried hard not to watch her. But it was so tempting. She was so tempting, even shrouded in her hooded cloak. He could still see her beautiful face, her expressive eyes. Worst of all, his gaze was always drawn back to those luscious, kissable lips. Deliberately, he turned his head away and stared out of the window. He was still lusting after her, in spite of everything. In spite of the fact that she had already shared the Russian Emperor's bed tonight, and had probably given satisfaction to Beck as well. He should be fleeing in disgust.

He forced his shoulders to relax and leaned farther back into the seat, letting the sumptuous velvet cushion his cheek.

And then he smelt it!

It was an exotic, foreign scent, full of dark, hard notes—an expensive perfume, of the kind worn by a man who wanted the world to know his power.

Leo sat up with a jerk of revulsion. Beck had reclined here. Leo had no desire to smell like the Baron's leavings.

Opposite him, the Nightingale coolly raised her eyebrows. 'You are in some difficulty, Lord Leo?' She sounded, for all the world, like a grand London hostess enquiring after one of her guests.

In spite of himself, he had to admire her. But he steeled himself to respond sharply, to retain the upper hand. 'I find the comforts of your carriage a little…overpowering, *madame*.' He sniffed ostentatiously at the purple velvet. 'It smells,' he said brutally, 'of the sewer.'

She blanched at his words, but she quickly recovered. 'It smells, I do not doubt, sir, of the previous occupant of that seat. I may tell you—though I note you do not ask—that he did not occupy it at my invitation.'

Leo felt a wave of relief pass through his body. Her liaison with the Tsar he could understand. But not with Beck. The man had probably been threatening her again. She was only a woman, after all, and unprotected here in this carriage, except by her useless, cowering maid. Perhaps he should offer to help her against Beck?

He realised, in that moment, that he had been frowning at the Nightingale ever since he had stepped into her carriage. He forced a slight smile. 'Madame Pietre,' he began, in something closer to his normal voice, 'if you have been troubled by the Baron von Beck, I remain at your service.'

She responded with a throaty laugh. 'I suggest, Lord Leo,' she said, after a moment, 'that it would be in both our interests if we maintained a thoughtful silence, at least until we reach the river. It will give us both time to consider the rights and wrongs of what we may have said.'

A tiny smile was playing around the corner of her mouth. More than anything, Leo wanted to lean forward and kiss it.

Chapter Nine

As the carriage drove down to the river, and the Prater island beyond, the air became cooler and sweeter. Sophie breathed it in, in long luscious draughts, as if she were savouring the finest wine. She had not looked at Lord Leo directly. She did not dare to. It was enough that she had told him about the Baron. She had weakened there, because she could not bear to have him believe she would welcome the advances of such a villain.

She would not excuse herself further to Lord Leo Aikenhead. Besides, she would be leaving Vienna in a few hours. They would probably never meet again, after tonight. A sudden churning in her stomach warned her that she was not totally unaffected by that thought. She feared Beck, for she knew he would ruin her if he could. She feared the Tsar now, too, for he had the power to ensure that Sophia Pietre would be spurned by the royalty and aristocracy of Europe for the rest of her life. But she did not fear Lord Leo Aikenhead. He might rail at her, but he would never do anything to hurt her. His bark was worse than his bite.

The thought of his bite, of his lips on her flesh, set her heart racing. Her skin began to heat. His lips… She dared to dart a single glance in his direction. He was gazing out of the window, his eyes distant, his body relaxed, his lips ever so slightly parted. Those lips… She had never before thought of any man's mouth as enticing, but his was. She was tempted to reach out and touch the tip of a finger to the tiny gap between his top and bottom lips, to feel the warmth of his skin, perhaps even the fleeting graze of his tongue. Would he taste her skin as a snake's flickering tongue tasted the air? And was he as dangerous?

Yes. He was. Any man was, as she had learned to her cost.

The carriage had crossed to the island and was pulling up at the end of the main tree-lined alley. Sophie did not move. Lord Leo rose, bowed as well as he could in the confined space, and jumped down. Then he let down the steps and stood back, holding the door for her to alight. He was smiling a company smile.

Sophie did not return it. 'I would ask you, Lord Leo, to walk on a little way. I shall join you shortly.'

His eyebrows shot up, but he said nothing. With a tiny bow, he turned and stalked off, leaving the carriage door swinging on its hinges.

As soon as he had gone, Sophie threw back her hood. With Teresa's help, she removed all the jewels from her hair and stowed them in the bottom of her reticule. 'Now,' she said, raising her hood once more, 'I can at least uncover my hair without appearing to be ridiculous before half the population of Vienna.'

Teresa murmured agreement. She still seemed bemused.

'Stand in the doorway now, please,' Sophie ordered. Shielded by the maid's body, Sophie rapidly pulled up her skirt and retrieved her hidden pistol. She checked it and put it into her bulging reticule. She would feel safer with it to hand. 'Thank you, Teresa. Stay here. I shall not be gone long.' She straightened her skirts. 'And call that sleepy groom. I need a man's hand to help me down.'

The Prater was Vienna's playground. Even at this time of night, and this late in the year, people were strolling around, enjoying the atmosphere of a capital city at play. Everyone in Vienna came here, from the highest to the lowest. There were great ladies in silken gowns and towering head-dresses of ostrich plumes wandering around on the arms of their escorts, with sullen servants a pace behind. There were fat, complacent merchants, with their gossipy wives and daughters, all grown rich on the profits of renting their property to the visiting foreigners. And there were working people, too, servants, and peasants and labourers, dressed in their best and bent on enjoying this extraordinary autumn and the benefits that the Congress had brought to their city.

The Prater garden itself was amazingly beautiful, particularly when lit by hundreds of lanterns. The long central avenue was lined with horse chestnuts, tall and venerable, yet still clothed in their whispering leaves. It seemed more like late summer than the middle of November.

Sophie breathed in the scents of trees, and leaves and good moist earth. This would be the last time she would walk here. Tomorrow, if she were rash enough to remain, she would surely open her door to the secret police, come to expel her. She would not give them that satisfaction. She would leave tonight of her own volition, and with her pride intact.

She dropped her head back to look up at the trees. They seemed immensely tall and graceful, dwarfing mere mortals below. Far above, their fine branches were interlaced against the dark star-spattered sky. It reminded her of a Greek myth she had been told once—a man and a woman whose love for each other was so deep, so enduring, that they begged the gods not to separate them in death. And the gods allowed them to die in the same instant. Both were turned into trees that stood together for ever, with their topmost branches entwined in a lovers' embrace. It was a beautiful story. Those delicate horse-chestnut branches, so far up against the sky, were a symbol of what real love could be.

She stumbled.

Lord Leo grabbed her by the arm to steady her. He did not speak, but the look in his face told her precisely what he was thinking. *If you walk along with your eyes on the sky, you will surely fall over your feet.*

Sophie straightened and extracted her arm. She walked on again, her heavy reticule banging reassuringly against her leg with every step. She had no wish to speak. She would continue to enjoy the trees and the soft glow of the lamps on the dark greenery and the even darker earth. For the last time. But she took the precaution, now, of keeping an eye out for obstacles in her path.

She heard his hurrying feet and then he was beside her again. Not touching, but close enough to converse, if that was what they eventually chose to do. Close enough to be acquaintances, but not to be lovers. Nor even to be friends.

* * *

It was as if she had erected a wall between them. Why? She accepted the advances of other men. Why not Leo? He was no coxcomb, but he had had enough success with women to know that most of them found him very attractive. Yet the Nightingale would not even permit him to touch her. Was it that she now considered herself to be above him, the exclusive property of the Tsar? That could explain it. And yet, he was not sure that it did.

He looked at her again, trying to apply his logical mind to what he saw and to prevent his confounded body from interfering. He saw a beautiful lady, apparently strolling nonchalantly through the Prater garden, admiring the scenery. She was, admittedly, rather strangely dressed, for her dark velvet cloak was pulled closely around her body, with its hood covering her hair.

He walked on slowly, trying to make sense of the confusion she created in his mind. In spite of everything, he still wanted her. If he once took her to bed, would that break the hold she seemed to have over him?

They continued to walk in silence. It was not a companionable silence, but the longer it continued, the more Leo felt their strife receding. He had said unforgivable things to her. He should not have done so, for he had no rights at all over her. If she chose to share Tsar Alexander's bed, or even—God forbid!—the Baron von Beck's, she had the right. She was her own mistress.

The irony of that word brought an unwilling laugh to his lips, but he bit it back. She *was* her own mistress. No one else's. No matter how many beds she shared. If Leo still wanted her, he would have to come to terms with that.

He glanced at her then. He had not turned his head. Neither had she, but he could see that she was watching him, out of the corner of her eye. Had her expression softened a little? Perhaps the beauties of this place were lessening her righteous anger against his appalling behaviour? It had been the thought of her with Beck. That image had burned itself into Leo's brain and fired his jealous fury.

But he had been wrong. She had told him, clearly enough, that the Baron was not her lover, and he had no reason to doubt her. As for the Tsar, no woman in the Nightingale's position could possibly refuse him. Few society ladies would have refused him either, if truth were told.

Leo allowed his long, leisurely stride to reduce the distance between them by half a yard. He saw from her quick sideways glance that she knew what he had done, but she walked on as if nothing had happened.

He edged a fraction closer still. She was gazing up at the trees again, and at the sky. He grabbed at the tiny opportunity she had offered him. '*Madame*,' he said softly, 'will you not consent to take my arm? Then you may gaze at the stars as much as you desire. I promise I will not let you fall.'

Her reaction was totally unexpected. She stopped dead, threw back the hood of her cloak and laughed. That joyous sound was directed up at the stars, as if she were communing with powers above and beyond them both. Leo did not dare to speak, lest he shatter the moment. He simply offered her his arm.

She looked down at the ground beneath her feet and,

fleetingly, at him. Then she laid her fingers on his arm. He felt as if a tiny, precious bird had alighted there, and that he was responsible for protecting it against the hunters of the world. A very precious bird. A nightingale.

They had been walking together for well nigh half an hour in almost complete silence. The only words spoken had been Lord Leo's invitation for Sophie to take his arm. Yet they were communicating. Without any words at all.

Sophie risked a quick glance up at him and then immediately looked back at the path. He was very much aware of her. As she was of him. She could feel the warmth of his flesh seeping through the layers of clothing, through her fine kid gloves, into her loosely perched fingers, and flowing up her arm to suffuse her whole body with heat. She longed to throw off her cloak, for it was now almost suffocating her. But under it, almost every part of her body was hung with jewels, gifts from admirers such as the Baron von Beck. She had had a perfectly good reason to wear them for that ill-fated meeting with Emperor Alexander, but she could not stomach the thought of Lord Leo seeing her so. He would think that she was indeed risen from the gutter. And she would be put to shame.

Other men might think of her as they would. But Lord Leo's opinion mattered. Too much.

'Madame?' he said enquiringly, looking down at her hand on his arm.

She followed his gaze. Her fingers, previously lying limp upon his dark blue evening coat, had curled into claws. Her nails were digging into his arm.

'Oh.' She made to pull away, but he was quicker.

He laid his free hand reassuringly over hers. And then he smiled.

She looked away. She could not endure the kindness in that smile, for she had not been kind. Yet she soon found herself looking back again, drawn by his magnetic gaze. He was still smiling. It might even have broadened a fraction.

'*Madame*, I know that something is troubling you. If a poor English gentleman may help you, I am totally at your service. Pray believe that.'

When she did not reply—for she could not—he continued, 'Shall we walk a little farther?' He steered her along one of the narrower walks, where there were fewer lamps and hardly any people.

She did not feel afraid. Not with him. They continued to stroll in silence, trusting companions now. Or almost so. Sophie allowed herself to enjoy the moment. It was her last with him. And her last in this wonderful setting, a place she had grown to love. She would miss Vienna greatly, not only for its beauty and the friendliness of its people, but because it rang with joyous music, the thing she loved most in all the world. Nowhere in Italy—not Venice, not Rome, not any other city— seemed to live for its music as Vienna did.

Without meaning to, she had allowed her steps to slow.

'You are weary, *madame*,' he said gently, giving her fingers the tiniest squeeze. 'There is a bench here. Shall we sit?'

She was not weary, but she nodded. Her senses were longing for one last moment close to this enigmatic Englishman. He was behaving like the perfect gentleman. He had even taken out a fine linen handkerchief and dusted the bench, before inviting her to sit. And he asked for permission before taking his own place beside her. But when he lifted her fingers to his lips, he simply gazed into her eyes and burnt his kiss through the fine leather. Just like before.

Sophie could not tear her eyes away. She wanted to frown him down, but her body so exulted in his touch that it refused to move even a fraction. It was as if she were floating, and the whole world were a lake of smooth, scented water.

He raised his head, but did not release her fingers. 'Forgive me. It seemed to me that permission was already given by your beautiful eyes.'

She bent her head to hide her face. What else could he see in her eyes?

He returned her hand to her lap, but continued to hold her fingers loosely in his own. His lips were almost against her hair.

'I have behaved in an appalling manner to you, Madame Pietre. I had no right—absolutely none. I apologise unreservedly. Can you forgive me?'

'It is forgotten,' she whispered. She bent her head even farther, her gaze fixed on her fingers. And his. This man affected her like no other. And he had humbled himself to her. She owed him at least part of the truth. 'You will not be troubled by my presence here any longer, Lord Leo. By tomorrow, I shall be gone from Vienna.' There, it was done. She felt cleansed.

His sharp intake of breath was very loud in the silent, deserted alley. There was a long pause. 'It is not for me to comment on what you may choose to do.'

She could not tell, from the flat tone of his voice, whether he was glad or sorry. They sat motionless. Then, in her lap, his thumb moved to caress the back of her hand. It was the most erotic touch she had ever experienced. 'Ah!' Her indrawn breath was part gasp, part groan.

'What is it?'

She threw her head back and looked him full in the face. His eyes were dark and fathomless, but his expression was a strange mixture of desire laced with concern. They gazed at each other, transfixed. Then slowly, very slowly, leaving her every opportunity to pull away from him, he brought his mouth down to hers.

His kiss was so gentle, so sweet, so gossamer-light, that she was not absolutely sure that he had touched her. Until he moaned in the base of this throat and drew her into his arms for a longer, deeper kiss.

Sophie could not think. She could only feel. And it was like nothing she had ever felt before. The wonder of it radiated out from her mouth, to her limbs, to her pounding heart. It tripped into a weird, staccato rhythm that no orchestra would ever manage to play. She gloried in it.

He deepened the kiss yet more, touching his tongue to her slightly parted lips. She dared to steal one hand around his neck, under his thick hair. So close now. This must be how it was meant to be between a man and a woman.

A loud, deliberate cough intruded into her fuzzy, floating thoughts. Horrified, Sophie pulled herself away and flung up her hood to hide her shame.

Lord Leo rose at the same instant and placed his large body between her and the new arrival. 'You are *de trop*, sir.' The threat was unmistakable.

'I...I seek Madame Pietre, sir,' said a younger voice. *'Madame?'*

There was no help for it. Sophie would not cower behind Lord Leo. She rose and threw back her hood once more. She knew her cheeks were flushed. Her lips were probably swollen and much too red, but she would face him down. 'I am Madame Pietre. What do you want of me, sir?'

The young man wore the distinctive white pelisse and dolman jacket of a Russian cavalry regiment. Her judgement had been wrong. The Tsar's vengeance was to be immediate. A shiver ran down Sophie's spine. She bit her lip, but she managed to straighten her shoulders and lift her chin. 'Well, sir?' she said proudly.

From under his pelisse, he drew out a long box, which he offered to Sophie with a courtly bow. 'I bring you this gift, *madame*, with the compliments of his Imperial Majesty. He begs that you will join him for supper tomorrow evening.'

When Sophie did not move, the officer pushed the box into her limp hand. Automatically, she opened it. The diamonds exploded with fire, even in the half-light of that narrow alleyway. The necklace was worth a small fortune.

It was all too much. Sophie glanced at Lord Leo. He was glowering at the Tsar's emissary who stood, uncertain, waiting for Sophie's response.

Yes, it was indeed too much.

She began to laugh. Not in joy, as before, but in anguish. She laughed so much that she had to put a hand to her belly to ease the pain.

'With your permission, *madame*...' Lord Leo was making no effort to conceal his anger. 'With your permission,' he said again, 'I will withdraw.' He sketched a slight bow. 'I am sure you may look to this young officer to escort you to your carriage.'

Sophie's laughter died. 'Lord Leo—' He was already halfway down the path, moving almost at a run, his shoulders rigid with fury.

The Tsar's officer was embarrassed, but he could not leave until she gave him her reply.

'Pray wait on me in the morning, sir,' she said. By then, she could be gone. 'I shall give you my reply then. In the meantime, since I appear to be alone in this place, I should be grateful if you would escort me back to my carriage.'

Sophie was relieved that the young officer did not try to join her in the carriage. As soon as he saw Teresa, he bowed and left. Sophie let her head fall back on to the soft velvet. She still could not decide what to do. 'Tell the coachman to drive around for a while, Teresa.'

Teresa did as she was bid and settled into her corner.

Sophie opened the Tsar's gift and gazed at it again in astonishment. This, from the man she had humiliated this very evening? But of course, no one else knew what she had done. *That* was the crucial difference. Whereas Lord Leo had been humiliated in public by being forced to watch as her supposed royal lover bestowed an extravagant gift on her.

She must not think about Lord Leo! She must think about herself, and the Tsar and Vienna. She took several long, deep breaths. If the Tsar was giving her jewels and inviting her to share his supper table, he was clearly still pursuing her. Was he piqued because she had refused him? Had any other woman ever done so? Probably not. So she could be sure the Tsar, at least, would not have her deported.

But what about the Baron? She had challenged him

to do his worst. He might well try. Then again, if the Tsar were truly enamoured of her, the Baron was unlikely to succeed. The Austrians would not act on the Baron's information while they were trying to win the Tsar to their side of the negotiations. For the moment, she was safe.

She continued to ponder, allowing the gentle swaying of the carriage to soothe her fraying nerves. She did not have to flee now. It was not a good time to go, in any case, for she had not planned where she would live or how she would keep her identity secret. Her jewels would not keep her for long. The moment she started to sing in public again, she would be recognised.

She could return to her Vienna apartment as if nothing had happened. Yes, why not? If Verdicchio quizzed her, she could explain that she had made tasteless and stupid decisions about which jewels to wear because she was nervous. He was unlikely to question that. After all, she would have returned to him, would she not?

And then there was Lord Leo. No, she would not think about Lord Leo Aikenhead. She would not! She had allowed him to kiss her; she had returned his kiss. But then her despair had broken through in shrill, bitter laughter, which he had taken as a personal insult. He must surely hate her now.

She would not think about him any more. It hurt too much.

She made up her mind. 'Tell the coachman to drive back to our apartment.'

Chapter Ten

'And where precisely have you been, *madame*?' Verdicchio snapped, the moment she appeared in the doorway. Anger was written in every line of his body.

'I have been with his Imperial Majesty, the Emperor of All the Russias, as you very well know.' She threw back the hood of her cloak.

He extracted his gold watch from his waistcoat and studied it closely. 'According to my information,' he said, in a deceptively gentle voice, 'you left the palace nearly two hours ago. I ask you again, *madame*. Where have you been?'

'You are not my keeper,' Sophie said haughtily. 'Where I go is my affair.'

'Your *affairs*, *madame*,' he responded immediately, 'are very definitely my business. Since I have arranged for you to keep company with the Tsar, I also require that you keep company with no one else. Do you understand me?'

This was going all wrong. Instead of accepting her explanations, he was trying to treat her like a menial. Fury exploded inside her. 'You do not own me. We work *together*. I sing, you play. I perform, you arrange engagements. I will not work with a man who tries to turn me into a whore.'

He took two steps towards her, his fists clenched. 'You will work with me because if you do not, I will make sure the whole world knows who you really are. Then you will not be able to make a living at all, even as a common whore.'

Sophie closed her eyes against the horror of it. Her common sense had deserted her. She had been betrayed by the memory of that devastating kiss, and by the reassuring weight of the Tsar's diamonds nestling next to her pistol. She had forgotten that Verdicchio could ruin her. And he would, if she crossed him.

There was nothing more to say. She drooped a little.

'I see that you have recognised your position once more, my dear Sophie. We have a partnership, but it is not a partnership of equals. You *do* understand that, do you not?' He was determined on her complete submission.

She nodded. 'Yes, Maestro.' He had won.

'And now, Sophie, you will deliver up to me all the jewels that you wore for the Tsar. Teresa, take *madame*'s cloak.'

Teresa scuttled across the floor to obey.

Verdicchio's piggy little eyes fastened on the emeralds and diamonds at Sophie's throat, and then on the jewels beneath her bosom, at her waist, on her arms and wrists. 'Very fetching. But a little ostentatious, do you not think?'

'I— It was to meet an emperor. I thought it…er…appropriate.'

'Did you, indeed? Well, Sophie, it is a singularly

tasteless display. I cannot imagine what his Majesty thought. In future, *I* shall decide what jewels you wear. Teresa will unpin them and bring me the jewel box. For safe keeping. Teresa?'

'Yes, Maestro?'

'Make sure you include everything. I seem to recall that *madame* was wearing a fortune in her hair, but she is doing so no longer. Take care that those items, too, are in the box when you bring it to me. If anything is missing, you will be dismissed from *madame*'s service.'

Teresa's groan masked Sophie's gasp of outrage. This monster would sink to any depths. He had black-mailed Sophie with threats to reveal her past, and now he was blackmailing her again with threats to dismiss her helpless maid.

Sophie took a step forward. She and Verdicchio stood almost nose to nose. This time she managed to raise her chin. She would not permit him to browbeat poor Teresa. 'I shall ensure, Maestro, that every item on your list is in the jewel box. If anything should be missing, you must look to me, not to Teresa.'

He raised his eyebrows and looked Sophie slowly up and down. 'If nothing is missing, I will have no reason to carry out my threat, will I?'

Sophie dropped the last earring into the jewel box and closed it with a snap. He would gloat over it all, but she was not prepared to watch him do it. 'Unlace my gown before you go.' She stood in the middle of her sumptuous bedchamber while Teresa undid the fasten-ings of her gown and of her corset beneath. The two women exchanged conspiratorial glances as the hidden pocket was revealed. Neither said a word. Sophie put both pistol and necklace beneath her pillow. She would find a better hiding place once Teresa was gone from the room. Some secrets were too dangerous for the maid to share.

Her silken wrapper provided cool relief to her naked skin. She was beginning to feel she could breathe again. 'Take the box to him now, Teresa. And arrange a bath in, say, half an hour. I should like to rest a little first.'

Teresa curtsied and left, carrying that infernal box as if it might explode.

Sophie slumped on to her bed and lay staring up at the canopy. She had made a stupid, stupid mistake. She had underestimated Verdicchio.

Why? She must have run mad for the moment. She would pay the price for that. Worse, Verdicchio was not her only enemy in Vienna. There was also the Baron von Beck. And, all too soon, the Russian Emperor. How much longer could she refuse him and retain his regard? It would not take long for thwarted lust to turn to anger, and a desire for vengeance.

She closed her eyes. She felt numb, betrayed, alone.

It was for Leo. For his kiss. The words slithered into her brain and offered their answer, like the serpent offering the apple to Eve. She tried to deny the message it brought. She tried to refuse it. But she could not. Lord Leo Aikenhead had kissed her hand, and her mouth. Twice. In that final embrace, Sophie had given him her lips, and her heart.

Dear God, she had fallen in love with an English aristocrat! She, a lowly opera singer, was in love with a man who wanted to buy her as his mistress. She felt as if her insides had become one vast, aching emptiness.

He did not love her. He could never love a common whore. He simply wanted to possess her. And for that, she had surrendered her chance of freedom. All she had now was a tiny purse of money, one fabulous diamond necklace and a pistol.

Two hot tears forced their way out and down her cheeks. She wiped them away impatiently. She was not weak! She would not give in. She would not!

She took a deep breath and sat up. She would not be beaten. The Tsar's diamonds would be safely hidden, along with her pistol. In the next few days, she would try to extract more gifts from him, gifts that she could conceal from Verdicchio. She had suffered a setback, to be sure, but she could start again from here. From now on, she would put her feelings for Leo behind her. She would not think of him, she would not meet with him, she would not speak to him. She would concentrate on her escape plan. One day, she *would* be free!

Leo had spent a sleepless night and a bad-tempered morning failing to put the Nightingale out of his thoughts. She had allowed him to kiss her. She had even responded to his kiss. But the next moment, she was accepting that diamond necklace from her royal lover. It was embarrassing enough to be caught kissing her, but the presentation of the necklace had been the outside of enough. In front of that Russian cub, too. All Vienna would soon be laughing at the story. Just as the Nightingale had laughed at the time.

Such behaviour was unforgivable, even from a whore.

Leo reminded himself that she was leaving Vienna. Indeed, she might already have gone. That was his one consolation. He would not have her, but neither would the Tsar. With an effort, he decided he would try to ignore the wrongs she had done him. He would forget her. In time.

The apartment was suffocating him, especially with Jack and Ben chattering over their leisurely breakfast. He needed air. He would go for a walk. He would walk until he was exhausted. Then, perhaps, he might be able to sleep tonight.

Two hours later, with only his body exhausted, he found himself in the square where she had lodged. How had he come here? He had certainly not intended it. The Honours' man was still lounging against the wall as if he had been planted. Leo was surprised. If the agent was still here, watching, it must mean that the Nightingale's departure had been delayed.

Leo strolled nonchalantly up to the man and asked him for the time.

The watcher made a great show of taking out his watch and consulting it. In an undertone, he said, 'She hasn't left the apartment yet today, sir. Nor has Verdicchio. A young Russian officer called earlier, though. The Tsar wanted to see her again tonight, according to the servants. Clearly very keen.' The man gave a lecherous wink. 'But she's put him off until the day after tomorrow. Clever. She knows how to keep a man dangling. Even an emperor. Maintains she already has engagements that she's not able to break. Believe that if you like! No, the Nightingale is playing a long game, in my opinion.'

'I had heard she was leaving Vienna today.'

'What? Oh, no, sir. There's no sign of packing. And the laundry woman has just gone off with a whole basketful of washing. The Nightingale wouldn't leave her petticoats behind, now would she?'

Leo managed just a brief nod. He strode off before his fury exploded.

She had lied to him. She had looked him in the face and lied to him!

She was, without doubt, the most treacherous woman he had ever met. She had whispered that she was leaving Vienna. He—gullible fool that he was—had swallowed her lies. And then given her the kisses she craved. It had certainly demonstrated her power over him. That must have been her purpose, for what other reason could there be?

If only he had not kissed her. Without that, he might have been able to put her out of his mind. But her kiss had been soul-searing. It had tasted like the kiss of an innocent, too. Astonishingly so, he now realised. Leo Aikenhead, renowned rake, lover of some of the most beautiful women in England, had been totally taken in by it. Sophia Pietre must be the most talented whore in Europe.

'Leo?'

'Jack?' Leo turned. Jack was looking anxious. 'What on earth is the matter? I told you there was no need to come after me.' Leo knew he sounded short-tempered still, but it was beyond his control.

'There's every need. Castlereagh sent an urgent summons for you. When you didn't return, I took it upon myself to go in your place. I'm sorry if you—'

'You did absolutely right, Jack.' Leo was relieved. Now he would be forced to focus on their mission. And Jack's new sense of responsibility was a blessing. Leo would have found it embarrassing to explain to the

Foreign Secretary that he had spent the night, and half the morning, trailing after a foreign whore instead of carrying out his duty to his country. 'What did his lordship want of us?'

Jack looked round swiftly. There was no one within earshot. 'We are on the brink of a crisis, Leo. In the secret negotiations, the allies are at each other's throats. Castlereagh fears there may be war.'

'And you will, of course, be present at the Imperial Riding School next week,' Verdicchio finished. 'Everyone will be there. The most beautiful ladies in Vienna are to partner the knights who will ride in the joust.'

Sophie raised a questioning eyebrow. He had a considerable hold over her, but they both knew he would be unwise to browbeat her now that he had won.

'Yes, yes,' he said hurriedly. 'The most beautiful *ladies* in Vienna. Everyone knows you are their equal in beauty. But sadly, no longer a *lady*. If they had but known who you really are, my dear, you could have claimed your place among them. Except—' he chortled '—that they would then have shunned you.'

That harsh truth did nothing for Sophie's plummeting self-esteem. In her country, the aristocracy was a class apart. The rule was absolute, and rigidly enforced. If an aristocrat dared to marry outside his class, both he and his children lost all status and privileges. By going on the stage—a far worse sin in aristocratic eyes—Sophie had forfeited her rank. There was no way back.

'None the less, my dear, you must certainly attend.'

'Very well, since you insist. What am I to wear?'

'The knights' ladies will be dressed in costumes of centuries ago,' Verdicchio said. 'But the other patrons will probably wear the colours of peace: blue and silver. You should do likewise. You must order a new gown.'

'And you will pay for it?'

'Now why should I do that? I am sure you can find a way, my dear Sophie, of persuading the Tsar to frank you for at least one new gown. Or perhaps he will give you some jewels to wear with it? Sapphires would look good. Or diamonds.' When Sophie shook her head, he continued, 'But if he does not, I am sure we can find something to suit in your jewel box. I am told that the knights' ladies are planning to wear almost all the jewels their families possess. You may need to do the same.'

Sophie said nothing, but her heart lifted a fraction.

'Have no fear. I will ensure that you do not disgrace yourself this time. Now, I have ordered the carriage for seven for tonight's performance. I hope that will suit you?' He sounded almost conciliatory.

'It will. Though I was planning to go for a drive today.'

'Why?'

'It is very stuffy in this apartment. My throat is feeling very tight. I thought a drive out in the fresh air, perhaps down to the Prater, would help. I need to be on top form this evening. There will be royalty in the audience.'

That clinched it. Verdicchio always insisted that Sophie must impress potential royal patrons. 'You are probably right. But do not tire yourself. And be back in good time to change for the evening. It will not do for you to feel rushed.'

Sophie smiled humbly. 'Thank you, Maestro. Your advice is wise, as always.' She summoned Teresa and, together, they made their way downstairs to the waiting carriage. 'Drive down to the river,' she said in a very carrying voice. 'I wish to take the air.'

As the carriage moved off, Sophie let out the breath she had been holding. So far, so good. Once they had turned the corner, she would change the coachman's orders. She had to do it now, before she lost her nerve. She had less than two days before her next meeting with the Tsar.

They walked back to their lodgings in silence, for the detailed information Jack had been given by the Foreign Secretary was much too secret to be discussed in the street. The servants, with the exception of Leo's valet, Barrow, were sent off to find their supper. Barrow was put on guard outside the door. The three Honours— King, Knave, Ten—took their places around the small table in their shared parlour.

'Lord Castlereagh is going to the theatre this evening,' Jack began. 'To hear the Nightingale's recital, as it happens. He asks that you wait on him around seven, at his rooms. I said you would.'

Leo did his best to ignore the mention of Sophie Pietre. The merest thought of her inflamed passions that he knew he had to master if he was to do his duty. 'Yes, of course. But in the meantime, you had better brief me on what you learned.'

'War.' Jack sounded very serious. 'That is what he said. You know him well enough, Leo. He is not one to exaggerate. He understands these great men.'

'Explain,' Leo said.

Beside Jack, Ben nodded too, serious but eager to know.

'You know—we all know—that everything here hangs on the decisions about the future of Poland.' Leo and Ben nodded. 'The problem, Castlereagh says, is that the Russian army now occupies Poland. Do you remember what the Tsar said, when he was in London? How he planned to give a liberal constitution to Poland? It was a lie. He told Castlereagh, in terms, that he would keep what he holds. There is no hope for the Poles. They will be swallowed by the Russian Empire.'

'Austria will like that no more than England does,' Leo said.

'True. But the King of Prussia supports the Tsar's plans. The Tsar has promised that Prussia will receive the whole of Saxony as compensation.'

'Austria will not have that,' Leo said sharply, 'and neither will we. Never mind the French.'

'That is the problem,' Jack agreed. 'Castlereagh has done everything in his power to wean the King of Prussia away from the Tsar, but he has failed. The Tsar is ready to go to war to defend what he holds in Poland. And Austria and France are ready to face him down.'

'And we?' Leo asked, wonderingly. Bonaparte was safely penned, and England had spent millions in doing it. Leo did not believe for a moment that the British government would sanction another European war. Not over Poland.

'Poland is a very long way from London,' Ben said thoughtfully, voicing Leo's concern exactly.

'Yes. But Castlereagh is adamant that the balance of power must be maintained in central Europe. The Tsar already has far too much influence over the Prussian

King. With Poland as well, he would be able to threaten all the other German states.'

'But what does Lord Castlereagh want the Honours to do?' Ben asked.

'Castlereagh hinted at something to do with Prussia,' Jack said.

'Ah, yes, I see,' Leo said. 'The Tsar needs the King of Prussia's backing for his aggressive line over Poland. If we can somehow drive a wedge between the King of Prussia and the Tsar, then the Tsar will not be able to threaten war.'

'What can we do?' Jack asked. 'These are two reigning monarchs, after all, and we are only penniless spies.'

Leo forced himself to smile confidently at both of them. 'You forget, my friends, that we are Englishmen, renowned for our guile and quick wits. I have no doubt that we shall find a way. The Honours have never failed before, have they?'

Jack and Ben shook their heads. They were no longer frowning. Part of Leo's assumed confidence seemed to have been transmitted to them.

Leo was very glad of it, for he had not the least idea how they were to accomplish such a mission. 'For the moment,' he said, 'I suggest you carry on as usual. Make a round of all our men on the streets and find out what you can. I shall wait on Lord Castlereagh, to see what plan we may concoct between us. I shall meet you here at eight o' clock or shortly after. Make sure that all the servants are out. Give them the night off, if you have to.'

'But won't you be going to the recital along with Lord Castlereagh?' Jack asked. 'Surely you're not going to miss a chance of hearing the Venetian Nightingale sing?'

Leo rose. 'I think not.' He almost spat out the final word. 'I have more important things to do.'

Chapter Eleven

Sophie was completely covered by her dark cloak and hood when she arrived at the entrance. She had even taken the precaution of leaving her carriage two streets away. That purple carriage was very fine, but much too distinctive.

A young diplomat led her into an empty room and left her alone. That only served to increase her anxiety.

Coming here had been her last gamble. The Austrians had spies enough here in their capital city. Her position with the Russians was impossible, because of the Tsar. And France, since its defeat, had sunk in importance. That still left the English, but after so many confrontations with Leo Aikenhead, Sophie could not bring herself to consider them. So what was left? Only Prussia. Only her native land. If she had not been so desperate, she would never have contemplated such a move.

A hidden door opened in the far corner of the room to admit the Prussian ambassador. There was another man in the shadows beyond the door, but the door closed on him. He seemed to be waiting. Who was he? And why was he there?

'Madame Pietre?' Ambassador von Humboldt bowed to her.

Sophie curtsied in response and took the seat he indicated.

The ambassador sat down behind the huge desk and smiled condescendingly at her. 'Now, *madame*. In what way may we help you?'

'That is not why I have come. I am here to offer to help *you*, my lord. Allow me to be frank. Vienna is full of informers and spies. We both know that every delegation here needs information on all the others. You will understand, I am sure, that I move in the highest circles. I am in a position to provide you with useful, nay invaluable, information. But the price is high.' She named an enormous figure, enough to keep her for more than a year. Then she smiled. 'Payment in advance, naturally.'

Fifteen minutes later, Sophie was triumphant. Her plan was working. He had accepted her services as a spy!

He opened a drawer of his desk and extracted a small leather pouch which he placed on the desk in front of her, rather than offering it. It seemed he was unwilling to touch the hand of a woman like Sophie—a whore, and now a spy.

The insult stabbed at Sophie, but she reached for the money. Without the advance, this whole charade would have been for nothing. She weighed the pouch in her hand and glared at him. 'This is nowhere near the advance we agreed.'

His smile was sly. 'We are happy to buy the information that we discussed, but it will be cash on delivery. Bring good information to your intermediary and he will pay you well. Fail, and you will receive nothing.'

'I am not prepared to deal on those terms.' She felt as though she were standing on thin ice that was starting to crack beneath her feet.

'Ah, but it will be better for you if you do, *madame*. Otherwise, I shall ensure that the Austrian chief of police is immediately forewarned of the danger you pose to the Austrian state.'

The ice had given way. She was floundering in freezing water, which could kill her. She grabbed the only available lifeline and said, bitterly, 'You leave me no choice, sir.' She rose and turned to the door by which she had entered.

'You omitted to ask about the identity of your intermediary, *madame*.'

So she had. She turned back. 'I am sure that he will be a man of your own stamp,' she said witheringly. She was furious with herself. Her carefully crafted plan was a failure. She had thought, naïvely, that she could pocket a huge advance and flee Vienna before her next meeting with the Tsar. She had reckoned without the penny-pinching ways of spymasters.

The hidden door opened slowly. The shadowy second man was revealed.

'May I introduce your intermediary, *madame*, the Baron von Beck?'

Beck laughed, in his sinister way, as he escorted her back to her carriage. 'Tonight's recital,' he said pointedly, 'will give you a chance to prove your loyalty to your new master, *madame*.'

'I have *no* master,' Sophie replied bitterly.

'As you will.' He shrugged his shoulders. 'But remember, *madame*, that if you do not deliver what you have promised to the Prussians, I shall take the greatest of pleasure in denouncing you. Now, listen to me. Lord Castlereagh is to attend this evening, and also Prince Metternich. Both of them have an eye for a beautiful woman. Your task, *madame*, is to find out what the English and the Austrians are planning to do. Especially about Poland.' He smiled nastily. 'I will call on you tomorrow morning to learn what you have discovered.'

'You cannot call on me. Verdicchio will suspect.'

'Oh? Why? Surely Verdicchio still counts me among your admirers, the men he tries so hard to milk for money and jewels?'

'Maestro Verdicchio is particularly insistent that I should entertain no one apart from the Russian Emperor at present,' she said calmly. It was the truth.

'Ah, yes, the Tsar. You will be seeing him again soon? In private?'

Sophie bent her head to hide her blushes. 'He has invited me to supper. In two days' time.'

'Then any meeting with me must be above reproach. Let me see... I shall offer to take you driving in an open carriage. No one can see any harm in that.'

Sophie knew she was beaten. She could not possibly refuse to meet the Baron. But could she obtain any of the information he sought? Castlereagh, in particular, was remarkably close-mouthed. What would the Baron do if she had nothing to offer him?

* * *

'I hope I am not inconveniencing you too much, Aikenhead.' Lord Castlereagh invited Leo to precede him into the imperial theatre. 'If I had not been delayed earlier, we could have completed our business in my office. However, there will be time at the end of the recital, and I know you for a man who appreciates fine music. Was it truly your intention to miss this event?'

Leo tried not to growl his admission that he had planned to be elsewhere. He had sworn to avoid that lying woman, but now they would come face to face all over again. Castlereagh was bound to speak to her after the performance.

'You are missing nothing of importance, I hope?' Castlereagh asked with a frown. They both knew what he meant. If Leo was supposed to be on a spying mission elsewhere, it was more than an inconvenience for him to attend the recital.

Leo shook his head. 'No, sir. Nothing of importance.'

Castlereagh's anxious look subsided. 'Excellent. Then let us enjoy the music.' They made their way into the theatre and the Foreign Secretary's box.

The music was indeed splendid, and Leo felt perversely glad that he was able to hear it. The choir and the ensembles and the orchestra were first class. And then, at the end of the recital, the Venetian Nightingale appeared, dressed in white satin and fabulous emeralds. She sang to make the heart swell and the tears flow.

In spite of what she was, and the insults she had heaped on him, Leo found her voice unutterably moving. If she were only a voice, and not also such a damnably alluring woman. It was impossible to separate his reactions to her music from his urge to throttle her, or kiss her into submission, the moment he was close enough to touch her.

The performance ended on her famous high pianissimo. The note floated out across the theatre into awe-struck silence. It became softer and softer, yet never faded completely. It was so pure, and so beautiful, that the whole audience seemed to be holding its breath. Even after the note ceased, the silence in the auditorium continued for fully ten seconds. Then the cries and the cheers erupted.

Beside Leo, Castlereagh let out a long sigh. 'What a voice. We are privileged, Aikenhead, to have heard her. The finest voice in the whole of Europe.'

Leo was too overcome to speak. He nodded.

One of Castlereagh's young secretaries entered from the corridor behind their box. 'My lord, Madame Pietre will be taking wine in the salon. I bring a cordial invitation for you and your guests to join her.'

Castlereagh rose immediately.

Leo was rather slower out of his chair. This was something he really did not want to do, but what excuse could be made to the Foreign Secretary? None. So he followed Castlereagh out of the box and along the corridor.

I will compliment her on her performance. Castlereagh will expect that of me. And so will she. Besides, she deserves at least that. But I will say nothing more. I will be distant. I will be cold. I will not respond to her charm or her beauty in any way.

She had sung better than she had dared to hope. It was all those years of experience, of course. To be successful, a singer had to learn to put any immediate troubles behind her, and to concentrate on her performance alone. Tonight, Sophie had done it. And she was proud of herself.

Now, Castlereagh would come, and she must begin her other task. For that, she had no training at all, and no experience. Oh, she knew how to flirt with men. She even knew how to extract gifts from them. But extracting information—important political and diplomatic information—was a different matter entirely. She had no idea at all of how to approach such a task. Yet she had no choice.

Without moving her head, she glanced quickly around the room. Yes, the Baron von Beck was there, lounging by a doorway, watching Sophie's every move. He would assess whether she was making enough effort to converse with the great men, to flirt with them, and to persuade them to confide in a woman they would judge to be beautiful but harmless.

A waiter passed with a silver tray of champagne. Sophie caught up a bubbling flute and took a long swallow. It was not wise, but she needed a little extra courage for the insane mission she was embarking upon.

You should have left Vienna when you had the chance. The voice in her head was insistent. And it was right. She had been unable to think clearly at the time. Her mind had been full of the glories of the Prater garden, and the even greater glory of being kissed, being desired, by the man she loved. She had blossomed in his arms like a flower opening to the sun. And even after he had stormed off, her body had continued to yearn for his touch. That had led her to make a grave mistake. If her brain had not been befuddled by thoughts of Lord Leo Aikenhead, she would have ordered the coachman to make for the border the moment she had the Tsar's diamonds in her pocket.

Now, her situation was as bad as it could possibly be. She was still expected to share the Tsar's bed; at the same time, she was being forced to spy on all the great men in Vienna. That was her own fault, too, since she had tried to lure the Prussian ambassador into her trap by boasting of the list of great men she knew. Her list had not included Leo, for she loved him too much to involve him in such a sordid charade. She could never think of betraying him. But now she would have to betray his country. It made her want to weep. It was wicked, but she had brought it on herself. Because she loved him. Her punishment was very hard.

As she set her glass down, a hush fell over the salon. Lord Castlereagh had entered. It was always so when his tall, elegant figure walked into a room. Everyone—even the highest—waited to see what he would do. On this occasion, he strolled across and bowed low to Sophie.

At his shoulder was the man she least wished to see. Leo Aikenhead. And his features were set hard as granite when he looked at her.

Lord Castlereagh raised Sophie's fingers to his lips in an uncharacteristically gallant gesture. He was not smiling, but there was a gleam in his eye that Sophie recognised. This man was a music lover and her singing had touched him. *'Madame*, I must tell you that your singing was extraordinarily moving. I thank you. It was an experience I shall not forget.'

Sophie bowed her head. 'You are most generous, my lord.'

He stood for a moment, frozen, gazing at her. It struck Sophie that he might still be hearing her music in his mind. Then he seemed to remember where he was. '*Madame*, may I present Lord Leo Aikenhead?'

Sophie looked up sharply. Leo sketched a tiny bow. Anything less would have been a gross insult. 'We are already acquainted,' she said quietly, speaking solely to Lord Castlereagh. She did not acknowledge Leo, or look directly at him. She could be just as cold, just as forbidding, as he. Pride was all that she could cling to now. In the face of his lacerating scorn, her love would shrivel and crumble to dust.

It was time. She focused all her attention on the British Foreign Secretary. She might have one minute, or five or ten, but Beck would be watching. For her own survival, she must seize this opportunity. She might not have another.

'It is warm here, do you not agree, my lord? It would be pleasant to take a turn around the room. Would you be so kind as to give me your company?'

Lord Castlereagh, the consummate English gentleman, smiled down into Sophie's face. 'It would be my pleasure. You will excuse us, Aikenhead?'

Leo's eyes narrowed. He bowed to Lord Castlereagh. Much lower, Sophie noticed, than the insulting bow he had made earlier, to her.

'I will speak to you later, Aikenhead,' Castlereagh added, drawing Sophie's arm through his.

'Of course, sir.' Leo's response was all politeness, but the fury in his eyes shot out towards Sophie like sparks from a spluttering fire. Her instinct was to cower away. If one of those sparks should touch her, his anger would burn her up.

* * *

His behaviour had been outrageous. He had intended to be cool and distant, to behave like a gentleman, complimenting her on her performance. But what had he actually done? He had insulted her, with that silent, arrogant bow.

Even now, watching her with Castlereagh was setting his thoughts and feelings all on end. He could not take his eyes off her.

She was flirting with Castlereagh, using all the wiles of the practised courtesan. The Foreign Secretary had said something to amuse her. Leo heard her musical laugh, clear and true as a bell, from the other side of the room. She was smiling up into Castlereagh's face and touching her fingers to his arm.

Leo felt that touch. The muscles of his arm contracted in painful response. She had touched him in much that way while they walked together in the Prater garden, before he had taken her in his arms and—

They had parted. Castlereagh had left her in order to speak to the French ambassador. She was alone!

Leo strode across the room before any other man could approach her. 'A word with you, *madame*.' He seized her arm and held it so firmly that she could not escape him until he chose to let her go.

He walked her swiftly into a shadowy alcove and dropped the curtain. Then he pulled her into his arms. The memory of that other kiss flooded through him like water thundering through a broken sluice. His physical reaction was basic and primitive. He wanted her— now—and his body was ready to prove it. It was telling him to kiss her until they were both trembling with passion, ready to couple right here on the floor.

His mouth descended on hers in a hard, possessive kiss, punishment for the torments he had suffered. Let her feel who was master!

The weight of his body pushed her back into the corner, so she could not escape. Leo put his hands to the sides of her head, to hold her steady as he deepened the kiss, demanding entry to her luscious mouth. Her whole body shuddered as she opened to him. She made a noise in her throat. Was it desire? Or was it fear?

Shocked, he broke away, gasping for breath. What the devil was he doing? Even in the gloom, he could see that her skin was pale and her eyes were wide. She must be terrified of him. '*Madame*, I—'

She touched a finger to her swollen lips. 'I think, Lord Leo, that we have *said* quite enough.' She pulled back the curtain and swept out without a backward glance.

Chapter Twelve

It was extremely late. The Honours were back around the little table in the parlour.

It had taken Leo hours to recover his self-control after his outrageous behaviour at the theatre. He was ashamed of what he had done. But he was not sure that he could prevent it from happening all over again the next time he laid eyes on her. Especially if he saw her in company with another man. She should be his. She should be his alone!

It would never be so. If he wanted to retain his self-control, and the respect of the men he worked with, he would have to stop himself from thinking about her, and avoid meeting her altogether. It was the only solution. He must focus on their mission.

'Keep your voices down,' he ordered. 'In case the servants are not yet asleep.'

Jack nodded. Ben looked over his shoulder as if he were expecting one of the servants to appear. There was no one, of course.

'I am sure that we can trust them all, even if they did

chance to hear something,' Jack said quietly. 'They have served us for years, and they are all loyal Englishmen.'

'I agree,' Ben said. He reached for the wine bottle, but managed to knock over Jack's half-full glass. 'Dammit!' He jumped up from his chair, cursing. Jack calmly mopped up the spill with a napkin, righted his glass and refilled it.

Leo leaned back in his chair, focusing on the byplay. Eventually, Ben sat down again, still apologising. 'It doesn't matter,' Leo said. 'You probably did us a favour.' He lifted his own glass, sniffed at it and grimaced. 'I know we're rather short of the readies, Jack, but couldn't you find something better than this?'

Jack merely grinned in response.

Now that Ben had been put at his ease once more, Leo turned to the serious issue. 'Our task, my fellow Honours, is to find a way of driving a wedge between the Russian Emperor and the Prussian King.' He paused and raised an eyebrow.

'Nothing *too* difficult, then?' Jack quipped. Then, seeing Leo's quick frown, 'Sorry, Leo.'

Leo determined to respond in kind to Jack's flippancy. 'Oh, you're right, Jack. It is certainly not the simplest task we have ever tackled. I did ask Castlereagh whether he had any hints about how we might approach it. He just smiled in that enigmatic way of his and said he was sure the Honours would do what was necessary. In other words, he had no ideas, either!'

Ben and Jack laughed. Then there was a long silence while they all racked their brains. 'We don't have direct access to either of them,' Ben began. 'Or not easily. So, whatever we do will have to be done through third parties.'

'Yes. Good point,' Leo agreed.

'We need someone we can use,' Jack suggested. 'A woman, perhaps?'

Leo stroked his chin, thinking of all the women in Vienna. Except one. 'Am I right in thinking that the Prussian King is enamoured of Countess Julie Zichy? And was she not also the Tsar's mistress at one time?'

'You're right about the Prussian King. I'm not so sure about the Tsar. Though he seems to have taken a new mistress almost every day since he's been in Vienna.'

'So…the Countess Julie,' Leo said again. 'What can we do there?'

'Well…' Ben narrowed his eyes and stared into the middle distance. 'It would not be difficult to start a rumour that she had returned to the Tsar's bed. The King would be bound to hear of it. But would he believe it? The Tsar is still bedding the Nightingale, after all.'

Leo's throat muscles clenched.

'That makes no difference,' Jack said quickly. 'Everyone knows the Tsar has several mistresses at once. Julie Zichy would be just one more.'

'We've been thinking about the women favoured by the Prussian King,' Ben said slowly. 'What about the Tsar's women? What if the Tsar thought that the King was seeking to cuckold him with one of his mistresses?'

'That's a possibility,' Jack agreed. 'The obvious one is the Nightingale. And she is already involved with the Prussians. One of my men told me just this evening that the Prussian ambassador has his eye on her.'

'No!' Leo's voice was so loud that both Ben and Jack looked across at him in astonishment. But it could not be true. The Prussian ambassador took his pleasures with women from the gutter. Whatever Sophie was, she was not that. 'No,' Leo said again, striving to speak in a more normal voice, 'it wouldn't work. The King has no interest in women outside the aristocratic circle. You know that's the German way. The rumour might circulate, but the Tsar would not believe it.'

Leo's throat was still tight. He was becoming rather hot. Was he flushing? He made a great play of reaching for the wine bottle and topping up all their glasses. He did not want to use Sophie Pietre in any way, even as the subject of a rumour. He knew he was incapable of behaving rationally where she was concerned. 'So we are agreed? We start the rumour that the Tsar intends to bed Countess Julie and that he will enjoy stealing her from under the King's nose.'

'That should do it,' Ben said.

'Good,' Leo said. He had to stop this discussion while he still had control. 'If you two set about planting the rumour about Countess Julie, I will make discreet enquiries about the Nightingale and, in particular, about any relations she may have with the Prussians. Are we agreed?'

They nodded.

'I have another idea,' Ben put in suddenly. 'About the Nightingale.'

Leo tried to swallow. 'Tell us,' he croaked.

'Since she is the Tsar's mistress, she probably learns all sorts of things from him. Pillow talk, remember? Well, what if we let the Tsar think that the Nightingale is a spy, planted on him by the Prussians? Now that *would* drive a wedge between them, would it not?'

'Ben, that's brilliant! It's bound to work.'

'No, it won't,' Leo snapped. 'Why would the Prussians wish to spy on the Tsar? He and the Prussian King are as thick as inkle-weavers.'

Ben was looking a little glum. Jack shrugged his shoulders. Leo began to feel he could breathe again at last. If Sophie were rumoured to be a spy, she would be in real peril. An aristocratic spy would simply be expelled, but Sophie had no such background to protect her. The Tsar could easily arrange to have her meet with an accident. A fatal one.

'That is *all* you discovered?' Beck had been leaning close, so that Sophie's whispered report could not be heard by his coachman. Now he leaned back in his corner and stretched his arms along the polished wood of the open carriage.

Sophie shivered and snuggled farther into her fur-trimmed pelisse. The golden autumn was ending. Nothing was the same any more, not since she had sold her soul to the Prussians and the Baron von Beck. Not since that demanding, heart-stopping kiss, and her angry parting from Leo.

'I am afraid, my dear Madame Pietre, that your night's work is not worth much.'

She leant a little towards him. 'Baron, I took the risk, even if the result does not suit you. How am I supposed to do better, when you will not tell me exactly what you wish me to find out?'

'Hmm. You may perhaps have a point, *madame*.' He ordered the coachman to stop. '*Madame* and I have decided to take a stroll along this path. Walk the horses. We shall return quite soon.'

As soon as they were out of earshot of the carriage, he said, 'You are right, *madame*. We must be more specific about what we want. But I warn you now that, if this information should become known, your future will be… Let us simply say that your future will be far from rosy. Do you understand?'

She wanted to rail at him, but she did not dare. 'Yes.'

'Good. Now, listen. The King of Prussia and the Tsar have reached an agreement about the future of Poland. The details need not concern you. Suffice it to say that both England and Austria mislike the idea. Austria will probably threaten war over it. We need to know if that threat is real.'

Sophie was astonished. 'Surely Austria alone cannot fight both Russia and Prussia?'

'How very wise you are, *madame*,' he sneered. 'No, she would need an alliance with England. So Castlereagh is the key. We need to know whether, if it comes to it, he will take England to war against us.'

Sophie took a deep breath and swallowed hard. 'That is an enormous task you would set me, Baron. It must be worth a great deal.' She looked him squarely in the face, challenging him to deny it.

He did not. 'If you bring us the information we seek, you will be paid even more than your first demand.'

War! These men were ready to go to war again, to shed the blood of thousands of common soldiers, just so that the Tsar could proclaim himself King of Poland. Sophie put a hand to her stomach. The very thought of it made her ill.

She sat down on the edge of her bed and dropped her head into her hands. How was she ever to get out of this fix? She had lied to the Baron once already, but she could not lie to him about this. She did not dare to tell

Beck that Castlereagh would go to war over Poland. Equally, she did not dare to say that he would not. She would have to try to discover the truth.

A moment's reflection showed her that it was impossible. Castlereagh would never let slip such vital information. And even if he did, Sophie could not be so wicked as to pass it on. This was no game. Lives depended on what was done here. She would have to play for time, in hopes of some other solution. Even the Baron could not expect instant results, not on something as important as this.

Teresa appeared in the doorway. She was wearing her travelling cloak. 'The carriage is waiting, *madame*. I have taken the precaution of packing a small valise for you, in case the Empress should ask you to remain overnight.'

Sophie looked up in surprise. With her worries about her spying role, she had completely forgotten that she was to drive out to Schönbrunn to visit the Empress Marie-Louise and her son. She smiled at the thought of him. He was such a merry little fellow. For this afternoon, at least, Sophie would be able to forget about the dark, dangerous side of her life. She would sing, and converse and play with the child as though she had not a care in the world.

Leo's spies had produced much, but none of it was good. The Nightingale had paid yet another visit to the Empress Marie-Louise at Schönbrunn. It was a very strange friendship—a woman who was daughter to one emperor and wife to another, entertaining a woman who was little better than a common whore.

Leo found himself bridling at his own use of that term. There was nothing common about Sophia Pietre.

She had an amazing musical talent, she had the manners of a high-born lady and she had enough charm to draw the greatest men in the land into her net.

While he could not fathom what might be going on between Sophie and Marie-Louise, he was much more worried about her link with the Prussian ambassador. One of the most trustworthy of the Aikenhead spies had reported that the Nightingale had actually visited the Prussian embassy. It was astonishing, if true. Even if she were about to enter into a liaison with Baron von Humboldt, she would surely never meet him at the embassy, where everyone, down to the most junior clerk, would be able to leer at her and sneer at him. It made no sense. If she really had gone to the Prussian embassy, it must be for some other, deeper reason.

Leo was finding it difficult to banish the notion that Ben had planted in his mind, of Sophie as a spy. Yet Leo had been right, too—it made no sense for the Prussians to be spying on the Tsar.

He shuddered. Maybe they had set her to spy on everyone? That was an even worse thought. He remembered, with a panicky lurch of his pulse, that she had been more than charming to Lord Castlereagh on several occasions now. The pair had walked apart, and Castlereagh had clearly been very taken with her. What man would not be? Yet Castlereagh was so devoted to his wife that he had brought her to Vienna. A liaison with the Nightingale was impossible.

The voice of doubt in Leo's mind would not be silenced. Castlereagh was faithful to his wife, but was he susceptible enough to the Nightingale's charms to tell her things that he should not?

Leo felt the beginnings of despair. He had been

unable to deal with his feelings for this woman, even when his only complaint was that she sold her body to great men. But if she was also spying for England's enemies, she was Leo's enemy, too.

The horror of it made him want to retch. If Sophia Pietre was truly spying against Leo's country, it was his duty to take every possible step to stop her, no matter what the consequences. For him. Or for her.

Sophie gazed down at the Tsar's tall figure, asleep on the bed. He was almost naked, but he looked peaceful and comfortable enough for the moment. She had truly played the whore with him, using his own vanity to persuade him to undress first. She had begged to be allowed to feast her eyes on his royal person in all its glory. She might even have used those very words. A real man—a man like Leo Aikenhead, who seemed to have no personal vanity in spite of his dashing good looks—would never have swallowed such tosh. But the Tsar had responded like a spoiled and pampered child. He understood, he said, that if she disrobed first, their passion would overwhelm them before she had a chance to fulfil her desire to gaze on him.

She leaned closer to loosen the fastenings of his breeches. It took too long—her fingers were clumsy and shaking—but in the end, she succeeded. She did not try to remove them, for he was too heavy to lift, but she thought that she had done enough. He would awake and find his breeches undone. He would think, she hoped, that his desire for her had been so urgent that he had not even stopped to undress fully. Perhaps it would make him feel more virile.

She turned to the Tsar's pier glass and forced herself

to master her trembling fingers so that she could fasten the tiny buttons of her bodice, for she was utterly determined that no one should see her looking anything but perfectly groomed. She glanced over her shoulder. He had not moved. He was deep asleep. She had at least half an hour to make her escape.

Her immediate tasks were simple enough. She would walk nonchalantly down to the waiting carriage and return to her apartment. Verdicchio would not probe for details. He would assume that Sophie had shared the Emperor's bed. And she would allow him to do so.

But what about the Emperor? Sophie's drug gave men vividly erotic dreams that confused their memories, and their bodies, too. The Emperor would awake to find his clothes and his bed in disarray, and clear signs that Sophie had shared it with him. He would probably assume that he had fallen asleep, exhausted by passion, and that she had simply slipped discreetly away. And even if he suspected the truth, he would say nothing. He was much too vain to admit that he had been gulled.

She straightened the tiny puff sleeves of her gown and the jewels at her throat. Then she crept back to the bed to stare down at him: the Tsar of All the Russias, the man who would be King of Poland, who would sacrifice countless lives in order to secure that petty bauble. And yet, he was just a man, weak, driven by his lusts, and overcome by the guile of a single woman.

Sophie glanced down at the poison ring on her finger. She must not forget. She picked up the Tsar's champagne flute from the table by the huge canopied bed, took it into the antechamber, and rinsed it in the iced water from the champagne bucket. She dried it carefully with her handkerchief. Then she poured a bare half-inch of champagne into the bottom of it, before restoring it to its original place. No one would know that the glass had ever held anything but pure champagne. The Tsar would see the empty glass and blame a mixture of champagne and sated passion for his long slumber and erotic dreams.

It had been a fine performance by a consummate actress. She had teased and charmed, making every step last as long as she possibly could, until the moment arrived when she could safely add the drug to his glass and wait for it to take effect. She had been clever there, cleverer than on the previous occasion. Then, he had been too intent on uncovering her bosom to care about drinking champagne. This time, she had flattered him into uncovering himself first, while drinking toast, after toast, after toast—to his beloved homeland, to the passions they shared, to Sophie's beauty. He had even stood in the bedchamber to toast the great bed they were about to share, before he fell onto it and passed out.

She lifted her own champagne glass from the table beside the ice bucket, raised it in a mocking salute to the bedchamber beyond, and took a tiny sip. 'My felicitations, your Majesty,' she whispered. 'May your dreams tell you that you have enjoyed the love of the Nightingale.'

Leo had been waiting for what seemed like hours, but he had seen the purple carriage go into the palace courtyard and he was determined to wait until it left. It would not prove anything, except that Madame Pietre was sharing the Tsar's bed. It did not prove that she was a spy. But all the other evidence pointed in that direction. That was why Leo himself was on watch. He had to see for himself what she did and where she went, for he was the only one who understood what she really was.

Thus far, Leo had not been able to persuade himself to confide in Jack or Ben. He was not sure why. Was it because neither of them was in the least attracted to the Venetian Nightingale? Instead of a beautiful, seductive woman, Jack and Ben saw a courtesan, a manipulator of men, a pawn to be used in their spying games. Even if she was England's enemy, Leo would not permit her to be treated in that way. If she had to be trapped, to fall, he would ensure that her end was honourable.

There was movement behind the gates. It was the purple carriage.

Leo pulled out his watch and squinted at it in the half-light of the distant flambeaux. She had been with the Tsar for over two hours. Long enough for—

He forbade himself to think about what the Tsar and the Nightingale might have been doing together in the imperial palace. Leo's relationship with her—if there had ever been one—was dead. He was here as a spy catcher, defending his country's interests. That was all. He must think of England. And duty.

The purple carriage passed within a few feet of his hiding place behind the wall of the Chancellery. The window glass was down, in spite of the wind. Had she felt the need for some air after the passion-filled heat of the Emperor's rooms? She was wrapped in costly furs, but the jewels at her throat peeked through, catching the light like fireflies from the depths of some shadowy bush. She was staring straight ahead, her thoughts apparently far away.

And a satisfied smile was playing around her luscious mouth.

Chapter Thirteen

'My wife reported the rumours about the Tsar and Countess Julie Zichy today.' Lord Castlereagh motioned Leo to a seat by the fireplace. 'That was a good notion on your part, but it will not serve, I fear.'

Leo did not try to conceal his surprise. 'Might I ask why not, sir? She is the one woman who is truly admired by both the Tsar and the King of Prussia.'

'Yes, she is. The King of Prussia is particular in his tastes, whereas the Tsar seems to be prepared to couple with almost any woman who looks twice at him. However, the Tsar has taken to his bed. It will be some weeks, I am told, before we see him on the dance floor again.'

If he was ill, he could not be bedding the Nightingale!

Leo was instantly ashamed of his own selfish reaction. 'How will that affect the negotiations, the problems over Poland?'

Castlereagh took a tiny pinch of snuff. 'Nothing can be done until the Tsar recovers. He insists on taking all decisions himself. So we are at a stand. I am not sure whether there is anything you can do, Aikenhead. Except to continue to sow the rumours against the Prussian King.'

'We will do our best, sir.' Leo thought for a moment. 'Do you know when, precisely, the Russian Emperor became ill?'

'Yes, I do, as a matter of fact. It was two nights ago.'

Leo's heart sank. Two nights ago the Tsar had shared his bed with Sophie Pietre. Could that have had anything to do with his sudden ill health? Trying to keep his voice light, he asked, 'Do you know exactly what ails the Emperor?'

'Not exactly, no. Does it matter?' Castlereagh asked. 'He is ill enough to have taken to his bed. With a fever. I sent to enquire after him, of course, and I was told that it was a simple recurrence of an old illness. That is all I know.'

Castlereagh rose from his chair, indicating that the interview was over. 'The Emperor will be much disappointed to miss the joust at the Riding School next week. My wife tells me that nothing like it has ever been seen, even here in Vienna. The twenty-four damsels have apparently borrowed jewels from every woman of their acquaintance, so that their gowns may be strewn with diamonds. I am glad to say that my wife has not lent any of hers,' Castlereagh added with a knowing smile.

Leo, too, had heard the rumours about beauteous women covered with jewels, prised from their settings in tiaras and brooches, and stitched to satin and velvet. 'But you will be attending, sir?'

'Of course. My wife and I will both be there, as will all the visiting royals, with the possible exception of the

Russian Emperor, if he is still indisposed. It will be a
spectacle that will be talked of for years.'

'Have you heard?' Ben bounced across the room the
moment Leo appeared in the doorway of their lodgings.

Leo was reminded of a large, golden puppy, with the
sort of huge paws and wagging tail that knocked down
everything in its path. 'Heard what?'

'The Tsar is ill.'

'I know. I learned—'

'He's been poisoned.'

'What?'

'Well,' Ben said, in a slightly more reasonable voice,
'that's the rumour I heard. He was struck down two
nights ago and cannot leave his bed. His doctors fear
for him. So I was told.'

'They fear for him, do they?' Leo grimaced. 'I have
just come from Castlereagh and that is not the tale I
heard from him. According to his information, the Tsar
is suffering from a recurrence of an old illness. He has
taken to his bed with a fever. There was no mention of
poison. None at all.'

'Oh,' said Ben, sounding deflated, even disappointed.

'I think,' Jack put in, over Ben's shoulder, 'that Ben
was overjoyed to have detected a real plot. He thinks—
he thought, rather—that the Nightingale administered
poison to the Tsar while she was sharing his bed.' Jack
raised his eyebrows and put his head on one side, which
gave him a rather comical look. 'It would have been a
splendid plot, if it were true. And, to be fair, we do not
really know what is wrong with the man, do we?'

'It is our job,' Leo said, as calmly as he could, 'to

sow rumours, not to believe those that are maliciously started by others.'

Ben and Jack nodded. Ben looked a little sheepish now.

'However, we do have good news. Lady Castlereagh has heard the rumour we planted about the Tsar and Countess Julie Zichy. If she has heard it, it will no doubt reach the Prussian King very soon. With luck, he will soon become jealous enough to be angry at his erstwhile friend, the Tsar. We are making progress on that front.'

'True,' Jack agreed. 'But while the Tsar is recovering from his…um…recurrent illness, he can't be pursuing Julie Zichy. The King will know that.'

'Yes, he will. But he will wonder, all the same. He must know that the Tsar has favoured a very great number of women since his arrival here.'

'And the Countess Julie is extremely beautiful,' Ben added.

'Yes. She is to be one of the twenty-four chosen damsels partnering the knights at the joust. Let us hope that the Prussian King will be watching very carefully, to see whether she favours anyone apart from her knightly champion. The closer he watches her, the more jealous he is like to become.'

The crowd rose from their places as a fanfare announced the entry of the twenty-four knights. Each was preceded by a groom carrying his banner and followed by a squire bearing his heraldic arms. Their dress belonged to a bygone age, when men wore shining breast plates and fighting helms. The knights were in four companies, their velvet tunics coloured to represent Austria, France, Hungary and Poland. Each man escorted a beautiful damsel, garbed in matching colour and sparkling with jewels. The ladies' national costumes were also of ancient style, though they had allowed themselves certain liberties in order to ensure that their best features could be properly admired. Some had slashed their sleeves, some had slit their skirts. Necklines were immodestly low. And every inch of the sumptuous fabrics they wore—satins and velvets, silks and laces and gauzy veils—was sewn with jewels.

Leo could not believe his eyes. It was beyond anything to see such displays of wealth. The ladies were wearing enough jewels to crown several monarchs. Watching the parade, he began to understand what Castlereagh had hinted at. Lady Castlereagh had probably been very wise to refuse to lend her own diamonds, for some of the fixings on the gowns were far from secure. Leo noticed a couple of stones falling from the Duchess of Sagan's gown as she walked in stately procession to her place in the gallery. Servants clearing up after tonight's festivities might find some excellent rewards among the dust and dirt.

The damsels took their places in the gallery, ranged together by colour. Red and blue and green and black. They shimmered in the golden light from thousands of candles set in the walls of the Imperial Riding School. And they were certainly basking in the admiration of the vast crowd. Leo had never seen women who looked so proud or so certain of their status.

A flourish of trumpets announced the arrival of the Austrian Emperor and all the other royal personages, apart from the Tsar. They paraded around the arena before taking their seats in their own gallery at the far end of the riding school. The royal ladies were also hung with jewels, but they were outshone, Leo felt, by the twenty-four damsels.

Heralds and trumpets announced the start of the spectacle. The cavaliers were on horseback now, each wearing a satin sash that had been tied around his waist by the fair lady he championed. The magnificent horses paraded round the ring, allowing the riders to dip their lances to the monarchs at one end, and to their ladies at the other. Some spectators cheered, others clapped. Many of the female spectators were whispering together and pointing, probably exchanging opinions about the champions and discussing whether they might make good lovers. In Vienna, anything was possible.

It was only when the display of horsemanship began that Leo saw Sophie. She was quite a long way from the front of the arena, with Verdicchio at her side. She was craning her neck to watch as the cavaliers used their lances to pierce rings and split suspended apples. Even from such a distance, Leo could see that her face was full of animation and that she was applauding every fine feat of horsemanship. He saw, too, that she had followed the lead of the twenty-four damsels. She was covered in jewels, not only in her hair and at her throat, but sewn to her gown and the lace wrap around her shoulders. Leo fancied she was making a point. The twenty-four damsels were indeed beautiful, but Sophia Pietre was more than their equal. Were it not for her humble origins, she would have been sitting among them. That abundance of jewels was her way of telling the world that she should have been in the damsels' gallery and acknowledged by all.

Leo felt a flicker of sympathy for her. She certainly

was beautiful, and it was no fault of hers that she was only an opera singer. She did what she must in order to survive. Did that include administering poison to the Russian Emperor? Had that been the reason for that tiny smile on her lips as she drove away?

He would not allow himself to believe it. Sophie was no murderess. He was quite certain of that. She could not be. Besides, what purpose would it have served? If she was simply the Tsar's mistress, poisoning him would remove a potential source of wealth and influence. Leo had seen for himself, in that simple leather box, just how much wealth the Tsar could bestow on a lover who pleased him. Perhaps she was acting for the Prussians? But that made no sense either. The King of Prussia was the Tsar's closest ally. If the Tsar died, the King would find himself friendless against much more powerful nations, like Austria and Britain.

Leo continued to conjure up argument after argument, but rejected every one. The rumour that Sophie was responsible for the Tsar's ill health was patent nonsense.

Enormous cheers heralded the end of the spectacle. Leo realised that he had been far away. How long had the joust continued? He did not know, but he had seen almost none of it. His thoughts had been fixed solely on the Venetian Nightingale and the threats surrounding her. He could only hope that the rumour had not spread too far in the hothouse atmosphere of Vienna for, if it did, it would harm Sophie's reputation even more. It was bad enough that she was known to be the Tsar's mistress, which was bound to provoke jealousy and disdain among the aristocratic ladies. But if they suggested for a moment that Sophie had administered poison, she would probably have to leave the city. The ill fame would follow her, and her career could be ruined.

They had not exchanged a single word since that encounter in the alcove, but he had to speak to her now, whatever her reaction, to warn her about what was being said. As the Tsar's mistress, she could surely arrange for his household to give out more reassuring information about his illness and his condition? Anything to scotch the rumours of poison.

'Madame Pietre?'

She was standing at the back of the ballroom, watching the dancing. Verdicchio stood close by her side, like a watchdog. Was he guarding the lady? Or all those jewels she wore? Leo fancied it was the latter.

'Madame Pietre, may I have the honour of this dance? They are playing a waltz.'

Sophie shot a quick sideways look at Verdicchio, but then she smiled up at Leo, as though his invitation were the most natural thing in the world. As though their last meeting had not consisted of that single, unbelievable kiss. He could almost taste her still.

'Lord Leo, how very kind. I should be delighted.' She laid her gloved and beringed hand on Leo's and allowed him to lead her on to the floor. She was wearing so many jewels that it was difficult to find a free spot on her gown where he could place his hand. Even the back of her gown was sewn with jewels.

They began to move together in the seductive rhythm of the waltz.

'May I say, *madame*, that you rival the twenty-four

damsels tonight? By rights, you should have been one of their number.'

She blushed hotly.

Leo resolved to behave like an English gentleman. 'Did you enjoy the display, *madame*? You seemed to be most enthusiastic.'

She nodded. Her shoulders relaxed a little. 'The riding was splendid. As one would expect from gentlemen who have been in the saddle almost since birth. The horses were particularly impressive, I thought. Each company so well matched, so fierce in the gallop, and yet so obedient to the heel and the hand. At times, they seemed to stop and turn on a penny.'

Everything she said was true, as far as Leo could remember from his vague impressions of the spectacle. It was interesting, however, that she had made no mention of the ladies. He decided to probe a little more. 'And what did you think of the ladies' archaic garb? It became them wonderfully well, I thought.'

'Yes. I think it did.'

An interesting response. Leo had given her an opportunity to make slighting remarks about the twenty-four exalted damsels, but she would not do so. Someone, somewhere, had taught her impeccable manners.

They continued to dance in silence as the music rose to a crescendo. It was the first time he had held her since that extraordinary kiss at the imperial theatre. This time, she felt exactly right in his arms, as though they were meant to be together. But Leo knew it could not be. She was the Tsar's mistress. And almost certainly a spy.

A great wave of self-disgust engulfed him. This woman was a spy and an enemy, and yet he could not stop thinking about the feel of her in his arms, about how right it seemed when they were together. If only he knew the truth. If she were merely the Tsar's mistress, he could find a way of dealing with it. It was her spying, the fact that she was an enemy, that carved at his gut.

The words burst out of him like red-hot lava from an exploding volcano. 'Are you spying for the Prussians, Sophie?'

Her shock was palpable. She stopped dead for a second in the middle of the floor, every muscle of her body taut as a bowstring. But she mastered herself again almost at once and allowed him to continue the movements of the waltz. It was unlikely that the other dancers had noticed anything amiss.

'In my country, Lord Leo,' she said very softly, 'we have a saying, that "like cleaves to like". Why do you ask such a thing of me? Is it, I wonder, that you yourself are a spy?'

As soon as the music ended, Sophie attempted to leave him on the floor, but he would have none of it. They had danced the rest of the waltz in festering silence, but he was clearly determined to escort her back to her companion. He did not offer his arm, or touch her in any way, but she could feel his hand hovering behind her back, just inches from her heated skin, steering her through the throng.

She was sure she had flushed bright red from head to toe when he asked if she was a spy. How could he possibly suspect? But he had been completely thrown by her counter-attack. Could it be that, in her haste to find an appropriately cutting response, she had lit upon the truth? Could Lord Leo Aikenhead be a spy?

Of course he could. Anyone in Vienna, no matter how illustrious, could be a spy.

They reached the edge of the dance floor. Sophie noticed a small group of aristocratic ladies standing with their heads together, as if they were sharing a delicious secret. One of them nodded towards Sophie and said something in an undertone. Another nodded eagerly. Sophie was in no doubt that they were discussing her. And whatever they were saying, it was not flattering.

Sophie tried to ignore the women, but as she and Leo pushed their way through the dense crowd, it was difficult to avoid hearing some of the whispered words. She heard 'nightingale' more than once. Once she heard, quite distinctly, the word 'poison'. And then it was repeated, in a group of young men who turned, as one, to stare at her.

Poison? Who had been poisoned? And what did it have to do with Sophie?

Leo took a quick step forward to place himself between Sophie and the group of young men. 'Come, *madame*,' he said, rather more gently than she expected, 'let me find you a glass of champagne.'

He took her arm and forcibly drew it within his own. He must feel her trembling. Did he know what it was they were saying? Did people really believe that she had poisoned someone? Who—?

The answer hit her with stunning force. The Russian Emperor was ill. Everyone knew that. Everyone knew also—or so she had thought—that it was a recurrence of an old infection. But it seemed that was not what they were saying. Someone had told the world that the Tsar had fallen ill after an assignation with the Venetian

Nightingale. That he was ill because she had poisoned him.

It was impossible! The drug was harmless. It gave
a man delicious dreams for an hour or two. Nothing
more. He would not even have the headache when he
awoke again.

The rumour was fizzing round the ballroom like a
flame up a fuse. Everyone was turning to look at her.
Some of the great ladies drew aside their skirts as
Sophie passed. Sophia Pietre was about to become an
outcast from Viennese society.

Leo guided her to a seat before summoning a waiter
with a tray of glasses. It was so like that earlier time,
almost their first meeting, when she had choked on
champagne. But this was different. He believed she
was a spy. That was certain. For all she knew, he might
also believe she had tried to poison the Tsar.

She could not face such accusations. Not from the
man she loved. She had to get away from here, from all
these people. From Leo Aikenhead. And from Vienna.

It was time. She had made her plans, and now she
must go.

'Have you seen the Nightingale?' Leo asked Jack.
She had taken barely a sip of her champagne before
pleading a slight headache and withdrawing to the
ladies' retiring room. Almost two hours had passed.
Had she fled the ball because of the rumours? It would
not be surprising. Yet Leo had expected her to be
prepared to face down her tormentors. Surely she was
too proud to flee?

'No, I haven't seen her. But I wouldn't be surprised
if she has gone. That rumour about the Tsar is every-

where now. They were talking about her quite openly. And in the most insulting terms.'

'It cannot be true. It makes no sense. I was at her side when she first realised what they were saying of her. She was horror struck.'

'Yes, she would have been,' Jack said laconically.

Leo scowled at him.

'You have to admit, Leo, that if she is guilty, she would be horrified to be found out. If she is not guilty, she would be horrified to be accused. Stands to reason.'

Jack was applying cold logic to the situation, an ability that had completely deserted Leo. Logic said that he should not follow her, but he knew he must. He had to find her and help her. 'She must have left the ball. I am going after her. We need to know the truth.'

Jack raised a sceptical eyebrow.

'Oh, not about the poison,' Leo said, hastily deciding on the tale he would spin to Jack. 'We know the truth about that. We need to know whether she really is a spy. I think… No, I'm almost sure that, if she has been spying for the Prussians, we should be able to recruit her to make her spy for us. The embassy could certainly offer her more than the Prussians will pay, however much that is. And we do need to know what the Tsar is thinking.'

'Once he's off his sick bed,' Jack said.

'Naturally,' Leo snapped. He forced himself to sound more measured. 'We have a little respite. The Nightingale cannot return to the Tsar's bed while he is sick. So we have time to persuade her that her true interests lie with us. And that, Jack, is what I am going to do.'

'What if she's left the city? She might have done. In fact, with all these rumours, there's every chance she'll be expelled anyway.'

'If she has left, I will follow her.' Leo's decision was made, almost without conscious thought, but he still had responsibilities as leader of the Honours in Vienna. 'You don't need me here for the moment, since nothing can happen until the Tsar recovers. You must take over if I have to leave. You and Ben have been doing most of the work, in any case, and if Castlereagh needs a report, you can give it to him.'

'What if he asks about you, Leo?'

'Tell him that I have left Vienna in pursuit of a spy, a spy who will, I believe, play a vital part in defending England's interests.'

Chapter Fourteen

'No, *madame*. You must go on. What if the maestro is following us?' Teresa tried vainly to sit up.

Sophie pressed the maid gently back down on to the lumpy seat of the hired carriage and continued to apply her dampened handkerchief to Teresa's feverish brow. The poor woman had been suffering for two days now and her fever was getting worse.

Sophie made up her mind. It would take several more days to reach Venice. If she insisted on continuing this breakneck pace, she was likely to be carrying Teresa's corpse into the serene city. 'No, Teresa,' she said, as calmly as she could. 'It is not necessary. Even if Maestro Verdicchio has decided to follow us—and even if he knows where we are bound—we have made excellent time. We can afford to rest for a day without any risk of being caught.'

'But, *madame*—' Teresa's voice was barely a wisp '—you cannot be sure. If he catches you, you will be in such danger.'

Sophie stroked Teresa's hand and shook her head,

smiling sadly. 'Believe me, Teresa, a day's respite will make no difference. And I must tell you that, although you seem to have endured the journey with the greatest fortitude, I am finding it sadly wearing. If I do not have some rest soon, I shall probably run mad with the rocking of the carriage on these abominable roads. It is enough to make anyone ill.'

In spite of her weakness, Teresa looked up with disbelief in her face. But Sophie did not care how many barefaced lies she had to tell. She would do whatever was necessary to persuade Teresa that their journey must stop.

Sophie produced some watered wine and forced a little down the maid's throat. After a little while, Teresa fell into a troubled slumber. Sophie rearranged their only cushion under Teresa's head and tucked her own velvet cloak around the maid's body, which was now starting to shiver. Teresa must have some rest, even though stopping here on the road, miles from any source of assistance, was dangerous.

They were passing through bleak countryside, for winter was certainly upon them. At least there had been no snow as yet, which was a blessing, and unusual for early December. But then, it had been a most extraordinary season altogether. There was nothing to be done about the gathering gloom, however. Sophie consoled herself with the fact that her hired coachman had promised to bring them to a reliable inn well before nightfall. She glanced out of the window. It truly was beginning to get dark. If he was to fulfil his promise, the inn could not be far away.

Even from his perch on the box of his rickety carriage, Leo could see no other vehicles. The road was so bad that it was a wonder that any vehicles at all could travel on it. But it seemed that Sophie's carriage had continued to make much better time than Leo's. He had been following her for almost two weeks now—at least, he was fairly sure he was following her—but he had not set eyes on her once. There had been tantalising mentions of a hired carriage carrying a beautiful raven-haired lady, but always at least a day ahead of him. Yesterday, he had learned that she was now three days ahead of him.

Leo rubbed his aching eyes and huddled into his greatcoat. The weather was becoming much colder now. It was no wonder that Sophie was making better speed, for she probably had enough money to pay for teams of the best horses, and a coachman besides, whereas Leo had had to buy this sorry excuse for a carriage and drive it himself. He looked down at the two wretched slugs he was driving. No other horses had been available at his last stop, even if he had been able to afford them. If he did not catch up with her soon, he would find himself penniless and stranded. Would she ever realise what she had done to him? In pursuit of Sophie Pietre, he might end up as a frozen effigy under the ice.

He shrugged his stiffened shoulders. He would not think about her, about the strange effect she had on him. He might have every reason to seek revenge against her, but he was following her out of duty to his country. Nothing more. To bring her back to Vienna, so that Castlereagh could use her against the Tsar. It was absolutely essential for England to thwart Russian ambitions, now that there was such a grave risk of another war.

Leo had resolved to even use force if he had to, though he doubted it would be necessary. She was a sensible woman. But would he ever catch her? It was all very well to make plans to take her back to Vienna, but if she reached Venice before him, she could easily disappear among its maze of alleys and canals. She must have friends, allies, who would hide her. He might never find her at all. All this effort might have been for nothing.

And he might never see her again.

His fingers tightened involuntarily on the reins, pulling at the horses' mouths. They slowed immediately, almost to a standstill. Leo swore, loud and long. These horses would barely go, but they were eager to stop. It took him precious minutes to get them moving again. At this rate, he would never catch her.

He could give up and turn back. He could just about afford a slow journey back to Vienna, though he might have to sell his watch and his signet ring.

This time his curses were directed at his own weakness. The Honours never gave up on a mission, no matter what the hardships. Besides, if he made it to Venice, he would be able to raise ready cash from the bankers there, though he would have to pledge his brother Dominic's credit in order to do so. He had never yet done that, not even when he was paying off young Jack's enormous gambling debts, but this was an emergency. Dominic would understand. Leo might need a great deal of money to employ spies, or pay bribes to find Sophie's hiding place.

It would be dark soon. At this time of year, the days were incredibly short. He would have to find an inn, or some other shelter for the night. He did not dare to drive on after dark, not on an unfamiliar road, and not when he had no idea how far it would be to the next change. Besides, he was becoming desperately tired.

Leo cracked his whip by the leader's ear. By rights, that should have encouraged the nag to greater speed. But it seemed that the beast was oblivious to any such threat. He plodded on at his own slow pace. Leo groaned. He might be spending tonight in an uncomfortable, unheated carriage.

Sophie had not dared to sleep for two nights, for Teresa needed constant attention as her fever mounted. Sophie dreaded the thought that she might fall asleep and wake to find her only friend lying cold upon the bed. Every time she felt herself beginning to weaken, she would rise and pace the floor, telling herself that she had to stay awake. Teresa needed her. And as Teresa had cared for Sophie over many years, so Sophie would now care for Teresa.

It was almost dark when she glanced out through the dirty, half-shuttered window. This was a poor apology for an inn, but at least the landlord had not refused them entrance. They had been lucky there. The landlord of a high-class establishment would have taken one look at Teresa's lank hair and sweaty skin and turned them from the door, no matter how much money Sophie had offered. This landlord had allowed them to stay because he wanted Sophie's gold, but even he was worried about infection. He had refused to allow Sophie to enter any of the public rooms—not that she wished to leave Teresa's side—and none of the inn servants would enter the bedchamber. The room had not been swept or dusted since their arrival. Food, water and logs for the fire were simply left in the passageway outside the door. Sophie had quickly become quite adept at tending the fire and looking to Teresa's bodily needs.

She passed the brown-speckled looking glass for at least the fiftieth time. She was still wearing the gown she had arrived in, though now it was stained and grubby. Her face and hands were reasonably clean, but her hair was escaping from its normal neat knot. There were wisps of it everywhere, framing her face with unruly, childish curls. She tried to smooth it back as she paced, but she would not sit down to comb it. If she ceased to pace, she would be asleep in seconds.

There was a soft moan from the bed. Sophie ran to Teresa's side, gazing at her maid's face, grey under the olive skin, and with blue sunken shadows round the eyes. Teresa's eyelashes flickered. Slowly her eyes opened. She looked lost and bewildered. 'Where am I?' Her voice was just a thread.

Sophie clasped Teresa's hand and raised it to her lips. 'Oh, Teresa,' she said, desperately trying not to weep. 'You are back with me.'

The maid smiled weakly. 'I…' she croaked.

Sophie jumped to her feet, wiping away one rebellious tear with the back of her hand. 'How stupid of me. You must be so thirsty.' She fetched water. Then she gently raised Teresa, so that she could swallow. 'Just a little more. There. Is that better?'

Teresa's eyes told her that it was.

'Splendid. You shall have more soon. But first, I think you should sleep.'

Teresa's eyelids were already drooping. Soon she was asleep.

Sophie sat for a long time by the bed, caressing the maid's hand. She touched her fingers to Teresa's forehead. Much cooler now, and no longer so damp. She was recovering. In another day or two, they would be able to go on.

A day or two? Did she dare to remain here any longer? What if…?

No. Teresa was much too weak to travel. No matter who might be on their trail, they could not leave until Teresa was stronger.

Sophie gently placed Teresa's hand beneath the covers and went to check her store of valuables. And her pistol. One day, soon, she might need to use it. Sophie set herself to cleaning and reloading it. She had to be sure that she could rely on it, for it gave her only one shot.

If Beck should follow me, I shall make sure that single shot counts.

After a few minutes, the pistol was cleaned and primed. This time, she laid it on the table where it would be readily to hand. Then she set about hiding her jewels in the concealed pockets that she and Teresa had sewn into her petticoats during the long, boring hours in the carriage. It was safer so. Her reticule could be stolen. And a single bulging pocket under her gown might be noticed.

Having taken care of the wealth on which they depended, and the weapon that would protect them, Sophie sat down on the hard chair in front of the dressing table. The foxed mirror showed her a pale, gaunt face and unkempt hair. She should wash and put her hair into some kind of order. She really should.

But just for a moment, she would sit here. Just for a moment.

* * *

The pounding on her door woke her with a start. Oh, God, she had been asleep. She was all confusion, unable to remember quite where she was and why. Except that she knew she should not have been asleep. The landlord was shouting in his almost incomprehensible dialect: something about a man, a man who was looking for—

Sophie sprang to her feet and grabbed the pistol. She had been found! It did not matter whether her pursuer was Beck or Verdicchio. If either of them sought to force her to their will, she would shoot them.

Pistol in hand, she backed away from the door until her legs were against the bed where Teresa lay, still deeply asleep. Sophie's body would protect the maid. She would not flinch from this. Using both hands now to steady the pistol, she pointed it at the door and waited.

The latch moved. But the door did not open. Sophie had kept it locked since their arrival. Perhaps the intruder would go away? Perhaps it was not—?

The lock splintered. The door flew wide, crashing into the wall with great force.

'Stand where you are,' Sophie cried, 'or I will shoot you down.'

The dark, muffled figure in the doorway stopped dead. Its red eyes stared. Then it started to laugh.

Sophie's hands began to shake. 'Leo?' she managed. 'Oh, thank God. I thought—' And then she slumped into oblivion.

Leo was not quick enough to catch her. Fortunately, the bed broke her fall, and most of her body remained balanced there, with only her legs dangling. Leo lunged forward and grabbed her before she could roll off the bed. The pistol, he noticed, had been cocked and ready to fire. With a grimace, he prised it out of her fingers, made it safe, and set it on the night stand.

A fiery piece, the Venetian Nightingale. Since he had been foolhardy enough to laugh at her, he was remarkably lucky not to have been shot.

From the open doorway, the landlord had begun babbling in some incomprehensible language, which might have been Italian.

Leo pushed Sophie a little farther towards the centre of the bed where she would be safe. Her maid was sound asleep on the far side, but there was plenty of room for two women.

Throwing off his greatcoat and muffler, Leo strode to the doorway. The door lock was in a sorry state, but the hinges were still serviceable. He would be able to ensure Sophie's privacy.

He tried French on the landlord, and then English, but without success. Then, racking his brains for his pitifully small store of Italian words, he demanded water and brandy. The landlord's response was a simple one. He narrowed his eyes and held out his grubby hand, palm up, in a universally understood gesture. With an oath, Leo delved into his pocket. There were precious few coins left, and he had to hand over several of them before the landlord gave a grudging nod and departed.

Leo pushed the door shut and placed a stool against it to hold it closed. He quickly surveyed the pitiful bedchamber. There was some used washing water in a bowl on the dressing table. Relieved, he crossed the room to rid himself of at least some of the dirt of the road. She must not lay eyes on him as he was now. Not again. But the sight that met him in the mirror was far worse than he could have imagined. It shocked him into laughing aloud. He looked like a filthy vagabond.

Yet Sophie had known him instantly. It was very strange. How had she recognised him through all this dirt?

He washed it off as best he could and dried himself with his muffler. He would not soil Sophie's own towels. He ran his fingers through his dusty, uncombed hair. That would have to wait.

He crossed back to the bed. The maid was laid out like a corpse, and almost as pale. So that was why he had caught up with them. The maid was ill—seriously ill by the colour of her—and Sophie had stopped to care for her. Of course she had. She would not abandon her servant when she was sick. She would tend her, even at some risk to herself.

He drew in a quick, shuddering breath. Sophie could not be sick, could she? He laid his cold fingers on her brow. Finding it was perfectly cool, he let out a long sigh of relief. She was not ill. He examined her more closely now. The gown she wore was filthy, and he guessed that her hair had not been combed for days. Had she been looking after the maid with no help from the landlord or his servants? It was certainly possible. There were black shadows under Sophie's eyes and her cheeks were gaunt. She looked utterly exhausted.

Following some strange inner urge, Leo laid the back of his fingers against her cheek and stroked gently down to her chin. Her skin was just as soft and just as perfect as ever. With rest and good food, she would soon recover her strength and her glorious bloom.

Food! Yes. He strode to the door and flung it open.

The landlord was already there, with a bottle in one hand, and his head cocked on one side, as if he had had his ear to the door. Leo growled at him and snatched the bottle from his hand. *'Agua?'* he snapped.

The landlord bent to pick up a large jug of steaming water from the floor.

Not what he had tried to ask for, but it would be useful. He motioned to the landlord to set it on the floor, just inside the door. Then, using a mixture of sign language plus the odd word, Leo gave the man to understand that he should bring food and water. Drinking water. Again, the landlord insisted on payment in advance and, this time, he took the last of Leo's money.

There was no obvious means of disposing of the dirty water from the basin. No doubt the landlord would charge to have it carried away. So Leo forced open one of the dirty windows and emptied the basin into the yard below. There were no shouts of outrage. Pity. Leo would have enjoyed throwing foul water over that money-grubbing landlord. Judging by the amount of dirt on him, it would have done him no harm at all.

Leo poured some of the fresh hot water into the basin and dipped the end of Sophie's towel in it. Then, while it cooled a little, he poured brandy into an empty tumbler. She had still not moved.

There was just enough space for Leo to edge one hip onto the bed. He put an arm under her shoulders and lifted her. He smoothed the damp towel across her forehead and mouth, and set the brandy glass to her lips. She moaned. That opened her lips just enough for him to tip a small amount down her throat. She began to cough and splutter as the brandy burned its way down to her stomach.

Leo waited until he was sure she was able to sit up by herself before he removed his arm and stood up. 'It's a sovereign remedy, you know.' He smiled down at her. Then he let his gaze roam around the spartan room in a very obvious manner. 'Besides, you do not appear to have any feathers to hand. To burn under your nose,' he added wickedly, in response to her obvious confusion. Adopting an expression of total innocence, he raised his hands, palms uppermost, in a gesture of helplessness. 'What else was I supposed to do?'

She stared dumbly at him.

Her eyes seemed to have grown huge in her drawn, ashen features. She was too exhausted to follow his teasing. He offered the brandy glass again. 'Come, my dear lady. You are exhausted. This will help you to recover.'

She raised a hand as if to push the glass away, but he would not permit it. He held it there, just in front of her face.

At last, with a tiny shrug of resignation, she took it and drank a little. She began to splutter all over again. 'Good God!' she croaked. 'What on earth is it?'

Leo retrieved the glass and took a sip. Whatever it was, it was confoundedly strong, much stronger than the brandy available in England. The landlord had probably made it himself. He set the glass down on the night stand. 'I beg your pardon, *madame*. I asked for brandy to help revive you. That—' he glanced at it with distaste '—is not something that any person of discernment should drink. I do apologise.'

She was still staring at him, wide-eyed. But there was a glow in her face now, a warmth that had not been there before.

It must be the effects of the spirit. He should be glad that she was beginning to revive. He allowed himself a mischievous grin. 'I do have to say that, vile though it is, it did the trick. You recovered remarkably quickly from your swoon.'

She continued to stare at him. Then, quite suddenly, she smiled. It was as if the sun had burst out from behind a blank, grey cloud. 'You are fortunate, Lord Leo,' she said, still with a slight croak in her voice, 'that I did not shoot you. Believe me, I intended to.'

That brought him back to earth with a jolt. He had to swallow hard before he could say, with a fair semblance of calmness, 'I have not the least doubt of it.' He reached for the pistol on the night stand and pocketed it. 'And so, if you permit—and even if you do not—I will take charge of your pistol.'

'You have no right—!' she began, but stopped short when he shook his head at her. Perhaps it was because he was still smiling ruefully at her. 'Oh, very well,' she finished. 'For the moment, at least. I admit that I am extremely tired.'

'I can see that,' he said gently. 'Will you tell me what happened?'

Sophie explained about her maid's illness and the days they had spent in this disreputable inn while Teresa's fever mounted and finally broke. 'She will recover now. In a day or two, we will be able to continue our journey. All she needs is rest and good food.' She was swaying a little. She needed rest, too. But before he could suggest it, she continued, 'You know how we came to be here. But why are you travelling to Venice so late in the year? And without your companions?'

Now was not the time to start an argument about

whether she would go on to Venice or back to Vienna to spy for England. 'Forgive me, dear lady, but I am not at liberty to discuss my journey. Not with anyone.' She frowned up at him. He saw the moment when she decided he must be on a government mission, and that further questions would be useless. He smiled down at her and changed the subject. 'I have ordered food and water from the landlord. At least, I think I have. The first time I ordered water for you to drink, and he brought a jug of hot water, for washing. So I cannot be absolutely sure what he will bring this time. Let us hope it is something edible.'

She gave a tiny laugh. 'His dialect is very difficult. I speak many languages, but—' she shrugged her shoulders '—even so, I find it difficult to communicate with him. But I dare say he will have understood a request for food. If you paid him enough, that is.'

Leo felt himself flushing. 'I did pay him.' He paused. He had no choice but to tell her. 'To be frank, *madame*, I paid him with the last of my ready money. If he demands more, I shall have to find some other means of paying him.'

'You have nothing?'

He shook his head. 'I have this signet ring.' He raised his right hand to show her the gold ring on his little finger. 'And my watch. I had intended to sell them to pay my way. But I doubt that our landlord will give me a fair price.'

'You are right. However, I have more than enough gold for the remainder of my journey and to make you a small loan, besides.' She raised her eyebrows. 'That is, if a gentleman such as yourself will stoop to borrow from a mere opera singer?' In spite of her exhaustion and her dishevelled state, she suddenly looked every inch the great lady.

Leo did not think. He simply lifted her hand to his lips and kissed her fingers. 'Madame Pietre,' he said, in the most serious tone he could muster, 'you see before you a penniless second son. A suppliant at your feet. I will most gladly accept any loan you are prepared to offer. And I promise, on my honour, that the money shall be repaid, with interest, at the first opportunity. The opera singer, the beautiful Venetian Nightingale, has taken pity on a beggar, and I assure you that he is humbly grateful.'

Her eyes widened in astonishment. They were shining, too.

Leo turned her hand in his and pressed a fervent kiss into her palm.

He should not have done it. It was clearly too much for her, in her weakened state. She gave a little gasp. Her eyes rolled upwards, and she fainted.

This time, however, Leo caught her in his arms, and held her safe.

Chapter Fifteen

The last thing Leo had expected was to be nursemaid to two invalids, one recovering from a fever and the other from exhaustion. Nor had he expected that, at the first sight of Sophie, he would instantly forget all his grievances against her, and focus his whole being on serving her and saving her from any peril that might threaten her. He could not understand what had come over him. He needed to fathom out his own reactions, but that would take time and tranquillity. He had neither. He was much too busy for anything but tending his charges.

He hurriedly swallowed the last mouthful of his bread and cheese and rose to check on his two invalids. The maid had not stirred at all. Sophie, still clad in her grubby gown, had been thrashing around and moaning earlier. Now, she appeared to be sound asleep at last, under the coverlet. Her breathing was steady, and regular. She would soon be well again.

Leo wished he had had the courage to remove her gown and her underthings, since that would have made her much more comfortable. But she would have been outraged to discover that he had undressed her. She might not be a lady, but he had promised himself he would treat her as if she were. He could think of no other way of proving that he had no intention of taking advantage of her. Would she believe it? Probably not. Not after some of the things he had said to her before.

His rebellious mind began to conjure up pictures—Sophie at her recitals, Sophie at the imperial joust, Sophie seated by his side in the Prater, Sophie in his arms—but he swiftly banished them. Such images would lead him to recall the insults they had exchanged and the wounds they had inflicted on each other. He could not bear to remember those.

He was here to make her well, and then to ensure she returned to Vienna, where England needed her help to prevent the outbreak of war. That task was vital. She must have no reason to think that Leo had any personal motives in this.

If he behaved as a gentleman should, she would have no cause for suspicions of any kind. He was a gentleman. So why was he finding it all so very difficult?

Sophie yawned and stretched luxuriously. She felt wonderfully refreshed, at last. How long had she slept? She had no idea.

It was very strange to have a man for a chambermaid, especially one who was a lord rather than a servant. But Leo had insisted that both Sophie and Teresa were too weak to do much for themselves. He had fetched food and water, he had tended the fire, he had even—to Sophie's considerable embarrassment—carried away the chamber pot. And yet he had always known exactly when he should leave the room, to ensure the two women had privacy when they needed it. It was as if he could read Sophie's mind.

She had loved him before, even when he was demanding to buy her body. Now, seeing at first hand how gentle and sensitive he could be, she loved him more. Was he sensitive enough to guess how she felt about him? She hoped not. It would be unbearable to be pitied, and that was all she could expect. No man of such exalted station would ever do more than dally with a woman of Sophie's station.

She wanted him. Of course, she did. Almost every time he looked at her, or touched her or simply spoke to her, her whole body came alive in a way it never had before. Every inch of her skin longed for his touch, his kiss. And low in her belly, there was a hot, melting ache. It had started the moment she first awoke, two days ago, to find him applying lavender water to her brow. Since then, it had grown and swollen like a flower bud ready to burst into life. She knew it was desire.

But she also knew that, if she permitted him to buy her as he had originally wished, their joining would be soiled and she would come to hate him. If only he wanted her for what she really was, rather than for what he believed her to be. If only… She gave up. Such daydreaming led precisely nowhere.

It was cold in this chamber, in spite of Leo's efforts with the fire. Sophie put on her thick wrapper and tied the belt around her waist. Then she went round to the other side of the bed to check on Teresa. She was asleep still, but she was clearly much improved. There was colour in her cheeks and her face no longer looked so pinched. That must be at least partly because of Leo's patient work with the feeding spoon.

A sudden thought struck her. How on earth had he paid for the food he had coaxed them both to eat? She vaguely remembered that he had said he had no more ready money. She had even suggested he accept a loan from her, hadn't she? But she had had no opportunity to give him anything. Apart from breaks to wash and to eat, she had spent almost two full days sleeping.

She was fully recovered now. She would dress and go out to find him. She would insist that he accept her money for the room and for their food. After all, only she and Teresa had actually used this room as a bedchamber. As soon as it was clear that neither of them was in any danger, Leo had left them to sleep alone. Sophie suspected that he had been sleeping outside in the stables, or in his own carriage. He was too much the gentleman to compromise them, even by sleeping here in a chair. He was—

The door swung open. Sophie realised that she had been so preoccupied with thoughts of Leo that she had failed to hear his knock. 'Lord Leo! You—'

'How interesting,' said a well-known voice. 'That was not at all the greeting I was expecting.'

Verdicchio! He had found her.

Sophie straightened and glared at him, but he ignored her and quietly closed the door. He had the look of a cat that had caught a mouse, pleased with himself, and ready to play with his new, living toy. Oh, God! Leo! What had Verdicchio done to Leo? Visions of Leo bleeding, perhaps dead, swam into her brain.

'Nothing to say, my dear Sophie? That is most unlike you.'

She pulled the belt of her wrap even tighter. If only she had her pistol! But it was still in Leo's pocket. She raised her chin and stared unblinkingly at him. She would not let him cow her. Not ever again. 'Why should I have anything to say to you? Our partnership, such as it was, is over. That is why I left Vienna.'

'Why you ran away, rather,' he said softly. 'But nothing has changed, Sophie. You are still mine. I bought you from your father fourteen years ago, and you are mine unless I decide to release you. Which, I may say, I shall not. Not while the Venetian Nightingale continues to be the singing toast of Europe.'

Sophie moved to put herself between Verdicchio and the sleeping maid. She would not yield to him. Not this time.

'A defiant piece, are you not? Absent-minded, too. Let me tell you again, therefore. If you do not return to me, the whole world will discover who you really are. It's a stark choice, I fear. Music and wealth, with me. Or the gutter, alone.'

'I would rather starve than return to you,' she spat.

He shrugged his shoulders. 'Very well. I will leave you to do just that.' He looked her up and down with narrowed eyes. 'But before I go, I will have the return of all the jewels you stole from me.'

She gasped. 'Never! They are mine. You have no right—!'

He moved more quickly than she had imagined possible. In an instant, he grabbed her and twisted her arms up behind her back. She cried out in pain.

'Quiet, woman! You are not hurt. But you will be, if you don't return the jewels. Where have you hidden them?'

Sophie bit her lip hard against the pain and shook her head. Those jewels were all that stood between her and starvation. She would not give them up.

He twisted her arms still higher, until she thought that her bones must break. Eventually, her self-control gave way and she gasped with the pain of it. 'Quite so,' he murmured, the satisfaction evident in his voice. 'Tell me where they are, Sophie, or I will break your arm.'

The door crashed open. This time, the figure standing there was neither muffled, nor red-eyed. Leo looked huge and menacing and intent on vengeance.

'Leo!' She had known he would come. In her heart, she had known.

'Release her.'

Verdicchio responded by hauling Sophie's arms even higher. She could not prevent the cry of real pain that escaped from her lips.

Leo became very still. He did not move from the doorway. For a long time, he stood, just staring at Verdicchio. When at last he spoke, his voice was so hoarse it was barely audible. 'I will give you precisely five seconds to let her go, Verdicchio. If you do not, I will kill you.'

Sophie felt a tiny slackening in Verdicchio's grip. He seemed to be holding her with only one hand now. The pain receded a fraction.

'You have no right to her,' Verdicchio spluttered. 'I paid for her. She is—'

'One.'

'—mine. She is mine!'

'Two.' Leo slipped his fingers into his pocket and withdrew Sophie's pistol. 'Three.' Very deliberately, he cocked it and aimed at Verdicchio's heart. 'Four.'

Verdicchio raised his free hand level with Sophie's head. He was holding a pistol of his own. And he was pointing it at Leo.

Sophie screamed and pushed back against Verdicchio with all her might. He staggered, losing his balance and his grip on her. She managed to haul herself free and launched herself forward to protect Leo.

She was too late. Two shots rang out, deafeningly loud in the confined space. Followed by an eerie silence. And then a loud groan of pain.

A puzzled Italian voice said, 'What is happening? I don't understand.'

Sophie spun round. Teresa was sitting up in bed, looking confused. And Verdicchio lay in a crumpled heap on the floor, bleeding profusely. Sophie ignored him. Only Leo mattered. She ran to him. He was still standing in the doorway, pointing the empty pistol at Verdicchio.

'Did he hurt you?' Leo asked.

'Are you hurt?' Sophie gasped in the same moment. Almost in the same breath.

It seemed that Leo was unhurt. He put his free hand on her shoulder and rubbed gently. But he did not take his eyes off Verdicchio. 'Nothing broken, I hope?'

'No,' Sophie breathed, leaning into his touch. 'Ah, that is so much better.'

He continued to rub. 'You will be sore, but it will soon heal, I expect. More than I can say for our friend here.'

From the floor, Verdicchio groaned, 'You have killed me. You will hang for this.'

'Shall I, indeed? I think I have witnesses, sir, who will swear that yours was the first shot.' When Verdicchio simply slumped a little more, Leo said, 'Madame, pray remove that pistol from his grasp. Make sure you do not cross my line of fire.'

Sophie hoped that her surprise did not show. Her pistol was empty now. Leo must know that. But of course, Verdicchio did not. Leo was bluffing, because Verdicchio's pistol might hold another shot.

She skirted the bed and moved behind Verdicchio to remove the pistol from his limp fingers. He was losing a great deal of blood. She could not tell precisely where he was wounded, but it looked very bad.

And then the truth struck her. It was just as Verdicchio had said. If Verdicchio died, Leo might hang for his murder. His life was in danger. He must get away from here! She must make him go!

Leo did not seem overly concerned about the risk. He simply held out his hand for Verdicchio's pistol. 'Hmm. Yes, there is a second shot with this one. A neat little item.' He pocketed Sophie's pistol and transferred Verdicchio's to his right hand.

Sophie's gaze was drawn to that lean hand. It looked odd, somehow. It took a moment or two for her to work out what had changed. And then she saw the pale mark on his little finger. He was no longer wearing his ring. Of course. That would account for—

'Now, be so good as to summon the landlord, *madame*,' Leo ordered briskly. 'I imagine he is not far away. Probably listening in the corridor just outside the door.' He glanced quickly over his shoulder, but there was no one in the doorway. 'Tell him to send for a surgeon. We must do all we can to save the life of this miserable worm. It is, I fear, our Christian duty.'

Sophie had expected Leo to resist her pleas to leave immediately. Surprisingly, he did not.

It had cost a large part of Sophie's reserves of coin

to persuade the landlord to keep Verdicchio at his inn and to send for the surgeon. But she grudged none of it. She was desperate that the man should not die. Not for his own sake—she had hated him as long as she could remember—but for Leo's. He was a foreigner in this land. The authorities might take delight in hanging him.

'I dare say he will recover,' Leo said as he swung the last of their bags into the boot of his carriage. 'And if he does not, it will be the fault of the care he receives. It is not a serious wound, I promise you.'

Sophie looked up at him with wide, questioning eyes. Could she believe that? There had been such a lot of blood.

'Up with you, now.' He put his hands to her waist and lifted her into the carriage where Teresa was already in-stalled, tucked up in Sophie's travelling rugs. There was even a hot brick for her feet, which Leo had heated in the open fire of the bedchamber. He seemed to think of everything.

Sophie willed herself not to put her hands to her waist, to touch the throbbing skin where he had held her. He must not know. Not ever. She took her seat as calmly as she could, waiting for him to climb in beside her. Being a gen-tleman, he would not crowd her. He would sit opposite, with his back to the horses. Too far away to touch.

She waited, but he made no move. 'Surely you are coming, too?'

He laughed, his eyes twinkling with good humour. 'Someone, *madame*, has to drive this apology for a vehicle. I think…' he nodded towards Teresa, and then to Sophie '…that, of the three of us, I am perhaps the best fitted for that task. Or did you have other ideas?'

'My coachman...' she began. Her voice tailed off. Leo was looking infuriatingly smug. And now she thought about it, Sophie realised that she had not set eyes on her coachman or her carriage for days.

'Your coachman decided that he was not prepared to risk further exposure to Teresa's fever. I'm afraid he deserted you almost a week ago.'

'Well! And I had paid him as far as Venice! Of all the—!' He shut the door before she could finish her tirade. Half a minute later, they were off.

After a few hundred yards, Teresa stirred in her corner. 'This is not a good carriage,' she said flatly. 'I think we are going to have an uncomfortable journey.'

Sophie patted the maid's hand. Teresa was often ill on carriage journeys. Since this vehicle swayed worse than most, she would probably have a difficult time of it. Sophie set herself to diverting Teresa's attention from her discomfort. If Sophie gossiped and told stories, perhaps the maid would not suffer too much.

Sophie was beginning to feel hoarse. She had been talking almost non-stop, trying to keep Teresa amused. And so far, it seemed to be working. Teresa had not been ill. Sophie refused to think about the effects on her voice. She did not expect to be singing in public again for a long time.

It would be dark soon. Leo would have to find somewhere to stop for the night. This road would be new to him, but now that they were nearing Venice, there must be more inns to offer rooms to weary travellers. They were bound to find one soon.

She let down the glass to call to him. Behind her, Teresa gasped as the chill air hit her. '*Madame*, it is freezing.'

Sophie ignored her maid and called out loudly enough to be heard over the wind. 'Can you find somewhere to stop for the night? It will soon be—'

'Get back inside,' he snapped. 'There's a carriage coming the other way. You must not be seen.'

'But what about you?'

'Do as I bid you, Sophie.' He was pulling his muffler up round his face as he spoke. Only his eyes would be visible now.

Sophie ducked back into the carriage, threw up the glass and covered both herself and Teresa with the travelling rug. To Teresa's muffled protests, she said only, 'Hush. Travellers. We must not be seen.'

She could hear the sound of many hooves now. The other carriage had a team of four horses to pull it. Someone important must be leaving Venice. Perhaps it was someone she knew? She might even recognise the carriage. She waited until she judged that the carriage had passed and then peeped out of the window.

Oh, yes, she certainly recognised it. It was a very fine vehicle indeed, and all its blinds were drawn. Its owner would be resting in comfort inside, while his servants bore the brunt of the bitter weather. That was very definitely his way.

She shrank back into her seat, shivering. The Baron von Beck. What was he doing here? And when had he gone to Venice?

It did not matter, she told herself sternly. The important thing was that she and the Baron were going in opposite directions. She need not fear him at all.

Her confidence lasted only seconds. Somewhere on the road ahead of the Baron was a disreputable inn where Verdicchio was being tended by the local surgeon. What if the Baron should stop there and discover what had happened?

Sophie was shivering even more now. She pressed her handkerchief hard against her lips. She must not cry out. Leo might hear. And Teresa would be terrified.

Sophie herself was already terrified. For Leo. Beck was just the kind of man who would delight in taking vengeance for the slights he had suffered at Leo's hands. And with Verdicchio shot, possibly dead, Beck would have just the ammunition he wanted. This was a very dangerous game they were playing.

Leo did not fear the Baron, of course. He had already shown that.

But Sophie feared him very much.

It was only on the second night that Sophie thought to comment on the weather. 'Even though it is nearly Christmas,' she said over supper, 'I expected it to be warmer this far south. I have never known it to be as cold as this in Venice.'

'Ah, but we are a long way from Venice, *madame*,' Leo said quietly. He seemed to be concentrating on the huge plate of food in front of him.

'Surely not? The inn where you found us was no more than four days from Venice. We should arrive there in a day or two, now.'

Leo began to laugh. And then he choked on his food. Sophie quickly poured him a glass of water, but he shook his head, still spluttering. He pointed mutely to his back. She rose from her chair and gave him several hearty thumps in the middle of his shoulder blades.

'Thank you,' he croaked. Then he began to laugh again. His eyes were dancing with mirth.

Sophie resumed her seat with dignity. 'I fail to see, Lord Leo, what you find so amusing in a chance remark about the weather.'

'I can see that you do, *madame*. Fail to see, I mean.' He laughed again, a great rollicking burst of mirth.

Sophie felt an urge to hit him again, on a rather more sensitive part of his anatomy. She glowered at him instead.

He made an effort to straighten his face. Then, he said slowly, 'For such a well-travelled lady, it is astonishing that you have not noticed.' He swallowed another laugh.

'Noticed what, may I ask?'

'Oh, you may, *madame*, you may. You have not noticed, I collect, that we are travelling north. Back to Vienna.'

'What?' Sophie jumped to her feet, overturning her chair. 'But we cannot! You know we cannot! In Vienna, they think I poisoned the Tsar.'

Leo said nothing. He simply rose from his place, set her chair back on its feet and waited for Sophie to sit down again. Then he resumed his meal.

Just like a man! Sophie wanted to curse him for his arrogant assumption that he could order her life, but she managed to resist the impulse. She was a lady. Ladies did not curse, even when provoked as much as this. 'When you have finished filling your belly, Lord Leo, perhaps you would be good enough to tell me why we are going back to Vienna?'

He swallowed his last mouthful, put his knife and fork neatly together on the plate and rose. Something appeared to have caught his attention, for he sauntered across to the window and stood there, gazing out.

Sophie was becoming increasingly impatient. She rose, too, and followed him to the window, but before she reached it, he turned and said, 'I fear you will not be celebrating Christmas in Vienna, *madame*. Indeed, we will be lucky if we manage another twenty miles. The weather has finally broken.' He gestured towards the window. 'Look. It is snowing.'

Chapter Sixteen

She had forgiven him.

Though not immediately. For three days, she had refused to speak to him at all. But then they found themselves stranded by blizzards at a tiny village inn where they were the only guests. She could not continue to ignore him there, not when he was so obviously a gentleman and her escort. Besides, even if Verdicchio did not die, it was crucial for Leo to escape from Italy. Vienna, where he had powerful friends, was the obvious destination.

Sophie was glad, in her heart, that Leo was taking her with him, in spite of his high-handed ways and the dangers she would face in Vienna. She would willingly endure many risks for a little more time in his company. One day, possibly quite soon, she would lose him.

The landlady of the inn was a little chary about offering them rooms, even though it was clearly impossible for them to drive any further. 'It ain't proper,' she said in her thick Austrian accent, 'for a gentleman to be driving a carriage.'

Sophie replied with the first story that came into her head. 'You are right, of course, dear lady. But we had no choice. The gentleman is my cousin—my English cousin—and we are bound for Vienna to see our sick grandmother. Unfortunately, our coachman became ill on the road and had to be left behind. It was impossible to find another, so Cousin Leo took on the role himself.' She switched to English. 'Is that not so, Cousin?'

Leo had just entered the inn and was busy knocking the snow off his boots. 'What's that? Oh, yes. Just so.' He grinned at her. 'Cousin,' he added, with wicked emphasis.

Sophie tried to ignore the effect of that grin on her rebellious insides. 'We hope you will be able to provide us with two bedchambers. One for myself and my maid, and one for my cousin. And a private parlour, too, if you have one.'

The landlady looked them over. The sight of Teresa's comfortable body and plain dark gown seemed to reassure her. 'Very well, *madame*. What name would it be, please?'

Ah. Sophie looked quickly around the sparsely furnished entrance hall, trying to think of names. 'I am Signora Tavola,' she said. 'My maid is Teresa.' She waved a hand in the direction of Leo, who was waiting expectantly by the door. She fancied he had not followed any of her conversation with the landlady. Good. Now was the time for a little revenge. 'And my English cousin is Mr Leo Lackwit.'

Leo's eyebrows almost disappeared into his hair. Luckily, the landlady was too busy calling for her serving maid to notice. 'Take the *signora*'s luggage up to the room at the front. The English gentleman will have the small room at the back. And light the fire in the private parlour next to the *signora*'s room.'

The maid curtsied and disappeared, laden with their bags.

'I have to warn you,' Sophie said, with relish, 'that my English cousin speaks no German. His education was sadly lacking, I fear. The recent wars, you will understand.'

The landlady nodded. Leo looked simply mystified by all this incomprehensible chatter.

'He does speak French, if that would serve?'

The landlady shook her head. 'German, and some Italian only, *signora*.'

'Oh, what a pity,' Sophie said, with satisfaction. 'That being so, I'm afraid Cousin Leo will have to rely on me for absolutely everything for as long as we remain here. Judging by the depth of the snow outside, I fancy that it may be some days before we are able to resume our journey.' Sophie assumed a grave expression. 'Poor, dear Grandmama. I do hope we may yet be in time.'

'*Signora*, a moment, if you please.' The landlady sounded agitated.

Sophie felt a flutter of anxiety. Had someone come after them, to arrest Leo? They had been stuck in this little inn for over a week now, plenty of time for pursuers to cover the ground. She rose from her chair by the parlour fire and hurried to the doorway where the landlady was standing.

'*Signora*, it's about your Christmas meal.'

Sophie's relief blossomed into a smile. In the panic of the moment, she had forgotten that it was Christmas

Eve. 'My English cousin eats whatever is put before him, as you must have noticed. I do not think you need concern yourself.'

'But there is no carp,' the landlady wailed, not in the least placated. 'There must be carp on Christmas Eve.'

Sophie murmured sympathetically while the landlady continued to bemoan the state of her supplies. 'The roads should have been cleared,' she said firmly. 'The men have failed in their duty to honest working folk such as us. How am I to run this house if I cannot get food, and if travellers cannot reach us? It is a disgrace.'

For Sophie, it was a blessing. She put a comforting hand on the landlady's arm. 'My cousin and I will eat whatever you are able to provide. And gladly. It is not your fault that we are marooned here. We feared it would be much worse, that we should be stuck in the snow drifts. Here we are warm and dry and very well served.' The landlady preened a little. 'We are lucky to have found such a splendid inn,' Sophie continued, 'and we are more than content to remain.'

'But what about your grandmother, *signora*?'

Oh, dear. Sophie had completely forgotten the dying grandmother. She schooled her features into a resigned expression. 'In practical terms, sadly, there is nothing at all we can do. No amount of worrying on my part will serve to clear the roads. So I am endeavouring to accept the fact that we may be too late.' She pretended to wipe away a tear.

'Forgive me, *signora*. I did not mean to distress you.'

Sophie smiled a watery smile and held it until the landlady had disappeared back down the stairs to her kitchen.

* * *

They had left the church behind them. Its bells had welcomed Christmas and fallen silent at last. The villagers had returned to their homes, calling out greetings to each other as they closed their doors against the cold.

Sophie and Leo walked slowly back to the edge of the village and the welcoming warmth of their inn. The only sound now was the scrunch of their boots on the crisp snow. Above them, the sky was huge and cloudless and filled with stars. Behind the village houses, snow-shrouded fir trees stood sentinel, motionless as guardsmen on parade. There was not even a whisper of wind.

Sophie sighed with pleasure. She felt a great sense of peace in this place, isolated from the outside world and from the dangers that threatened there. She found herself wishing that the roads would never re-open. She glanced up at Leo, wondering what thoughts were going through his mind. Did he feel the same?

He flashed a smile at her and tucked her arm more closely into his. He had insisted that she take no risk as they walked, though he must have known perfectly well that the firm fresh snow was not at all slippery.

Sophie had been happy to accept his excuse and his arm, for it was almost the only time they had touched since their arrival in the village. Leo had been scrupulously polite throughout, but Sophie knew that he was deliberately avoiding her whenever he could. He had to join her at mealtimes, of course, for they were supposed to be cousins. But the rest of the time, he was nowhere to be seen. She had no idea what he did all day. She had asked him, once, and received some mumbled excuse about seeing to the horses. Feeble, indeed. The inn had servants to do such menial chores.

Tonight, walking arm in arm, he was more relaxed than he had been since their flight from Italy began. Was it the coming of Christmas? The service had clearly affected him deeply, even though she doubted he had understood a word of it. The tiny village church had been crammed with people, all singing with gusto. Sophie had been asked to sing, too, for the whole village had heard her practising at the inn. She had chosen her favourite German carol, *'Stille Nacht'*, which she had sung very quietly, and unaccompanied. She had put her whole heart into it. It was probably the most moving performance she had ever given, anywhere. And it was for Leo.

'May I say—' Leo stopped to clear his throat. 'May I say, *madame*, that your singing tonight was utterly perfect? I have never heard anything so beautiful.'

His words set up a glow around Sophie's heart. She would treasure them, always. 'Thank you, Lord Leo,' she replied softly. She wanted to say something more, to build on this unexpected closeness, but it was too late. In ten paces, they would be back inside the inn.

The landlady took Leo's heavy coat and Sophie's fur-trimmed pelisse while they both removed the snow from their boots. 'There is a fine fire in your parlour, *signora*, if you would please to go up?' The woman was beaming at her in a peculiar way. What was going on?

Sophie went upstairs to change her boots and her gown. Then, curious, she made her way to the private parlour where Leo was to rejoin her. From the corridor, it looked a little odd, as if it was lit only by the flickering firelight. She stepped into the room. 'Oh!' she cried. 'How wonderful!' The landlady was standing proudly beside a small Christmas tree covered in tiny white candles. It reminded Sophie of the millions of stars in the midnight sky outside. So very beautiful.

A moment later, she heard Leo's indrawn breath behind her. Was this tiny wonder new to him? She had been told that English Christmas customs were bizarre and uncouth. She turned, smiling, to explain, but he shook his head at her. Silence. His eyes were wide. She was sure she could see a hundred tiny reflections dancing there.

'You approve, *signora*?' The landlady's words broke the spell.

Sophie started, then beamed at the woman. 'Happy Christmas, dear lady.' She handed over the money she had prepared. 'And thank you for the tree. It is perfect.'

The landlady risked a quick glance at her palm. Her mouth opened and her eyes widened. It was a hugely generous gift.

But Sophie had not finished. She handed over silver coins for the other servants, too. She said they were simply gifts to celebrate Christmas, and to thank the little inn for the splendid service she and Leo had received. But in truth, they were thank-you offerings for the days they had spent together in the peace of this place, and for the days they might still have to come.

The landlady's thanks were effusive, but eventually she left them alone.

Leo looked about him. He had become a little uncomfortable, Sophie thought, now that he was alone with her. He was trying to find an excuse to leave, but she would not permit that. Not until she had finished what she had set out to do. She crossed to the fireplace and lifted the jug of mulled wine that sat by the hearth. '*Glühwein*, Lord Leo? It is wonderfully warming after a midnight walk through the snow.' Without waiting for his answer, she poured two glasses and offered one to him.

He looked a little taken aback, but he could not refuse without appearing impolite. In all their time on the road, he had been scrupulously, infuriatingly polite.

Sophie raised her glass in a toast. 'Happy Christmas, Lord Leo. And may we all reach Vienna well ahead of any pursuers.' She grinned. 'Even in your amazingly uncomfortable carriage.'

It was the ice breaker she needed. He laughed and drank. 'Excellent. As good as any mulled wine I have ever tasted.'

'I should imagine so,' Sophie replied, sipping her own wine and savouring its comforting warmth. 'It is one of the traditions in these parts, along with the tree.' She nodded towards the twinkling candles. 'And there is another tradition here on Christmas Eve. After church, we exchange—' She stopped short. That would not do. 'We give gifts, as you just saw me do to the landlady and her servants.'

'Charming.' He downed the last of his *Glühwein* and crossed to the fire to refill his glass.

Sophie took another tiny sip, set down her glass, and straightened the skirts of her red silk gown. It was her favourite because it became her so well. The fabric shimmered in the firelight, glowing with deeper reds and golds and purples. The tiny gift that had been hidden in her bodice was now held tightly in her fingers. She fixed her gaze on his back and waited.

He turned, his glass halfway to his mouth. 'Is something wrong, *madame*?'

'No, Lord Leo. Nothing at all. But it is Christmas

Eve, and I have a gift for you.' She opened her clasped hands and showed him what she held.

His eyes widened, but he did not move. Then, 'My ring!' He set down his glass and came forward to take both her hands, cupping them around the gold. 'You have brought me my ring.'

Sophie took a deep breath and sighed it out. His touch was so very special. She smiled up at him. 'You used it to pay for food for us, and to pay my debts. I simply redeemed it.' She pulled one hand from his to offer the ring to him on her palm. 'Pray take it, Lord Leo. It is yours. My Christmas gift to you.'

He did not take it. He took Sophie instead, into his arms, into an embrace so tight that she could hardly breathe. Then his mouth was on hers, touching, seeking, demanding that she respond to him. The coldness and distance between them was melting like snowflakes sizzling in the heat of the fire. It was the closeness she had longed for, with the man she loved.

His arms were around her now, one hand tangling in the knot of hair at her nape, the other stroking down her spine. His touch through the fine silk was magical, bringing her whole body alive with need. If only she could tell him how much she longed for him, but she could not, for her mouth was still stopped by his burning kisses. She felt as if her whole body was smiling at him, through every pore. She forgot her desire for words. He was going to make love to her here, by the light of a blazing fire and a tree full of candles. It was their moment. They would be together now. She could give him her true gift. Herself.

Her hair came free of its pins and tumbled down her back. She heard a low rumble of satisfaction in his throat, behind his kisses. She felt it, too, for the vibration travelled through his mouth to hers, and down to the core of her. Then the weight of her hair was lifted by caressing fingers and laid against the skin of her throat.

His kiss continued, unbroken, all the while. It seemed he could not let her go. He was stroking the side of her neck, first with a lock of her hair, and then with his fingers, skin against skin. His butterfly touches were creating a burning line, beginning at the lobe of her ear and dipping lower, down to her throat and then to her breasts. She could feel them heating, straining against the ruby silk, waiting eagerly for the moment when she would open to him. She wanted him so much. She wanted him now. She moaned softly into his mouth.

That single sound changed everything.

He thrust her from him, so roughly that she staggered back. His eyes were still black with passion, but it was passion overlaid with horror. 'Oh, God!' It was a groan of despair.

Sophie stared at this sudden stranger. Her whole being ached for him, and he was rejecting her. How could he? His desire had been at least as strong as hers.

He ran his fingers through his hair and closed his eyes tightly. He was like a man who had woken from a nightmare and did not know where he was, a man who was afraid to look around him, afraid of what he might see. His shoulders drooped for a moment. He was ashen under his weather-beaten skin. 'I ask your pardon, *madame*. My behaviour to you was not that of the gentleman I claim to be.' He took a deep breath, raised his chin and looked into her face. 'I promise you that you will be conveyed to Vienna without any further injury to your peace of mind.' He bowed low and made for the door.

Sophie stooped quickly. 'Lord Leo.' She was using her training to master the underlying shiver in her voice.

He turned back. His face was a picture of anguish.

Sophie stretched out her hand. The ring she had dropped was now suspended between her forefinger and thumb. 'You have forgotten your gift.'

His eyes widened, but he responded automatically.

Sophie let the ring fall into his palm and abruptly turned her back on him. Let him take it and go. He had touched, and then rejected, her real gift. And it was clear that he would never wish to touch her again.

At last! Leo could see Vienna, the roofs sparkling pristine white under a recent dusting of snow. In an hour or so, they would all be back in the city, back where it had all started.

He was not tempted to urge his team to greater speed, for he still had not decided what he should do. In spite of the bitter wind, he was glad to be alone on the box, with time to make up his mind.

He could not take Sophie back to his own lodgings. Jack and Ben would be there, and both of them viewed Sophie as little better than a high-class whore. These weeks of travelling together—and being snowed in for days on end—had proved to Leo that she was nothing of the sort. That incident at Christmas had been solely Leo's fault. His behaviour then had been a disgrace. By contrast, her behaviour was that of a well-born lady, and her manners were at least as good as his own. How had she acquired them? That was a mystery that he had not, so far, managed to unravel. He had the impression, though, that she had been bred to behave like a lady from a very young age. So why had she become an opera singer? No lady would ever stoop to that.

There had been that tantalising hint from Verdicchio that he had paid for Sophie. How could that be? Who could have sold her? And even if that were true, why would she have stayed so many years with that blackguard?

He gave up. He would not be able to solve the mystery, except by asking Sophie herself. Perhaps, one day, she might trust him enough to tell him the truth? He doubted that. Not after the way he had assaulted her on Christmas Eve. Not once he told her what he wanted her to do.

For the moment, however, he had to decide where to take her so that she would be safe. Instinct told him the Tsar would have recovered by now from his recurrent illness and that the rumours of poison would have been forgotten. If Leo was wrong there… No, it was more than six weeks since the Tsar had fallen ill. If he had died, they would have heard news of it on the road.

It should be safe to take Sophie back to her own apartment. The servants would probably be gone, but she would still have Teresa to take care of her. Leo would drive her there in this nondescript carriage and bundle her into the building shrouded in her cloak. She could stay hidden indoors until he was sure that the danger from those wicked rumours was gone. Then she could emerge once more, as herself, the foremost singer in Europe. That was enough. He did not dare to think beyond that.

Having at last settled what he would do, Leo grasped his whip to spring the horses, but the handle caught on his little finger. His ring was sticking out through a tear in his driving glove.

He let his grip relax again and leaned back on the box, rubbing the ring with his thumb. He treasured it. Now, more than ever. It had originally been a twenty-first birthday gift from his brother Dominic. Leo had had to trade it to that scurvy landlord in return for food for Sophie and her maid, but he had missed it sorely after. And then, on Christmas Eve, when they were snow-bound in that remote alpine inn, Sophie had shyly returned it to him.

That moment was like nothing he had ever experienced before. Time had seemed to stand still. Sophie had looked so ethereal, standing opposite the fire with the flames reflecting deep red shadows on her ebony hair. She had offered her gift a little hesitantly, and yet her eyes had been glowing, as if she could feel how much it would mean to him. Leo had been too over-whelmed to speak.

Even now, he could hardly believe that she had done it. In all the turmoil of their flight from the scene of Verdicchio's shooting, she had noticed that his ring was gone and had then found a moment to bargain with the landlord for its return. She was... He swallowed. She was thoughtful and generous to a man who had done nothing to deserve such generosity.

He remembered how their hands had clasped around her tiny gift. It had felt like a joining—there, just the two of them, standing together in front of the fire. He should have recognised that he was being driven by the emotion of the moment and the return of a treasured possession in the most unexpected way. But he had thrown himself on her instead, driven by his basest instincts. If her single groan of protest had not penetrated his lust-befuddled brain, he would have taken her there on the floor like an animal.

He had promised himself, as a matter of duty, that he would bring her back to Vienna. He had sworn that he would escort her like a true gentleman. On that one night, he had failed. But he had kept his vow for every night thereafter, though it had well-nigh killed him, watching her supping at his side, and knowing that she was asleep in a bed just yards from his own. Once back in Vienna, his vow would be fulfilled. There would be an end to the nights of torture, but without the curb of his oath, his own driving passions might overcome him once more. If she touched him now, his whole body would go up in flames.

The truth was that he still wanted her desperately. It was more than the desires of his body. He had seen her courage, her selfless devotion to her stricken maid, her ability to endure hardship without a word of complaint. He had recognised, finally, that she was an admirable woman. If it were not for her calling, she would be a fit mate for any man.

But it was her very calling that had made her into the weapon Leo must use to foil the Tsar's plans to annex Poland. Without her, Russian ambition would set Europe ablaze once more. It was Leo's mission to persuade her. Yet the thought of using her sickened him now. He would be sending a woman he admired to the bed of a man he had come to despise. In the name of duty.

Chapter Seventeen

Sophie was pacing the floor. She could not help it.

After all these weeks in Leo's company, she could not stop thinking about him, even though he had become increasingly insistent on keeping that infernal distance between them. He still desired her. She knew that. She saw it in his eyes, in unguarded moments when he thought he was unobserved. But he was stubbornly, mulishly determined not to yield to it. Just like a man.

Had it ever occurred to him to consider Sophie's desires? His kisses by that Christmas fire had been fierce and demanding, to be sure, but Sophie had welcomed them. He must have known it. And yet he had stopped, horrified. Was it his own weakness that shocked him? Or hers?

She had thought she understood men. But she did not understand Lord Leo Aikenhead. He was all contradictions. He was afraid of his own desires, but he was supremely unconcerned about the risks to his own life. That, plus his tender concern for her welfare during the remainder of their hideous journey, had finally overcome her fury at his rejection of her. She had told herself that she had every reason to hate him. But she loved him.

The sight of Vienna's walls had forced her to choose. And the strength of her love had overwhelmed all her puny, petty anger. This was where Leo was most at risk now, where his enemies would seek to have him arrested and executed. This was where she had to do everything in her power to protect him.

'*Madame!* You must stay away from the window. What if someone should see you?'

Sophie shook her head. Teresa's thoughts seemed to be all for Sophie and the rumours that she had poisoned the Tsar. But Sophie cared only for Leo. There were other roads from Venice to Vienna. What if news of Verdicchio's shooting had travelled by one of those? There could be officers on the way to arrest Leo at this very minute.

Where was he? He had said he was only taking the horses to the posting house. So why had he been gone for so long? She clenched her hands together until her nails were almost piercing her flesh. He must have been taken. She would never see him again!

Teresa's sharp cry pierced Sophie's despair. 'He is here, *madame*!'

Sophie heard Leo's light step on the stairs. The door was flung open.

'Leo!' In that moment of blessed relief, she could think of nothing but the fact that he had returned to her. She flung herself into his arms. 'Oh, Leo. You are safe.' She reached up to touch her lips to his in a tender kiss, filled with all the love and longing she felt.

His body remained totally rigid. Was he rejecting her embrace? Again?

But then her doubts vanished, for he pulled her even closer against his chest, wrapped his arms round her and tenderly kissed the breath from her body, as though she were more precious to him than all the world. It was an illusion—it must be—but for the moment she was more than willing to believe in it. She leaned into him. She drove her fingers into his thick hair in order to pull his mouth even closer, to give him the access that both of them craved.

It was not enough. This time, she had to show him that her longing was at least equal to his. Hesitantly at first, she touched her tongue to his. Then, emboldened, she ran it along the inside of his lower lip. He groaned, low in his chest. He deepened the kiss yet more. Sophie thought it would never end.

It was Leo who broke it, when both of them were gasping for breath. But he did not let her go. He was staring longingly at her, his eyes black with desire. Sophie knew that her eyes must be a mirror of his. She wanted this man. Oh, how she wanted him!

No words were spoken between them. Leo simply lifted her into his arms and carried her to her bedchamber, pushing the door closed with his boot. He settled her on top of the bed with such care that she might have been made of the most delicate porcelain. Then he lay down beside her, not touching at first, just looking into her face.

'So beautiful. So very beautiful.' He touched the back of his fingers to her cheek and slowly stroked down to the point of her jaw and beyond, till his hand was resting lightly on the side of her throat. 'Oh, Sophie. I cannot tell you how much I desire you. In truth, it has been so since I first saw you at that country inn.'

The memory of his kindness then warmed Sophie's heart. She loved this man. He truly desired her. Surely that was enough?

She had made her decision. Very gently, she laid her fingers on top of his. The pulse of her throat was beating against his skin. Deliberately, she lifted his hand and placed it on her breast.

His sharp intake of breath seemed very loud in the empty room.

She looked down at his hand and then back into his eyes. 'Kiss me, Leo.'

At Christmas, he had thought that the ring was the most precious gift he had ever received. But he had been wrong. Though it had taken him hours to discover it, he had finally confirmed that she was no longer in danger. That knowledge was worth more than any ring. And now, most precious of all, Sophie, beautiful Sophie, was offering herself to him. Without payment, without reward. Simply as a gift. He had wanted her for so long that it was impossible to reject her now. This would be a moment of mutual surrender. And they would glory in it.

He was bereft of words to tell her of his longings. All he could do was to show her, with his body, how much he valued what she was offering him. He kissed her first, for that was what she desired of him. And he was determined that, in this joining, she should have everything she desired.

He kissed her mouth. He kissed her face. He kissed her from the pulse below her ear to the hollow of her throat, and then down to the valley between her breasts, obscured still by the heavy silk of her high-buttoned travelling gown. She had offered her breast to him with her own hand, and he longed to put his lips to her skin. But there seemed to be a thousand tiny buttons, from the neck to the waist. He would undo them all, one by one, gradually exposing her glorious flesh to the touch of his fingers, and of his lips. This would be a slow, slow seduction. By the time he had removed her gown, she would be more than ready.

He began to kiss her in earnest now. A long kiss. A button. Another kiss. A button. He had barely reached the top of her breasts when she was moaning into his mouth. But he would go no faster. It took a long, long time for the buttons to be undone and her gown to be peeled slowly down her body. Underneath, she wore heavy winter petticoats, and a light corset over a creamy silk chemise.

He sat up on his haunches to feast his eyes on her. 'Ah, Sophie,' was all he could say.

She reached for him. At first he thought she wanted to kiss him again. But no. She was pushing at the lapels of his coat, trying desperately to remove it. A silver button pinged across the bed. She ignored it and pushed harder. Knowing she could never succeed this way, Leo touched a finger to her cheek, then undid the remaining buttons himself and shrugged it off. He was not sure where it fell, for she was already busy with the buttons of his waist-coat. He helped her with that, too, and it joined his coat. His cravat was dispatched with one urgent tug. And then she put her hands to the front of his shirt.

'Sophie,' he gasped, making to help her.

Too late. With a single bold move, she ripped it from his shoulders. 'Yes,' she said, laying her palms flat against his naked chest. 'Now I have you, Leo.'

The touch of her fingers on his skin made his

thoughts run wild. He wanted to throw up her petticoats there and then, and drive into her.

'Oh, Leo.' He thought he detected a quiver in her voice. 'I need you so.'

His brutish desires vanished on the spot. This was a moment for seduction, for a gentle, loving union.

He lay down beside her once more, glorying in the feel of her fingers on him. She was exploring the skin of his chest with a peculiar innocence, as if she had never before lain with a half-naked man. He remained motionless, holding his breath, while she pushed her fingers through the hair on his chest and ran the tips of her nails around his nipples. It was excruciating. It was wonderful.

Then, before he lost all control, he put his hand to the laces of her stays and loosened the cords so he could remove them. Now, through the fine silk of her chemise, he could see her nipples thrusting up towards him, beckoning his mouth. It was more than he could stand. He bent to take one nipple in his mouth, trapping her hands between his naked skin and her silk, sucking gently at first, and then harder until she groaned beneath him. It seemed that his name was the only word she could utter.

As he moved his mouth to the other breast, he untied her petticoats and pushed them down to her knees. She wriggled her feet out of the tangle of silk and wool, and the petticoats fell to the floor with a dull thud. Now, there was only her chemise. And her stockings. He ran his hand down one naked thigh to the wisp of lace above her knee.

He lifted his mouth from her breast. This was something beautiful. Something he had to see and remember.

He pulled himself away, just enough. She looked more beautiful, more desirable, than any woman he had ever known. Her lustrous hair had come undone and was spread over the golden coverlet in an ebony cloud, like sea foam blown by a gentle wind into the softest of waves and curls. Her cheeks and her throat were flushed. Her chemise was transparent where he had kissed her, and her long, slim legs, clad in silk and lace, had parted as if to welcome him.

Not yet. Not yet. He grasped the lower edge of her chemise and began to roll it up her body. She did not move, but her gaze was fixed on his face. The flush on her throat became deeper still. When he reached her breasts, he slipped his fingers under her shoulders and raised her from the bed, so that he could pass the chemise over her head.

She smiled languidly when he laid her down once more.

He could not bring himself to move. He was mesmerised just looking at her beauty, at the longing and the desire, in her face. This astonishing woman, who could have any man in the world, wanted him. She wanted Leo.

She waited and watched. Her eyelids drooped and lazily opened again. Her eyes seemed to be glistening. Very slowly, she ran the tip of her tongue along her lower lip and raised her arms to him. 'Now, Leo!' she said with melting intensity. She dropped her gaze to his waist and lower.

He was no longer in any doubt. He threw off the rest of his clothing and covered her body with his.

She put her hands to his face and her lips to his. Then, with a sudden movement, she wrapped her legs around his hips. It was now!

With a single, fierce stroke, Leo buried himself inside her hot, luscious body. Moving within her, he heard, as if from far, far away, a long low groan of satisfaction. He went over the edge into blissful oblivion.

He pushed the coverlet to the floor, pulled the bed-clothes out from under their naked bodies and tucked the blankets around them both. 'My beautiful Sophie. You must not get cold.'

She snuggled into the crook of his arm. She wanted so much to be part of his warmth, to be close to his body, now that they were no longer joined. Without him, she felt incomplete, for their union had been magical. She had thought she was about to touch the stars. Almost, she had. But then it had ended.

She had expected pain but, in truth, there had been very little. Had she cried out when he entered her? She was not sure. Probably not. Leo was a kind man. If he thought he had hurt her, he would not now be lying on his back, gently caressing her cheek.

She refused to think about how much longer they might have together, or whether she might lose him to the law. In this moment, he was hers. She turned her head to touch a kiss to the lobe of his ear. That brought a rumble of pleasure in his throat. Encouraged, she began to nibble.

'Enough, sweetheart. You know better than that.'

Better than what?

'You are very demanding, my dear Sophie. But a man needs a little more time to recover. Even with a lover as delectable as you.' He pulled himself up on to the pillows a little and glanced round the room. It was very bare, for very few of her possession had been unpacked. 'I see you have some wine there.' He nodded towards the side table.

'Would you like a glass?'

'Later. First, I…' He fiddled with the bedclothes, settling them more closely around them both. 'First I have something to ask you. Something very important, Sophie.' His voice seemed to have sunk half an octave.

She pushed herself round so that she was lying on top of him, looking into his face. His eyes were troubled. 'Tell me,' she said simply.

'Sophie, you were worried about those rumours. About the Tsar. I heard at the inn that he is fully recovered. There is nothing to concern you any more. Indeed, I am sure that his Imperial Majesty will be eagerly looking forward to seeing you again.' He had stopped meeting her eyes.

'I…I had not thought of that.'

'Sophie, if he asks for you, I believe you should grant his request.'

You are asking me to share another man's bed? She wanted to scream the words, but no sound came out. Suddenly, her body ached all over. The core of her felt as if it were burning with pain. She swallowed hard. 'Why?' she said at last.

His response came so quickly that it must have been prepared. 'Because the peace of Europe depends on it. We think the Tsar may be prepared to go to war to keep Poland. We need to know whether he means it. We believe you are the only one who can find out.'

Sophie rolled off him, but he reached for her and pulled her back against his body. She did not resist, but the warmth was gone. It was as if her body had instantly been encased in a block of ice. She could not bring herself to speak.

'Will you do it, Sophie? It could mean the difference between peace and war. And you know how many have already died.'

'Yes, I do know,' she said hoarsely. 'It is not an easy thing you ask of me, Leo, but…' She shrugged and pulled away from him so that she could stand up. 'You asked for wine. I think perhaps we both need a glass.' She sauntered across to the table by the curtained window, letting her hips sway provocatively as she walked. She needed to keep his attention on her body and the reactions of his own while she poured.

It took a few minutes, for she had to be careful. Her hands were beginning to shake.

When she walked languorously back to the bed carrying the glasses, she could see that his attention was focused on her body, rather than the wine. She knelt on the bed beside him and pushed a glass into his hand. Then she sat up to stretch her back and lift her naked breasts to his ardent gaze. 'A toast, then,' she said calmly, 'to this enterprise of ours. In hopes that I may provide you with what you seek.'

She raised her glass and touched it to Leo's. As she drank, she watched him closely to be sure he did the same. A long, long swallow. There was no mistake. She could see his throat working strongly.

Now, it was simply a question of waiting.

'Sophie.' Leo still felt relaxed and sleepy. He had been dreaming wonderful, ecstatic dreams. Without opening his eyes, he reached out a hand. The place where she should have been was cold and empty.

He sat up with a start. Where was she?

It was only then that he registered how late it was. How long had he been asleep? Had he been so exhausted from days of driving that a single glass of wine could knock him out for hours? He must be losing his famously hard head.

But he had no time to worry about that. He scrambled off the bed and began to pick up his clothes from the floor. He needed to wash. He could not appear in public smelling of a lady's boudoir. He looked around the room again, more carefully this time. Apart from the furniture and the tray of wine, it was empty. There was no basin, and no ewer of water. And every trace of Sophie had vanished.

Although she had gone—for some obscure female reason, no doubt—her maid might well be in the apartment still. He could send her for water. It should not take long. If he hurried, he would not be too late to wait on Lord Castlereagh. He started for the door, but a glimpse of his naked flesh in the pier glass reminded him that he was in no fit state to present himself to a middle-aged Italian abigail. He would wrap himself in one of the bed sheets.

He was turning back for it when he caught the full reflection of his body in the glass. Good God! What was—? Surely not? He looked down at his naked flesh and then back at the reflection. No, it could not be. It was impossible. It had to be impossible.

He strode back to the bed. They had lain together on top of the gold silk coverlet, too eager for each other even to slip between the sheets. If it was here, he would find it.

He threw the pillows to the floor and spread the crumpled coverlet across the full width of the bed. The mark was unmistakable. Here, on the golden silk. And on his body. Blood. Sophie's blood.

He stared at the stain in disbelief. And then he sank to the floor, with his head in his hands.

Chapter Eighteen

Sophie was relieved when Teresa finally appeared with the hired carriage at the far corner of the square. Waiting under the portico had been very dangerous, for it was always possible that Leo might recover from the drug before she could get away. She did not dare to think what he might do if he found her here.

Her common sense reasserted itself. He would have no reason to think she had drugged him. And as for her running away, why should she not? Any woman would be nauseated by the thought that Leo had seduced her purely in order to cozen her into spying on the Russian Emperor. That absurd idea brought a hollow laugh to her throat. Leo still assumed that Sophie had shared the Tsar's bed. If only he knew! She would never be alone with the Tsar again. And as for Leo…

She shook her head, furious at her own weakness. How could she love a man who tried to manipulate her so callously? She had thought him kind and gentle and thoughtful. She had thought him honourable when he had defended her, first against Beck, and then against

Verdicchio. But what he had done tonight, in her own bedchamber, was not in the least honourable. It was the action of the vilest blackguard. It was sordid.

She climbed into the carriage without waiting for help from the groom. She had no desire to be touched by any man.

'Where to, *madame*?' It was the coachman.

She did not know. She knew only that she could not return to that apartment. She would never be able to face the scene of her betrayal, where she had given her heart and her body to a man who had scorned both her gifts. 'Drive to the Prater,' she said, grasping at the memories of peaceful solitude beneath the horse chestnuts. 'I wish to take a walk.'

She sat back in one corner. Teresa made to speak, but Sophie shook her head. She needed silence. She surveyed the interior of the carriage, which was clean enough, but not especially comfortable. Unfortunate, since they might find themselves spending the night in it, for want of any alternative lodging. She refused to think about that. She would walk in the clear air of the Prater. It would allow her to order her thoughts and make plans.

The carriage was moving very slowly. The horses were probably sluggards of the first order. Sophie closed her eyes, and tried again to relax.

At that moment, the carriage slowed even more and the door was opened. What on earth...?

'Good evening, *madame*,' said the Baron von Beck. 'You permit?' Without waiting for an answer, he jumped in and took the seat opposite Sophie.

Good God! Again! The man must be in league with the devil! How else had he known where to find her? Had he been spying on her apartment?

'We have matters to discuss,' he said ominously, reaching for the check-string. The carriage stopped completely. 'Get out, woman!'

Teresa shrank from him.

'What I have to say to your mistress is not for your ears. Climb up on the box.'

'No!' Sophie cried. 'She will freeze!'

'I doubt that.' He leant across to throw open the door on Teresa's side. 'She is too well upholstered for the cold to reach her bones.' After a final pleading look at Sophie, Teresa almost tumbled out.

The Baron's long fingers grasped the leather strap and pulled the door closed. 'Now, *madame*, it is time to talk terms.'

'And so your journey to Venice to bring back the Nightingale was not necessary after all, Aikenhead. Though it was certainly an excellent scheme at the time. Once Britain, France and Austria had agreed to the secret treaty to stand against the annexation of Poland, and to put an army in the field, the Tsar and his Prussian ally backed down. I can tell you, in strict confidence, that the danger is now over.'

Leo swallowed hard. What he had done to Sophie had been unforgivable. Now, doubly so. He felt guilty, nauseated, dishonoured. But he dared not show it. He forced himself to maintain a semblance of self-control in spite of his inner turmoil. 'Most gratifying,' he muttered. 'When I left Vienna six weeks ago, Russia was in a position of strength, and our allies were in disarray.'

'Aye.' Castlereagh lifted the crystal decanter to refill Leo's glass. 'And so it was. But France played a very clever game. And the Austrian Emperor was shrewd enough to see the dangers and take a stand.'

'With your encouragement, sir, I am sure.' Leo raised his glass to the Foreign Secretary.

Castlereagh's normally impassive face cracked for a moment. There was just the hint of a smile at the corner of his mouth. 'Thank you, Aikenhead.'

Leo took a swallow of his wine. It began to warm his shuddering insides. 'What would you have us do now, sir?' he asked, trying to keep his voice flat and unemotional.

'I have no specific orders for you. Knave and Ten have been very useful in your absence. No doubt they will be able to brief you. I must tell you, however, that I am recalled to London to account for my actions before Parliament.' There was a thread of bitterness in his voice. His enemies in the House of Commons must have been making mischief again. 'At least I am taking them one prize they want—the Congress's joint declaration on the abolition of the slave trade.'

'That was a great achievement, sir, but I am sorry to hear you are leaving. Your wise counsel will be sadly missed here.'

Castlereagh smiled, quite broadly for once. 'The Duke of Wellington is on his way from Paris. He will, I fancy, be a more than adequate replacement for me.'

Leo was shocked. He had thought the Duke was to remain as British Ambassador in Paris. But on reflection, it did make sense. Britain needed her most capable man here in Vienna, where the future of Europe was to be decided. 'I shall look forward to meeting his Grace again,' Leo said quietly, but it was not true. The Duke was known to dally with courtesans as readily as with aristocratic ladies. Leo could already picture the scene: the famous victor bowing over Sophie's hand and leading her away for an amorous tête-à-tête.

Leo continued to mull over the dark possibilities as he walked down the stairs from Castlereagh's apartment and into the crisp cold air of the January evening. What could he possibly do? How could he ever make amends for the wrong he had inflicted on her? He had taken her innocence, treating her like a practised courtesan, when she was nothing of the kind. She had invited him to her bed—that was true—and she had been willing. But she could not have expected *that*. For all his experience and his good intentions, he had been rough and brutal. It must have been a searing and horrifying moment for her.

And then, to cap it all, he had asked her to share the Tsar's bed again. Again? There could be no *again*. What was he thinking of? It did not matter that she had spent two evenings alone with the Russian Emperor. With his own eyes, Leo had seen the proof that the Tsar had not bedded her. The only man who had bedded Sophia Pietre was Leo Aikenhead. And he was thoroughly ashamed.

'No, I will not!' Sophie spat her refusal at the Baron. She had had enough of being used by men.

'Dear me.' The Baron leaned back against the cushions and idly inspected his fingernails. 'It seems, my dear Sophie, that you do not learn, in spite of the number of times I have taught you. Let me make it perfectly plain: your master, Verdicchio, sold you to me, along with the secret of how he came by his wound. You are mine, as you were his, to do with as I will. And if you do not comply, I shall find myself obliged to take certain information to the Austrian secret police.'

'I care nothing for that. I will leave Vienna. There is nothing for me here.'

'Indeed? I think you mistake the information I have in mind. It was not your spying activities I planned to betray, my dear. Oh, no. It will be Lord Leo Aiken-head's murder of Maestro Verdicchio.'

Sophie's heart stopped in her breast.

'You understand now, I see. Remember, then, that murder is a capital crime. If you do not obey me, Lord Leo will die.'

Sophie closed her eyes. What on earth was she to do? The choice was between betraying Leo and succumbing to the Baron's vile lust. She could not let Leo die, no matter what he had done to her. But the Baron… The thought of his fingers, his body on hers…

She clapped her hand to her mouth. 'Pray stop the carriage, Baron. I must have some air.'

He laughed, but reached to pull the check-string. 'As you wish, *madame*, but it will not change the situation. Take a walk, by all means, but then bring me your answer.'

Sophie flung open the door and climbed down. Her legs felt like jelly. 'Teresa!' she called, but the maid was already getting down from the box and running to support her. 'Let us walk. I need clean air.'

They walked, slowly at first, and then a little faster. The same thoughts went round and round until Sophie felt her head was spinning.

Verdicchio is dead. Leo will be executed. Or I must yield to Beck. Verdicchio is dead. Leo will be executed, or I— No. No, I will not meekly accept the Baron's choices. There must be another way. There must. If I see Leo, tell him to flee Vienna, surely then he would be safe? He could return to England. Yes! They would never come for him there, because his brother, the Duke, would protect him.

Her thoughts began to arrange themselves in some sort of order then. She would tell Beck she accepted his terms, but she would try to gain enough time to warn Leo. It was unlikely, surely, that the Baron would insist she go to him tonight? He was a man of extravagant tastes. He would want to make special preparations for his triumph over Sophie Pietre.

She straightened her back and removed her arm from around Teresa's shoulders. 'I am quite recovered now, Teresa. Think nothing of it. A momentary weakness only. Come, we must return to the carriage.' She marched back, leaving Teresa straggling in her wake, and climbed in. Teresa climbed back onto the box and, in a matter of seconds, the carriage was on the move again.

'I can see that you have made up your mind, *madame.*'

'I have, sir.' She would not agree too easily. He would suspect double-dealing if she did. 'I can testify that the death of Maestro Verdicchio was no murder. Lord Leo fired in self-defence, and to save me, only after Verdicchio himself had fired.'

Beck laughed softly. 'Your word means nothing against mine.'

She let out a long, despairing sigh. 'Yes, I understand that the word of a mere opera singer has no value.' She pursed her lips and swallowed. 'Lord Leo defended me. As a matter of honour, I cannot allow him to die. Therefore, I have no choice. I accept your terms.'

He smiled a thin, contemptuous smile. 'I rather thought you would. Indeed, I have already made preparations.'

Sophie raised a haughty eyebrow. Inside, fear clawed at her.

The Baron's smile broadened. He puffed out his chest a little. 'Baron Hager was kind enough to agree that I might rent his apartment in the Mariusplatz. I would not have you live in surroundings less beautiful than you, my dear.'

Sophie pretended to be impressed. 'The Mariusplatz? Those are not apartments, Baron, but palaces.'

He preened a little. 'Yes, perhaps. But the setting for our…er…union must be sumptuous, do you not think?'

'That is for you to say, sir. And when shall you enter into possession of this palace?' She prayed that it would not be soon. Surely Baron Hager would have to vacate the rooms? A few days, a week?

'My friend the Baron is very understanding of my needs, my dear. The palace will be available at noon tomorrow. If you do not object, I think that you should take up residence in the afternoon. What do you say?'

She allowed herself to laugh. He would expect that. He would even take it as a compliment to his guile. 'Given the agreement we have just made, Baron, I see no cause to object to your timetable. But now, if you will excuse me—' she looked pointedly at the door '—I have calls to make this evening. With my maid in attendance.'

'Leo.'

'What is it?' Leo's response was a growl. He continued to refill his brandy glass. The bottle was already more than half-empty. He planned to finish it.

'There is a carriage down in the square,' Jack said. 'The groom has brought a message. He says it is urgent that you speak to the passenger in the carriage.'

'Who is he?'

'I have no idea. The blinds are drawn and the groom would not say.'

Leo crossed to the window to look down at the carriage in the square. It was a nondescript, hired vehicle, not much better than the one he had bought to follow Sophie to Venice. The passenger could be anyone, though he was unlikely to be a man of substance. 'Oh, very well.' Leo slammed his glass down. 'I will go. Though I do not see why you could not have dealt with this, Jack.'

'The passenger insisted that—' Jack began, but Leo stormed out and clattered down the stairs without waiting for a word more.

Leo was stoking his anger. This man had better have something good to sell, or Leo would make him suffer for his insolence. He marched across the square and hauled open the carriage door. 'Well, sir?'

The figures inside recoiled from Leo's snarling anger. Two women. And one of them was the lady he had so grievously wronged.

'Lord Leo,' Sophie said in a low, rather strained voice. 'How delightful to see you again.'

Leo remembered enough of his manners to sketch a bow.

'Quite,' she said. She indicated the seat opposite. 'Would you be so kind as to give me a few moments of your time? Teresa?'

The maid rose and climbed down from the carriage.

Sophie wanted to speak to him. Alone. After what he had done to her, he could not deny her the opportunity to berate him. Indeed, if she had her pistol to hand, she might decide that only shooting was a good enough punishment.

In the circumstances, he could not blame her.

'Lord Leo,' she began, once he had closed the door and taken his seat, 'I have come to warn you. Verdicchio is dead. The Baron von Beck—' Leo started at the name. 'I see you remember him. We passed him on the road when we left the scene of the shooting.'

'But you said noth—' Leo stopped short and shut his lips tightly together.

Sophie knew he had been about to accuse her. He would have said that, by failing to tell him about Beck, she had put them both in grave danger. She knew it perfectly well. And she was trying to make amends. 'Beck is threatening to denounce you to the Austrian authorities. He says they will execute you. Leo—' She pulled herself up. She was gabbling. She forced herself to speak slowly, and formally. 'Lord Leo, you must leave Austria. You should return to England where you will be beyond their reach.'

He did not look as worried as he should be. In fact, he did not look worried at all. 'Madame Pietre, I am sensible of your…er…kindness in coming here to tell me this, but there is no danger, I promise you. Did Beck tell you that Baron Hager would arrest me?'

'Baron Hager?' Sophie echoed wonderingly.

'Yes. He is the Austrian Emperor's chief of police. I can assure you, *madame*, that Hager will not arrest me. Why would he take the word of a Prussian over the word of an Englishman, especially one who has the protection of Lord Castlereagh?'

'Beck was certain that he would be believed,' Sophie said. 'He said my testimony in your favour would be valueless.'

Leo frowned. His mouth had set into a grim line. 'They might dismiss your evidence, *madame*—though they should not—but they would certainly not dismiss mine.' He raised his chin and looked directly into Sophie's eyes. 'Though I am in no real danger, I am greatly honoured that you should seek to help me. It is more than I deserve, after the way I used you.'

Sophie did not know what to say. Was he apologising? And for what, exactly? She raised her eyebrows, trying to look suitably haughty. 'You speak as if I am your chattel, sir. I am not.'

He had now begun to look deeply embarrassed. 'I owe you the most abject apology, *madame*, though I know it is inadequate. My behaviour to you was unpardonable. I shall always regret it.'

Sophie could no longer tell what she felt about this man. She did not acknowledge his apology. She could not. In her confusion, she could not decide whether to be pleased or angry that he had made one. Instead, she said rather stiffly, 'I came here to warn you, sir, and I have fulfilled my duty there. If you would please to get down, I shall be on my way.'

With one last, long look into her face, he nodded, bowed and left the carriage, closing the door quietly behind him.

She slumped in her seat. She felt as if someone had beaten her all over with a cudgel. Her very bones ached.

It was only when the carriage was in motion once more that she made the connection. Baron Hager. The man who was renting rooms to Beck, and who was so good a friend to that villain that he would move out at almost no notice. Beck's intimate friend was the Austrian chief of police!

She saw, on the instant, what she had to do. Leo might think he was not in danger, but Sophie knew better. Beck was capable of any wickedness. The threat from him had to be removed. And Sophie's quick brain had just discovered the ideal method.

She pulled the string and gave the coachman new, and precise, directions.

Chapter Nineteen

Where the devil had she gone? She seemed to have vanished into the air.

He should not have left her alone in that carriage without another word. He had been feeling guilty and embarrassed, but that was no excuse. What mattered was that Sophie had come to him, to warn him about Beck. He had not deserved that. Could it be that she had some lingering feelings for him? Unlikely. She would have come because she was an honourable and fair-minded woman who cared for the welfare of her fellow creatures. Even for men like Leo, who treated her like a whore.

He continued to pace slowly around Sophie's deserted apartment. The furniture was still in place, of course, since it belonged to the landlord, but there were no personal belongings to suggest that anyone had ever lived here. No ornament, no glass, not even a cushion. Nothing.

He stopped outside her bedchamber. He had lain with her behind that forbidding door. And he had—

He groaned aloud, but he forced himself to turn the

handle and enter. He had to face his demons. Once across the threshold he stopped, closing his eyes. He could remember it all. Every kiss, every touch. He breathed deeply. The room smelt of dust, and stale air and…and just the faintest hint of Sophie's perfume. Or perhaps he was imagining it? When he inhaled again, trying to capture that elusive scent, it was gone. As if it had never been.

Damn, damn, damn! Everything was his own fault! There had been so many signs—if he had not been too arrogant to read them. He had thought on many occasions that she behaved like an innocent, that she had the manners of a lady. But he had dismissed those notions, cynically putting them down to her skill as an actress. Why had he not followed his instincts? They had been telling him the truth. He was sure, now, that she *was* a lady. And she had certainly been innocent. Until, that is, she had invited him to her bed, welcomed him into her body and suffered under his lust. He deserved to be horsewhipped.

He opened his eyes and stared at the bed. The coverlet was gone. But he could still picture it, spread across the mattress, accusing him.

He needed to find her, to try to make amends. Somehow. But it was too late. She was gone.

The sight of Schönbrunn's rococo façade, sparkling gaudily against the snow, provided solace to Sophie's lacerated soul. Here she could hide from all the men who were pursuing her. Even the Baron von Beck could not reach her here. Schönbrunn would be a safe haven until Beck was removed from Vienna.

Sophie gazed out across the drifts of pristine snow

and inhaled a long breath of crisp, cold air. She allowed herself a tiny smile. It had been a clever plan.

The Prussian ambassador had been incensed to learn that his trusted spy was intimate friends with the Austrian chief of police, for the Prussians saw Austria as a powerful adversary at the Congress. Beck would never be trusted again by his own countrymen. In his fury, the ambassador had sworn to have Beck forcibly removed from Vienna.

The problem was that the removal had not yet taken place. And while Beck remained at large in the city, both Leo and Sophie were in danger. Leo could take care of himself, as he had made abundantly clear. But Sophie had no one to defend her now. Leo had been her only champion, and she had dismissed him in a cold and final way. She had not accepted his apology, and he would never forgive her for that.

She tried to tell herself that it did not matter, that she was unlikely to see him again, but her heart turned over at the thought. She had allowed her pride and her hurt to drive her tongue. She wished now that she had not, but it was too late for remorse. That encounter in her carriage could not be undone. She had no choice but to go on with her life. Alone.

She would lie concealed at Schönbrunn until she was sure that Beck was no longer a danger. No one in Vienna would suspect where she was, for Marie-Louise lived in seclusion, and Sophie had let it be known that she was leaving the city for good. Neither Beck, nor Leo, nor anyone else would wish to look for her.

'You missed a grand spectacle, Leo. Can't imagine why you didn't want to come.'

Leo threw a malevolent look at Jack and continued writing his report.

'All those sleighs, and the high-stepping horses to pull them. Such a pace they set, once we were out of the city. And there was even a Turkish band on a huge sled at the back.' Jack was obviously too excited by his day out to notice that Leo was in no mood for idle chatter. 'At Schönbrunn, there was even skating on the lake. One of the embassy fellows was doing all sorts of jumps, and spins and turns. The Austrian Empress was most impressed. I thought the ex-Empress Marie-Louise would be there, too, but she'd gone away for the day. Quite deliberately, I was told. Apparently, she prefers to live like a recluse. Silly of her, really. She even missed the performance of *Cinderella*, in the private theatre. I don't know much about music, but I thought the singing was splendid.'

'*Cinderella*, the opera?' Leo held his breath, waiting for Jack's answer. Was it possible that…?

'Mmm. The heroine wasn't half as beautiful as the Venetian Nightingale, though. *She* would have made a Cinderella worthy of any lucky prince.'

'I'm surprised she wasn't there,' Leo said, trying to sound nonchalant.

'Yes, I was, too. I even asked about her. But no one has seen her for at least a week. They say she's left the city.'

Leo returned to his report and stared down at the jumble of meaningless words it now contained. 'I expect she has,' he murmured hoarsely. It had been stupid to hope.

The door opened with a crash. Predictably, it was Ben.

'What now?' Leo said crossly. 'Can't you see I'm trying to work?'

'You won't want to work now, Leo.' Ben was beaming at them both. 'The Duke has arrived. He's gone to meet Castlereagh.'

Leo jumped to his feet. Duty! He must present himself for new orders. He strode across to the mirror and began, a little nervously, to straighten his cravat.

'Now we'll show 'em,' Jack cried. He sounded like a child, bested in some game, who had just seen how he could win the next round. 'The Tsar won't be up to any of his tricks now Wellington's here.'

Two days passed before the Duke of Wellington was ready to receive Leo. Wellington and Castlereagh had spent the time closeted together, presumably so that the Foreign Secretary could brief the Duke about everything that had happened and about the continuing risks the Tsar might present. Leo had rather expected to be kept waiting. Wellington had a very sharp brain, but even he would need time to absorb months of diplomatic manoeuvrings.

The Duke received him alone, sitting behind the desk. He was simply dressed, in a plain blue coat, fawn pantaloons and boots. His manner was brusque and to the point. 'Too much intrigue going on here, Aikenhead. And not nearly enough trustworthy men to police it. Remind me. How many of you are there?'

'We are three, your Grace, plus the locally recruited men.'

'Local recruits are no good. Not for this. Three? Is that all? I fancied there were four Honours.'

'There are. But my eldest brother was in Russia when we left for Vienna.'

'Ah, yes. Getting acquainted with his new wife.'

'Wife?' Leo echoed. So Dominic had married Alex after all.

The Duke laughed sharply. 'Aye. You tell me that you did not know?'

Leo shook his head. He had expected it, but he had not known for sure. He did not attempt to explain to Wellington. Dominic would have tried to send news home, but he had no reason to send to Vienna, for he did not know that Leo and Jack were there. And the mails from Russia were uncertain at the best of times.

Wellington's mind was already elsewhere. He had begun to drum his fingers on the desk, and he was frowning into the middle distance. Leo knew he must wait for orders.

They were not long in coming. 'We're devilish short-handed here in Vienna, Aikenhead, but there's danger-ous unrest in France. King Louis has put up the backs of most of his people with his high-handed edicts. You know what the French are like. Given any half-decent excuse, they will throw the white cockade in the gutter and hoist their tricolour again. Either that or start shouting for their beloved Emperor!'

Leo said nothing. What might the Duke want the Honours to do?

'We need first-hand information about what is going on in the south of France. Having the Honours here in Vienna is a godsend, for there are so very few agents we can trust. The Honours shall go.'

Leo's heart sank. It was bad enough that he had so far been unable to trace Sophie, but if he had to travel to France, he would never find her.

Wellington was staring at him. Did his anguish show in his face? If anyone could read Leo's inner turmoil, it would be the Duke. Leo pulled himself up a little straighter. He had no choice here. It was a matter of duty to his country. 'We can leave immediately, sir. Do you have specific orders for us?'

'Gently, my boy, gently. Victorious battles are fought after careful planning. This is no exception. Tell me, first, about your younger brother. How much does he rely on you in this murky trade the Honours ply?'

Leo thought for a moment. He needed to be fair to Jack. 'Of late, your Grace, he has needed very little direction from me. I was— I had to leave Vienna for some weeks over Christmas, and Jack ran our enterprise here very well. I believe Lord Castlereagh will bear me out on that.'

Wellington nodded. A tiny smile touched his mouth, but instantly disappeared. 'Castlereagh said as much. Glad to have it confirmed.' He looked up at Leo. 'That being so, I think we may risk splitting our forces. Your brother and young Dexter will travel to France. You will stay here. Three of you would be too conspicuous, in any case. And I need a dependable man here in Austria. You have done well so far in delivering information. Now, I need more.'

Leo's mind was full of questions. And renewed hopes. What did the Duke want him to do? And with this gift of extra time, was there any chance that he might find Sophie?

They were alone when Leo handed Jack the sealed packet. Ben had gone out to organise transport. 'Here are your final orders. Commit them to memory, and then burn them. There must be nothing to link either of you to England if you are caught.'

Jack was looking more serious than Leo had ever known. And grown up at last. Leo found himself wondering whether he and Dominic had wrapped the boy in cotton wool for too long. Jack needed to have an opportunity to prove himself. Well, this was certainly such a chance. It was supremely dangerous, but it could be the making of him.

'You should—' Leo stopped short. Jack must make his own decisions now. 'Um…have you thought about which route you will take?'

Jack grinned. 'Yes, but we haven't decided yet. I thought I would ask your advice.' His eyes were dancing. He knew perfectly well what Leo was about.

Leo clapped him on the shoulder and returned the grin with interest. 'I'm not sure my advice will be worth much. I was the one who was snowed up, remember?' Nevertheless, the two of them bent over the maps and considered the risks of the various routes.

'Time is what matters,' Jack said with decision. 'I shall consult Ben, of course, but I think we must take the most direct route.' He stabbed a finger on to the map. 'This one. Do you agree?'

'It's not my decision, Jack. But in your place, I would do the same. The sooner you arrive in France, the sooner you'll be able to get back to England with the information the government needs.'

Jack nodded and held out his hand. Leo shook it warmly. Then, feeling a little self-conscious, he pulled Jack into an embrace. 'Take care, brother. I mean that. Dominic will have my hide if you don't come home safe. Ben, too.'

'Don't worry, Leo.' Jack sounded as devil-may-care as ever, but his eyes were hooded. 'I can pass for a

Frenchman just as easily as you or Dom. You know I can. And unlike you two old reprobates, I look so young and innocent that all the girls and their mamas confide in me. You'll be astonished at how much information I can glean. I'll prove it when I get back to England. Wait and see.'

'Pray God it's so. But what about Ben? His French is not good enough to pass for a native.'

'He won't need to. We have it all worked out. Ben is to be a German. That will account for the foreign accent. His French is fluent enough apart from that.'

'And his German?'

'He has enough to get by.' Recognising the incredulity on Leo's face, Jack added, 'As long as we don't encounter any real Germans, that is. But I'm sure we won't. Not in that part of France. It's full of rustics.'

Leo couldn't help but laugh, in spite of the worry churning his gut. Blast the boy. He was so eager to prove his mettle. And he would, too. Leo was sure of that. Lord Jack Aikenhead—charmer, gambler, spy— was growing up at last.

Leo had continued to visit Sophie's apartment on an almost daily basis. He had even managed to acquire his own key by bribing the concierge. It had achieved nothing. She had never returned. And that elusive hint of her presence, that scent he had detected on his first visit, was gone for good. The rooms had remained deserted, with dust settling ever thicker on once-polished surfaces. Every visit brought pain and a sense that the gulf between them was growing.

But somehow, he could not stay away. It had been the scene of his greatest delight. And his greatest betrayal.

Leo let his mind wander as he walked across the city for yet another visit to that apartment. Jack and Ben had been gone for some weeks. The weather had been milder of late, so there was a good chance they would have arrived safely in France. Leo refused to consider the many things that might go wrong. Jack was a sensible fellow and a seasoned spy. He would not take unnecessary risks. He—

Leo stopped dead, unable to believe his eyes. That man outside Sophie's apartment. It was— It couldn't be! Leo ducked behind a small dividing wall and peeped out. There could be no doubt. The man standing in the portico of the building was Verdicchio, the man who had died from Leo's bullet!

Leo's mind was racing. He could not quite remember how he had learned of Verdicchio's supposed death. Had it been one of his own spies? Or Castlereagh? He racked his brains.

And then he remembered her, just as she had been, sitting alone in her hired carriage. It seemed a lifetime ago. But it was Sophie who had told him Verdicchio was dead. She had lied to his face.

The realisation came like a punch to the gut that almost doubled him over with pain. She had lied to him. She had lied to persuade him to leave Vienna. That was the one thing she had asked him to do. She had said he must leave before Beck denounced him as a murderer. Did that mean she was in league with Beck? No. Impossible. The very idea was nauseating. She might plot with the Prussians to remove Leo from Vienna, but she would never work with Beck. Not willingly. She—

Some tiny part of Leo's brain had been watching

Verdicchio all the while. The man was pacing up and down in the shadows. He must be waiting for someone. Could it be—?

Just then, a heavily cloaked figure came out of a side alley and sidled up to Verdicchio. Alas, it was not Sophie. It was the Baron von Beck.

It had taken Leo precious minutes to get close enough to hear their conversation. He had expected to find it difficult to follow, in Italian or German. But it seemed that the common language between these two villains was French. Leo listened eagerly.

Beck was getting angry. 'I bought her from you,' he was saying. 'You have no rights over her now. She is mine.' He gripped Verdicchio by the lapels and shook him like a dog with a rat. 'So where is she?'

'Let me go. I can't breathe!'

Beck loosened his grip, but did not let go completely. 'Tell me where she is, or you will cease breathing for good.' He tightened his grip again to underline his threat.

'I…I don't know.' Beck's grip tightened a little more. 'I don't know.' Verdicchio's voice had become very shrill. 'But I…I suspect…'

Beck's eyes narrowed. 'Well?'

'How much is it worth to you?' Verdicchio asked with sudden bravado.

'Nothing. Except your life.'

The maestro crumpled. Only Beck's grip prevented him from falling to the ground. He whispered something inaudible.

In his hiding place, Leo tensed. He could not hear. He had to know!

'What?' Beck leaned closer to Verdicchio's face. Verdicchio must have spoken again, for the Baron's face cleared suddenly.

At that moment, an officer and a small detachment of Prussian soldiers marched straight across the square to the portico, as if they knew what they would find there. The officer saluted. 'Herr Baron von Beck,' he began, before continuing in German that was too difficult for Leo to follow. But his purpose soon became clear. After less than two minutes, the Baron was marched away under escort. He had been arrested by his own people!

A strange sound broke the silence the moment the soldiers left the square. It was Verdicchio. And he was laughing.

Leo's temper exploded. He covered the distance between them in a few angry strides. He seized Verdicchio by the lapels, just as Beck had done. 'You villain,' Leo snarled. 'I should have killed you when I had the chance. What have you done with her?'

Verdicchio did not seem to be afraid any more. 'The Baron has relinquished his claim on her,' he said calmly. 'She is mine again.'

'No!'

'But yes. She herself will admit it, I promise you. I am about to go to Schönbrunn to retrieve her. She belongs to me.'

'She does not! She is to be my wife, and I warn you that I will kill any man who harms a hair of her head.'

Verdicchio's mouth fell open.

Leo placed his hands around the man's scrawny neck and tightened his grip a little. 'Do you feel that, Verdicchio?'

The man's eyes goggled. He managed to nod.

'Good. Then I suggest you swear to me now, on your life, that you will leave Vienna and never trouble Madame Pietre again.' He brought his face very close to Verdicchio's. 'Swear. Or I promise that you will have no life beyond this day.'

Verdicchio swore.

Leo had no idea how he had arrived back at his lodgings. He supposed he must have walked, but he had no memory of doing so.

His mind was fizzing with the revelation that his own angry tongue had spoken. He was going to marry Sophie. Of course he was. He would make Sophie his wife because he loved her. He had been in love with her for months, perhaps from the very beginning. But in spite of all his vaunted experience with women, he had been too much of a fool to recognise his own feelings.

She was at Schönbrunn, only a few miles from Vienna. She had been there all this time. So very near. He would ride out there and find her, wherever she was hiding. And then he would ask her—plead with her, if necessary—to become his wife.

She would accept him. She would. For she must love him. Why else would she have given him her innocence? She had welcomed him with such passion, such burning desire. She would not be able to refuse him now, not if he kissed her as he longed to do.

He took the stairs three at a time. There were several hours of daylight left. He could change and ride out to Schönbrunn. If she was there, he would find her.

He was smiling as he flung open the door.

'My lord! At last!' His valet was looking extremely anxious.

'What's the matter?'

'You are summoned to attend on the Duke. Immediately, my lord. The messenger came an hour since.'

Panic gripped Leo. Had something happened to Jack? He tried not to let his fear rule him. 'Sounds like some kind of emergency,' he said lightly.

'That it is, my lord. Boney has escaped from Elba.'

Chapter Twenty

Sophie was happier than she had thought possible. It must be the beauty and serenity of Schönbrunn, and the company of the little prince. She had always longed for children of her own, but that was an impossible dream, for marriage was not for her. Any child she had would be a bastard. Much as she loved children, she did not want that. Even with Leo…

She touched a hand to her flat belly. If Leo had given her a child, she would have loved it for his sake. But she knew for certain now that there would be no child. It was for the best. She, of all people, knew that a child with no father was destined to suffer its whole life long.

She moved a formation of soldiers across the battle-field set out on the magnificent inlaid floor of the oval Chinese room. She had become much more adept at battle tactics during these weeks at Schönbrunn. The young prince had commended her more than once recently. His mother was looking on indulgently from the chair where she sat, sewing. Unlike Sophie, Marie-

Louise did not crawl around on the floor, even to play with her son. It was beneath her dignity.

The boy waited until Sophie had finished marshalling her men. Then he shook his head. 'You will lose them, *madame*. My cavalry will cut them down.'

Sophie had to laugh. He sounded like a sage old warrior, rather than a small boy. He was just reaching for his cavalrymen when the door opened to admit his governess and Marie-Louise's major-domo. Maman Quiou-quiou looked anxious. The man looked very grave.

The Countess curtsied and immediately swept the child into her arms.

'Madame!' Marie-Louise protested indignantly.

The Countess reddened, but did not release the child. 'He must not hear, your Majesty.' She dropped another hasty curtsy and fled from the room, carrying the little prince.

Marie-Louise sprang up from her chair in outrage.

Sophie scrambled to her feet and tried to straighten her crumpled skirts.

The major-domo ignored Sophie. 'Your Imperial Majesty,' he said pompously, 'I have grave news. About the Emperor.'

'Papa?' Marie-Louise paled and put a hand to her throat. 'Tell me.'

'Your Majesty, your husband, his Imperial Majesty the Emperor Napoleon, has left Elba and raised his standard in France.'

Sophie could not believe her ears. Escaped? And raising his standard? There would be war all over again. She looked from the major-domo to Marie-Louise, who seemed to be frozen where she stood. Her face had gone sheet-white, apart from a bright red spot on each cheek. She looked as though she might collapse at any moment. Sophie ran to her and offered a supporting arm. 'Your Imperial Majesty. Pray sit.'

'Do not call me by that name,' Marie-Louise said in a hollow voice.

Not an empress? 'I beg your pardon, your Imperial Highness,' Sophie ventured. It was the correct mode of address for an Austrian Archduchess.

The major-domo had not moved. 'Your imperial father sends word that he is distressed at these tidings, and concerned for your welfare, your Ma—' He frowned briefly. 'Your Imperial Highness, the Emperor asks that you remove, with the prince, to the imperial palace in Vienna.'

That request—or was it a command?—seemed to affect Marie-Louise as news of her husband's escape had not. She drew herself up to her full height and looked down her nose at the major-domo. 'I shall not remove to Vienna. I shall remain at Schönbrunn where I am mistress of my own household.'

Sophie was astonished. She had never heard Marie-Louise make such a bold statement before. Particularly not when it meant crossing her father.

'Now leave us.'

The major-domo bowed himself out. Would he send Marie-Louise's message to her father? Emperor Francis was quite capable of sending a troop of soldiers out to Schönbrunn and bringing his daughter back by main force.

Marie-Louise began to shake. 'I will not go,' she whispered. 'He wants to imprison me in Vienna. I will never be free again.' She threw herself into Sophie's arms and began to sob in great whoops of anguish. 'He will come to take me away,' she said between gasps.

'Your papa?'

'Yes. No. Either of them. They both want me. But neither of them loves me. No one loves me.' She broke down in a gale of bitter weeping.

Sophie had never seen such distress. She found herself blessing the governess for removing the child before he could see it. Unlike Sophie, the Countess had served the Bonapartes for years, and it seemed she was shrewd enough to guess how Marie-Louise would react. The weeping was getting worse.

Sophie urged Marie-Louise towards her bedchamber and helped her to remove her gown. Eventually, she managed to persuade her to don her nightrail and climb into bed. 'I will send for a tisane,' Sophie said, stroking the hair from her brow. 'It will help your Imperial Highness to sleep, I am sure. Things will be clearer once you have had some rest.' Sophie made to rise, but Marie-Louise would not let go of her hand. The tisane would have to wait.

Marie-Louise was too weak to speak. Sophie sat holding her hand, stroking it gently. After a few minutes more, Marie-Louise's softer, slower breathing showed that she had fallen asleep.

Sophie crept back to the oval Chinese room. It was empty, except for the dozens of painted lead soldiers arranged across the floor. It was about to begin again. She could not bear the thought of all those dying men. And for what? For the clashing ambitions of Marie-Louise's husband and father. Plus his power-hungry allies.

She clasped her hands. She wanted to pray. But she

could not. She was too full of anger against these hateful, ruthless men. Bonaparte, the Tsar, the Austrian Emperor, they were all the same. She sank into the chair where Marie-Louise had sat and dropped her head into her hands. That poor woman, used by the man she had married, and used by her own father. Just as Sophie had been used by her father. All men were wicked. There was not an honourable one among them.

There is Leo, said a tiny voice that refused to be crushed. Leo was an honourable man. She could not deny that, even to herself. And much as she had tried to struggle against it, she still loved him. What would he do when war began? Would he fight? Oh, God! He might be killed. She had a terrifying vision of Leo's body, broken and bloody on the ground.

She clasped her hands together once more and bent her head. This time, she did pray.

'I'm sorry I had to send you to Budapest, Aikenhead. I'm afraid there was no one else I could rely on for that mission. You did well. But now I have another mission for you. Again, I can offer you no help, but I don't imagine that there will be any real danger this time. Let me explain.' Wellington waved Leo to a chair.

That was most unusual. Leo sat rigidly to attention, ready to spring to his feet at a word.

'You know, I am sure, that Bonaparte's wife and son are living in seclusion at Schönbrunn. That palace is not defensible. I spoke to the Emperor about it while you were in Budapest. I suggested most strongly that he remove his daughter and grandson from Schönbrunn and bring them within the safety of Vienna's walls. But I was unable to persuade him. He will not insist. He invited her to come to the city, but when she refused, he would not agree to have her forced.' Wellington shook his head in disgust. 'There are times when a man—an emperor especially—must exert his authority.' He cleared his throat loudly.

Leo fancied the Duke had not intended to make that last comment. At least, not aloud.

'So it seems that Bonaparte's wife and her son will remain at Schönbrunn. I want you, Aikenhead, to go out there and protect her.'

One man? To protect a palace? Leo was astounded, but he said only, 'Are you expecting her to flee, your Grace?'

'No. Where would she go? In any case, she has made it very clear that she has no intention of returning to her husband. She had a fit of the vapours at the very thought of it, I understand.'

'I see.' In truth, he did not see. He could not think straight. He could think only that he was to go to Schönbrunn, at last, and that Sophie was there. That he would see her, speak to her, ask her to—

'I do not expect an attack, and I do not expect Marie-Louise to make any move to join her husband. But a wise general learns to expect the unexpected. At the first hint that she may be in danger, you are to bring her and her son to Vienna. By force, if you have to. Do I make myself clear?'

The interview was at an end. Leo rose smartly to his feet and bowed. 'Absolutely clear, your Grace. You may depend on me.'

Leo had been so determined to be ready to leave at first light. His pistols were quickly cleaned and loaded. He had acquired a sword, for he had no idea how many enemies he might have to face at Schönbrunn. He still had Hector, his hired gelding, but one riding horse could not carry Leo, his valet, and all their baggage. So Leo was forced to spend precious hours trying to secure a carriage and horses. He found there was more than a whiff of panic in Vienna now. Many of the foreign visitors were already fleeing, in hopes of defending their lands and property. Without using the Duke's name, Leo probably would not have succeeded in finding any transport at all.

When he eventually returned with the carriage, he found that Barrow had spent his time packing a vast array of clothes, so that Leo would always be properly dressed to attend on an emperor's daughter. Absurd! But Leo humoured the man—he had often been useful in a tight corner—even though he doubted there would be much time for such empty ritual. He was likely to be spending most of his waking hours trying to ensure the security of Schönbrunn.

And to win a commitment from Sophie.

He was desperately fighting the urge to think about her, about the confrontation to come. She might refuse to be alone with him, or to listen to the passionate declaration he so wanted to make. He tried to tell himself that he would succeed, that he would find a way to persuade her. He must succeed.

But first, he had to reach Schönbrunn and do his duty by Marie-Louise.

The sun was well up by the time Leo drove the carriage out of Vienna, with Hector tied on behind. Church bells were ringing cheerfully. Since it was Palm Sunday, the people were flocking to church. Leo suspected that they would all be on their knees, begging for deliverance from the French monster who had defeated them so often before.

One of the embassy secretaries hailed the carriage just as it approached the city walls. Leo halted his team. The man might have further orders from the Duke.

'Aikenhead, have you heard? Bonaparte has reached Grenoble. Thousands are flocking to his standard.'

Leo swore roundly. 'But surely the royalist troops will arrest him? King Louis sent Marshal Ney, did he not?'

'Marshal Ney has defected to Bonaparte, with six thousand troops. Bonaparte is on his way to Paris, at the head of an army of twenty thousand.'

No wonder Vienna reeked of panic. The situation could hardly be worse. 'Will Louis fight to hold the city?' If he did not, then another war was certain.

The secretary's incredulous expression gave Leo his answer before the man had said a word. 'King Louis has already fled.'

The door of the Chinese room was flung open. 'Your Majesty—' The major-domo had forgotten his mistress's rules. And he had lost his dignity. He appeared to be in total panic. 'Your Majesty, you must flee. Now!'

Marie-Louise screamed and jumped to her feet.

'Armed men. In the parade court. They have come for you. And your son.'

Marie-Louise screamed again, even louder, but she did not move.

'*Madame*, you must flee!' The major-domo was shouting now.

Still she did not move. She was staring at the man

as though he were an apparition. 'But I— Where can I—?' She looked round wildly. Her son's governess was ashen and seemed to by paralysed with fear. The other ladies-in-waiting were no better.

Sophie could see that this was no time for etiquette. She grabbed the little prince from the floor and pushed him at his mother. 'Come, your Highness. I will help you.'

Marie-Louise made no move to take the child. Instead she burst into howls of terror. She tried to speak, but her words were incoherent.

Sophie longed to slap her. She turned to the major-domo. 'How soon?'

He shrugged his shoulders. He was old and frightened. He would be useless against young, armed men.

Sophie made up her mind. It might be impossible to save Marie-Louise, but she could certainly save the child. 'I will take him,' she said resolutely. 'Delay these men as much as you can. I will try to get the prince to Vienna.'

Marie-Louise was staring blankly at Sophie. Had she understood?

'And you,' Sophie ordered the major-domo, 'send to Vienna for help. We need soldiers.'

The man straightened, trying to recover a little of his lost dignity. 'I have already done so, *madame*.'

Sophie clung to that tiny shred of hope. If she and the child could hide, or find horses to start out on the road, they might not be taken. Clutching the child to her bosom, she raced up the hidden Kaunitz staircase to the upper floor and through the labyrinth of interconnecting rooms. Ahead of her was her own bedchamber. She rushed inside. Where was her pistol? Was it loaded? She set the boy down. He was gazing up at her, wide-eyed.

He had not said a single word, but he watched while she scrabbled around for her gun. It took precious minutes to load it, for her hands were not steady. She pushed it into her pocket.

'And now, *mon prince*, we are going to play a game of hide and seek.' At his quick nod, she caught him up again and ran out. She dared not go down by the Kaunitz staircase for Marie-Louise was there in the Chinese room. It was the first place the kidnappers would look. Instead, Sophie raced to the farthest corner of the palace where the rooms backed onto hidden servants' quarters and stairways. At last she found the doorway concealed in the wall. She had never been behind it and did not know her way. She must trust to instinct. And luck. And her own determination to save this child.

She launched herself through the door and down the steep stone steps beyond.

Leo tossed the carriage reins to Barrow and flung himself onto Hector's back. The messenger from Schön-brunn was already disappearing in the direction of Vienna. Help would come. But would it come soon enough?

'*Los, Hector!*' Leo set his heels to Hector's flanks. 'Follow as fast as you can, Barrow,' he shouted over his shoulder. 'I will try to hold them.'

He could see Schönbrunn in the distance, glistening like an iced cake in the afternoon sun. Spring had arrived at last. But with it had come precisely the danger that Wellington had feared. Bonaparte had sent his agents to kidnap his wife and son.

Leo lay low along Hector's neck, encouraging him to

greater speed. The unaccustomed sword was slapping against his thigh. He would use it if he had to, though he had had no practice since his arrival in Vienna. But against a troop of armed men, two pistols would never be enough.

Hector's huge stride ate up the ground. Once, he stumbled on the uneven road surface, but Leo held him up. They had been galloping dangerously fast, but it had to be done. They had almost reached their goal. Leo turned the tiring horse up the long road to the palace gate and urged him to one last effort.

A group of riderless horses stood by the west door along with a small closed carriage. Leo jumped to the ground and cocked a pistol, but there were no men guarding the horses. Just one stable lad. Leo ignored the boy and ran into the palace. Which way to go? He stopped, listening. In the strange silence, he heard the sound of female wailing from somewhere on the floor above. He raced up the staircase and towards the sound. It led him to a small oval room full of Chinese objects and helpless, weeping women.

'*Madame*, where is your son?'

Marie-Louise took one look at a man with a pistol in his hand and shrank back into the arms of her women. 'No!' she screamed. 'Don't kill me! I beg you!'

'I am here to defend you,' Leo snapped. 'Where is your son?'

'He…he…'

An older woman stepped forward. 'That singer took him.'

Her words stabbed at him. 'Madame Pietre?' Leo croaked. 'She has taken him?'

'She said she would save him!' Marie-Louise

cried, between hiccupping sobs. 'She said she would protect him.'

Yes, she would do that, even at the risk of her own life. Leo was filled with desperate fear. Sophie. Sophie had put herself in danger. He must rescue her. 'The attackers? Do they know she took the boy?'

'I…I had to tell them,' Marie-Louise sank to the floor and covered her face with her hands. 'They terrified me. They were going to kill me.'

'I doubt that,' Leo retorted.

'How dare you say such a thing?' The older woman stepped between Leo and Marie-Louise. 'Her Imperial Highness—'

'Her Imperial Highness may just have sacrificed the life of her own son. And of the bravest woman in Austria.' He strode from the room. Outside in the gallery, he stopped, but this time he could hear nothing. Where would she go? Sophie was no fool. She would know there was no time to escape from the palace. She would try to find somewhere to hide.

He rushed back into the Chinese room, grabbed one of the younger ladies by the arm. 'Show me the way to the servants' stairs. Quickly! If you want to save that child!'

'This is a good spot,' Sophie said, trying to smile at the boy. 'Look. You may hide in this broom cupboard. You will not be afraid of the dark, will you, my prince?'

He swallowed and shook his head bravely.

'Your mama will be proud of you.'

'And my papa?' he said eagerly.

'He will be especially proud.'

He managed a tiny, hesitant smile. 'But you, *madame*, where will you hide?'

Sophie looked rapidly round the gloomy cellar room. It had only one door. If they were discovered, they would not be able to escape. So she must hide, too. There were no cupboards large enough for an adult. 'Behind that chest there,' she said, pointing. 'Now, shall we each creep into our hiding places? We must be very quiet. And whatever happens, you must not come out until I come to find you. Or your mama, of course. Can you do that?'

He nodded.

'You promise?'

'Word of a Bonaparte,' he said proudly.

Sophie gulped and pushed him into the cupboard. She closed the door very gently, praying that he would not be so frightened that he would cry out. She delved into her pocket for her pistol and slid down behind the huge chest in the corner of the room. It was well away from the prince's cupboard. If the soldiers found them, she would draw their fire. She would tell them that the child had been taken by…by one of the servants. Anything to stop them opening that cupboard.

At first she crouched, but after a few minutes her legs began to ache with the tension and the waiting. She dropped on to her knees. That was better. She could make herself even smaller this way. She was almost sure she could not be seen from the doorway.

She continued to wait, holding her breath. She heard the sound of booted feet on the stone floor outside. Not many. Two men, perhaps? Or three? She closed her eyes and crouched lower. She had only one shot. And once she had used it, she had no defences at all.

A French voice echoed terrifyingly around the stone walls. 'You there. Come out,' it ordered.

It was a bluff. He could not possibly see her. She did not move.

'Come out, or I will shoot.'

Chapter Twenty-One

Leo was lost. So many stairs. So many rooms. Where were they? He was losing precious time.

And then he heard the shot. Oh, God! Sophie!

His heart was pounding and he was gasping for breath, but he raced towards the sound as if the devil was on his tail. He had a pistol in each hand now, and he was more than ready to use them.

'Sophie!' She was in the far corner of a large stone cellar room. A man in a crumpled French officer's coat was hauling her to her feet. She was clutching her arm, and blood was seeping out between her fingers. 'Sophie!' he cried again, starting into the room.

'Behind you, Leo!'

It was too late. He whirled round to see two more men, each holding a drawn sword. One of them caught him unawares, knocking the pistol from his left hand. It skittered across the floor. Leo did not stop to think. He simply fired his second pistol. The man fell, screaming and clawing at his shoulder. Leo just had time to drop the empty pistol and draw his own sword before the second man was upon him. From the corner of his eye, he saw that Sophie was wrestling with her captor. She was hurt! He needed to go to her!

The second opponent lunged at him. The man was no expert with a sword, but he had clearly learned some underhand tricks in Bonaparte's battles. And he was exceedingly strong. Leo parried desperately, the force of the blows jarring up his arm. He tried to counter-attack, but he was not quite fast enough. He cursed his lack of practice. Step by step, he was forced backwards, as he tried to dance out of reach of the Frenchman's vicious slashes.

Leo stumbled over the uneven floor and almost fell. Only instinct saved him. His left hand went back to grab the stonework and restore his balance; his right whipped his sword across in a great sweeping arc. His adversary leapt back, out of range by inches.

Leo was almost inside a huge stone recess. As he pushed himself back upright, his free hand touched a heavy wooden staff. He seized it. It was an axe!

He pressed forward again, sword in one hand, axe in the other. The man, surprised, took his eye off Leo's sword to glance at this new weapon. In that fateful second, Leo thrust forward and sank his blade deep into the flesh of his opponent's sword arm. Sword and man dropped to the floor.

Leo spun back round to face the officer in the corner. 'Let her go, you devil!'

The man was struggling to unsheathe his sword, for Sophie had thrown her full weight on his arm and was fighting him with all her remaining strength. Her sleeve and her skirt were stained red with blood.

Ice settled around Leo's heart. This could be a fight

to the death. 'Your men will live, sir,' he growled, 'but if you harm that lady, you certainly will not.' He dropped the axe and sprang forward, sword raised. His arm had stopped aching. He was no longer short of breath. He was going to best this man.

With a huge effort, the Frenchman dragged himself free. Sophie fell to the ground with a smothered cry, clasping her hand to her injured arm.

Sophie held her breath, refusing to acknowledge the pain. She knew she must do nothing to distract Leo. He had overcome two opponents, but the officer was a fine swordsman. Even she could tell that, as the two men fought doggedly round the cellar, each seeking for a weakness and a chance to strike.

Leo seemed to be tireless. The Frenchman was soon gasping for breath, though he continued to thrust and parry with neat, precise movements. But Leo could have been playing a game. His blade flashed like quicksilver in the dusty half-light of the cellar. He had become as sure-footed as a mountain goat. He seemed to be a different man, now that he was fighting Sophie's captor. Her heart swelled as she watched. He looked…he looked invincible.

Sophie allowed herself to sink slowly down on to the floor and lean back against the stone wall. Its cool support eased her aching body. But now there was a hard lump under her thigh. She offered up silent words of thanks and very carefully reached under her skirts for the pistol she had dropped, never once taking her eyes from Leo's dancing figure. If this Frenchman looked to be winning, Sophie would shoot him. She would not let Leo die.

But there was no need. Leo had pinned the man

against the wooden table and was going to disarm him. It was over!

Leo touched the point of his sword to the Frenchman's throat. 'Yield.'

'That will not be necessary,' said a new voice from the doorway.

Sophie looked round, aghast. There were two more armed men there. And one of them had a pistol.

Leo had not moved. 'Yield,' he repeated.

The officer smiled. 'You are outnumbered, sir,' he said calmly. 'If you do not put up your sword, my men will attack you.' When Leo still did not move, he added, 'You *and* the lady.'

Leo's sword was withdrawn a fraction. He glanced across at the two newcomers, and then at Sophie.

He was going to surrender in order to save her. No! Sophie rose to her feet, resting her injured arm against the wall in order to keep her balance. She pointed her own pistol at the officer. 'If your men take one more step into this room, sir, I will shoot you.'

The officer looked round, took in the picture of a bloodied female with a pistol, and laughed shortly.

Leo's sword returned to rest against his throat. 'Best not to laugh, sir, for the lady is a crack shot. Now, tell your men to lay down their weapons and sit against that wall with their hands on their heads.'

The officer paused. Had he believed Leo's boast about her shooting ability? Sophie could see that the Frenchman was trying to assess the odds. One man and one woman, injured, against three men. But the men at the door did not have a clear shot at Sophie. Leo and the officer stood in their line of fire.

'Very well. Lay down your weapons, men,' the

officer said at last. His men obeyed Leo's order. 'Have no fear,' the officer said proudly. 'Our comrades will soon be here, and then we shall certainly have the upper hand again.'

'I doubt that,' Leo said curtly. 'Sophie, keep your gun on this man. If he moves an inch, shoot him.' He turned and knelt down on the floor, scrabbling about under the table. When he stood up again, he had a pistol in his left hand and his sword still in his right. 'Now, sir,' he said in a confident voice, 'go and join your men. You are all hostages for the good behaviour of those who may come after you. If they should attack, you will die.'

The officer's face fell.

Leo crossed to the door and risked a hasty glance into the corridor. Empty. Then he forced one of the Frenchmen to bind the hands of his fellows with their own cravats. The third man was still to be bound. Could Sophie…? No, not with that injured arm. 'Sophie, keep your pistol trained on them while I tie up the other one.'

She nodded and took a step forward. The determination on her face was frightening.

It was done in a trice. Leo put down his sword and slid an arm round Sophie's waist, helping her to a stool. 'We must bind up your wound.'

'No. There is no time. And it looks worse than it is. It is only a graze, I promise you.'

His instinct was to overrule her, to cosset her. But then she looked up at him with overbright eyes. She must be exhausted, but she would not give in. He owed it to her to respect her decision. And there was another message there, too. He raised an eyebrow and was rewarded with a tiny nod. Somehow she had ensured the child was safe, but she would not speak of it until this was over.

He smiled encouragingly at her and turned back to his captives. He must not let down his guard. The rest of the kidnappers might arrive at any moment.

One of the injured men was unconscious. The other one was groaning.

'May I tend to him, Leo?'

What an amazing woman she was. He found himself laughing. 'Would it make any difference if I said you must not?'

She shook her head and went to kneel beside the bleeding man.

But the sound of many running feet stopped her. Leo rammed her pistol back into her hand and pushed her behind his body. Pistol and sword in hand, he faced the open doorway.

He waited, his heart racing. The pounding feet were coming nearer. The end would come soon now. 'I love you, Sophie,' he said in an undertone.

He felt her glorious body lean into him for a second, transferring her living warmth. 'And I love you, too,' she whispered.

They had been Austrian soldiers.

Sophie had almost fainted with relief at the sound of German commands, but she forced herself to stay in control. It might not be over yet.

The young cavalry officer was very correct. He even bowed to Sophie. Meanwhile, his soldiers were marching away the three uninjured Frenchmen. 'Where is the prince, *madame*?' he asked in French.

She shook her head. Not until she knew all the

danger was over. 'What of her Imperial Highness? She was in the oval Chinese room, with only women to protect her. Is she safe?'

'She is, *madame*. And we have all the attackers. You may surrender the prince now. Archduchess Marie-Louise and her imperial father will be much in your debt.'

Sophie shook her head once more. 'He must not see.' She waved a hand at the two injured men on the floor. 'He is such a little boy. It is enough that he heard everything.'

'She is right, Captain,' Leo put in brusquely. 'Can you get some of your men to carry these fellows upstairs? They need attention in any case, and they cannot receive it here.'

The captain gave the order, and the two men were carried out. One was still mercifully unconscious, but the other screamed when he was lifted.

Sophie clapped her hands over her ears. The movement reminded her of just how much her arm hurt, but she ignored it. She must fetch out the little prince. He would be so very frightened by now. She started towards the cupboard and stretched out her hand to the handle.

'Sophie.' Leo stopped her with a gentle hand on her good arm. 'You are bleeding. He must not see you so. Let me fetch him.'

'No. No, Leo. I promised him that I would come for him. Or his mother would. He trusts me. I have to do it myself.'

He did not try to argue. He simply shrugged off his coat and placed it round her shoulders so that it covered all the blood. 'Now go to him,' he said, smiling proudly at her.

* * *

'You have been proclaimed a heroine, you know.' Leo grinned at her.

Sophie struggled to sit up, but it was too painful to move without help. She felt a fraud. It really was only a minor flesh wound, as the Emperor's doctor had confirmed when she arrived at the palace. She had had no choice but to join Marie-Louise there, for her old apartment had been re-let.

He slid his arm behind her back and lifted her higher on her pillows. 'You need rest and good nursing, the doctor says. With luck, you will be recovered in a week. Which is just as well, for I am arranging our wedding for two days after Easter. You have eight days to make ready.'

She had been right about Leo. He *was* an honourable man, but his honour was misplaced. 'There will be no wedding,' she said flatly, avoiding his eyes.

He fussed with arranging the bedclothes around her. Then he glanced over his shoulder at Teresa sitting in the chair in the corner. She was asleep. 'My darling Sophie,' he said softly, 'what makes you think you have a choice over this? You were foolish enough to confess that you love me, as I love you. I am afraid that is the end of the matter.'

'Oh, Leo, you are impossible. Your brother is a duke. You cannot marry an opera singer. You know you cannot. But if you…if you truly want me, I will be your mistress.' There. She had said it.

Leo muttered a very strong expletive. And then he bit down so hard on his lip that a tiny drop of blood swelled up like a crimson pearl. She wanted to reach out and stroke away the hurt, but she did not dare. If she touched him, she would never be able to refuse him, as she must.

'Sophie, we love each other. You are a lady and—'

'I am an opera singer,' she hissed. 'They think me a whore!'

'You are a lady, Sophia Pietre, and you are going to be my wife. If you do not agree, I swear I will follow you around Europe until you do. Sophie, darling Sophie, say you will marry me!'

It was so very tempting. 'Leo, I cannot. I… Since you have laid your heart at my feet, I will tell you the truth. All of it. And then you will agree that marriage between us is impossible.' Hoarsely, hesitantly, she told him of her true birth, as daughter of the Baron von Carstein, of how her father had sold her in return for money to pay his gambling debts, and of the life she had lived as the chattel of Maestro Verdicchio.

'Your father *sold* you?' His voice was hoarse with emotion. 'Oh, my dearest one, how you must have suffered.'

He made to put his arms around her, but she did not dare to accept his comfort, heart-warming though it was. She shook her head. 'A woman so dishonoured could never be accepted as part of German aristocratic society. The rules are absolute. Anyone who breaks them is cast out, and becomes worse than nothing, worse even than an opera singer. I was born a lady, Leo, but when my countrymen learn who I am, I shall be treated as if I had been born in the gutter.' She raised a hand to stop the protest that had clearly risen to his lips. 'No, Leo. It is impossible.'

He had taken a pace backward, but was now smiling at her in a very superior, masculine way. 'Very well.

Then I shall have to make your life a misery, as I threatened to do. You will never be free of me. Every hour, every day, I shall find a way of reminding you that you love me, and showing you that I love you more than life. You need someone to love you, to cherish you, Sophie, to compensate for the horrors you have endured. I am the man to do that. What's more, I shall enlist the aid of my brothers. They won't care what the Germans think, any more than I do. Why, my brother the Duke has just married a lady who served in the Russian cavalry. Do you think such a man will object to a sister-in-law who has appeared on the stage?'

Sophie shook her head in disbelief. 'Oh, go away, Leo. I am too tired to deal with your fanciful stories. Russian cavalry, indeed. You must be foxed.'

'I swear to you that I am not.' He put his hand to her cheek and caressed her skin, slowly and tenderly. 'Dominic has married his cavalry lady. And I…I wish to marry my reluctant mistress, to make her my willing bride. I need you, Sophie. I could not live without you now. I want to take you back to my home, where you will be honoured for the amazing woman you are, and where we can love each other for the rest of our days. Say you will marry me, Sophie.'

She was about to speak, to refuse him again. But then he bent his head and put his lips to hers, gently, lovingly, in a kiss that demanded her surrender, and then offered his own. And when he raised his head and looked pleadingly into her eyes, her heart spoke for her. 'Yes, Leo. I will.'

It was to be the most magnificent party, hosted by the Duchess of Sagan in honour of the Duke of Wellington, who was to leave Vienna on the morrow. The monarchs would all be here. Even the Tsar.

Sophie was shivering too much to move from her seat in Leo's carriage. 'I cannot go in there, Leo. They despise me. They will cut me.' She passed the back of her hand over her parched lips. 'Why did I ever let you persuade me to come?'

He put an arm round her shoulders and drew her into the warmth of his embrace. 'You are Madame Sophia Pietre, my betrothed. And tomorrow, you will become Lady Leo Aikenhead, my wife. No one will dare to cut you. Besides, you are the heroine who saved Marie-Louise and her son, remember? They will welcome you with open arms.'

She shook her head. 'The Tsar will be there. You know what he tried to do to me. And what I did to him.' They had told each other the truth about their activities in Vienna, no matter how sordid. And Sophie's tale had included every detail of those fearful encounters with the Russian Emperor. 'He will never accept me. And no matter what he does, you cannot call him out.'

She was right. It was impossible to challenge a monarch. In truth, it was the one encounter Leo feared. But all these people had to be faced, even the Tsar, as Leo had known when he announced their betrothal. His only concession, in deference to Sophie's fears, had been to continue to use her Italian name.

Leo kissed her lingeringly, prolonging the embrace until she responded and the tension in her body began to soften. She clung to him, moaning a little in her throat. He was tempted to order the carriage back to his lodgings, but he refused to listen to the raw urgings of his body. There would be time for that. Tomorrow, after they were wed.

'Come, my love. The woman who would face down armed soldiers single-handed will surely not be overset by the biggest bunch of reprobates in Vienna?'

To describe a monarch so was quite absurd. Sophie began to laugh.

'Exactly so, my love,' Leo said. 'And now, may I help you down?'

The door was opened as Leo reached for it. The unmistakable figure of the Duke of Wellington, magnificent in the red-and-gold uniform of a field marshal, was holding it for her, the stars on his coat sparkling in the light of the flambeaux. He bowed and offered his gloved hand to Sophie. 'My dear Madame Pietre, will you do me the honour of allowing me to escort you inside?'

Behind her, she heard Leo's muffled laugh.

'I realise I am cutting you out, Aikenhead,' the Duke said lightly, 'but you will have this lady all to yourself from tomorrow. Tonight, she shall be fêted by all Vienna. Everyone wants to thank her. *Madame*?'

The Duke's welcoming smile was very reassuring. Sophie put her fingers in his and stepped down. Wellington tucked her hand into the crook of his arm and started for the entrance. 'By the way, Aikenhead,' he said over his shoulder, 'have you decided who is to give the bride away tomorrow?'

'No, your Grace. We had thought of asking—'

'Excellent, excellent. Madame Pietre, would you object very much if I volunteered myself for that task?'

Sophie was sure the Duke was trying not to grin. She could hardly believe what she was hearing. The great general, *le vainqueur du vainqueur du monde*, wanted to give her away? 'I—' She choked and had to clear her throat. 'I should be honoured, your Grace.' No one would dare to cut her after this.

'Splendid. It shall be the last thing I do before I leave for Brussels. Except for— I shall want a private word with you before the ceremony, Aikenhead. A matter of business, you understand, dear lady,' he added, for Sophie's benefit, before leading her up the staircase to the reception hall, with Leo following in their wake. Sophie could almost feel Leo's delight radiating from him. It warmed her heart. Her greatest fear had been that he might be embarrassed as a result of who she was, and what she had been.

The Duke led Sophie straight to the Tsar. This was the moment she had dreaded. She sank into a deep curtsy and waited.

A gloved hand reached down to raise her to her feet. 'Madame Pietre. How delightful,' he said calmly. There was no spark of hostility or even recognition in his eyes. It was as if their encounters had never been. 'You are lucky, Duke, to have such a beautiful lady on your arm.'

'The lucky man, your Majesty, is Lord Leo Aikenhead, who is to marry Madame Pietre tomorrow.'

The Tsar nodded to Leo, who bowed. 'My congratulations, Lord Leo,' he said with a smile. 'I wish you both every happiness.'

Sophie almost believed he meant it.

A moment later, the Tsar seemed to have forgotten everything but the coming war with Bonaparte. He put a hand on Wellington's shoulder, looked round at the assembled company, and said loudly, so that everyone could hear, 'Duke, it is for you to save the world again.'

Chapter Twenty-Two

❦

They had finally succeeded in breaking away from all the well-wishers at the wedding breakfast and returning to Leo's lodgings. They were alone at last.

Leo insisted on carrying her up the stairs to his apartment. Over her protests. He particularly insisted on carrying her across the threshold. 'It is a poor apology for a lodging, my love. Not the luxury you are used to.'

She wrapped her arms even more tightly around his neck and nuzzled the line of his jaw.

'Mmm. I take it, Lady Leo, that you do not object to these poor surroundings?'

She shook her head, still feathering tiny kisses on to his skin.

'I'm afraid that, for the moment, we are rather short of ready money.'

She pulled away a little to stare at him.

'Ah, you should have been more careful about your choice of husband, my lady. If you thought to marry a fortune, you were mistaken, I fear.'

'Leo, you know perfectly well that—' He silenced

her with a kiss, and she melted into him. When the kiss ended a long time later, she found that he had carried her into his bedchamber and was about to lay her down on his bed. She shivered in anticipation. This time, it was not wrong. This time, they were man and wife.

'You really do not care, do you?' He raised his eyebrows at her.

She allowed herself to sink back into the pillows and shook her head. 'No, I do not. Why should I? You may not be exactly rich, but I am sure you will not allow me to starve.' She grinned up at him. 'Besides, I have—'

He stopped her words with a finger across her lips. 'Do not concern yourself, my love. It was just that I could not resist the chance to tease you a little.' He stretched out beside her on the bed. 'The truth is that I had to raise a great deal of money, at very short notice, just before we left London. I had no choice, unfortunately. It was a debt of honour.'

Sophie's indrawn breath hissed between her teeth. Her eyes were wide with horror. It was only then that Leo realised what she must think. This was a woman whose whole life had been ruined by her father's gambling and his callous treatment of his only child.

He put his palms to her ashen cheeks and turned her face to his. 'Forgive me, my love. That was a cruel thing to say to one who has suffered so much. Have no fear. The gambling debt was not mine. It was Jack's. I have very little taste for gaming. And now that I have you—' he dropped a tiny kiss on her mouth '—I can think of much pleasanter ways of spending the time. Don't you agree?'

Much relieved, she did agree. And to prove it, she drew his body to hers and kissed him with every ounce of the love and longing she felt. His response was immediate and equally passionate. Soon they were tussling with buttons and laces, kissing and laughing as they struggled to remove each other's clothing.

Sophie's silk-and-lace wedding gown was finally removed and discarded. Then her petticoats slid to the floor with a thump.

Leo stopped dead, his teeth about to nip the tender flesh of her upper breast. He raised his head and gazed into her eyes, looking puzzled. 'That's the second time. A lady's petticoat should drift to the floor like falling leaves, not with a clunk like a tossed boot.' He reached an arm over the side of the bed to retrieve it.

Sophie caught him back. 'I was trying to tell you earlier, Leo, but you would not let me. You assume I come to you with nothing, but it is not so. I still have most of my jewels.'

He had gone very still, his whole body tense. He must be remembering just who had given her those jewels: the Tsar, the Baron von Beck and others of his ilk. Why had she not thought of that before? Better she had thrown them in the Danube than remind him of her sordid history.

'Leo, oh, Leo—'

'Sophie, *I* can give you jewels, I promise you. You have no need of these.'

He was withdrawing from her. He thought she had kept them because— 'I never had any intention of wearing them, Leo. How could you think that of me? I planned for you to sell them, just as we did on our journey back from Italy. You need money. My jewels will provide it. But if you do not want them, I—'

'I do not,' he said sharply. Then, seeing the hurt in her

eyes, he went on, more gently, 'They are a terrible reminder of just how much you have suffered, my love. I would have you forget all that.' He stroked her hair back from her temple. The angry tension was leaving him.

Sophie leant into his caressing hand. 'Do as you will with them, Leo. Now that we are together, the hurt they represent is healed. You have healed it. By loving me.'

His eyes widened at her words. For a moment, she thought she saw a gleam of moisture there. Then he put his mouth to her hair and said softly, 'I could not bear the sight of them, I admit. I was jealous of all those men who had sought your favours, even though I know very well that you rejected them all. With your permission, I will sell them and we can use the proceeds to do some good in the world. What say you, my love?'

'It is a better solution than mine, Leo. I would have thrown them in the Danube.'

He laughed then, and the darkness between them fled, like night before the rising sun.

It had been a long, wakeful and wondrous night. A joining more perfect, more fulfilling that he had ever imagined.

Leo turned his head a fraction to gaze at his beautiful wife. She was still asleep, her glorious ebony hair spread starkly against the white linen pillow. He reached out to wind one silken strand around his fingers. He would not touch her skin, for fear of waking her, but this he could touch. He kissed the curl of hair, reverently. Her scent filled his nostrils, that same scent which had always seemed just out of reach, every time he had paced her empty apartment. Now, he would have his fill of it.

She moved in her sleep and the strand was pulled from his hand. She gave a little mew of pain.

Leo drew her into his arms and kissed her hair, where the poor misused curl joined her scalp. 'Did I hurt you, my darling? Forgive me.'

She smiled up at him. 'Good morning, husband mine. Did you sleep well?'

'Sleep? I remember very little of that, my lady. But I did have a most…um…refreshing night.' He grinned at her and was delighted when she responded by sliding her arms round his back to stroke the tender skin of his waist and hips. She felt so soft and inviting in his arms. And as her wicked fingers slipped lower, his body was beginning to respond again.

He had to tell her, before the desire overcame them both again.

He laid a hand over hers and held it still.

She frowned up at him. 'Am I not to be permitted to touch you, sir?'

He caressed her frown away with his free hand. 'You may do exactly as you will with me, wife, but first there is something I have to say.' She had relaxed again. Her eyes were wide, luminous, full of banked passion. One touch and she would be ablaze again. As would he. He managed to resist the temptation she presented. 'Sophie, Wellington informed me this morning, before he led you to the altar, that he has recommended me for a barony.'

'What? But you already have a title.' She was puzzled.

'A courtesy title only. This will be a real title. One that I can pass to my heirs. To our children, Sophie.'

Her mouth made an O, but no sound came out.

'And so, my love, you will now have another change

of title. From Lady Leo Aikenhead to Lady...er... Something Else. The precise name has yet to be decided.'

'You wretch, Leo,' she protested. She had recovered in an instant. She was a strong, wonderful woman. 'How can you do this to me? I am only just beginning to get used to calling myself Lady Leo Aikenhead. Am I to be plain Lady Aikenhead in future?'

'You could never be *plain* anything, Sophie.' He looked long into her eyes, enjoying the rosy blush that spread gradually over her cheeks, throat and bosom. When, eventually, she refused to hold his gaze any more, he cupped her jaw with a gentle hand. 'Forgive me, love. I did not mean to make you feel uncomfortable, though what I said is true. Even as Mrs John Smith you could never be plain.'

She closed her eyes and shook her head, her delicate skin moving within his palm like a caress.

'Mmm.' He sighed out a long breath. 'I cannot tell you, my love, what the touch of you does to me. Even when you would upbraid me for saying things I should not.'

At that, Sophie opened her eyes wide to find that Leo's face was now so close to hers that their lips were almost touching. She had only to raise her head from the pillow, just the merest fraction, and they would be kissing and then, ah, then, the journey to bliss would begin all over again.

She remained totally still for a long moment, savouring the feeling of anticipation. Swirling, melting anticipation, and deep, enduring love.

When she could stand it no longer, she made to lift her head. But as she did so, Leo moved too, maintaining the same distance between them so that they breathed each other's scent, their lips so tantalisingly close, yet not quite near enough to touch. She began to strain towards him, but he continued to pull away. It was as if a steel bar joined their two bodies, linking them together, yet forever holding them just an inch apart.

'Leo! Please!' It was a gasp of longing. She could not bear it any more. She reached out to clasp him in her arms.

He was before her. He put his hands to her shoulders and held her even farther away, so that he could see all of her and feast his eyes on her face. 'A moment, my sweet. There are things I have to ask you. Important things. You know I cannot think straight if I kiss you. One touch of your lips and I am lost.'

'As am I,' she murmured, so softly that he barely heard her.

The words stirred his desire even more. In a moment, he would no longer be able to resist the temptation she offered. She was already his, and his alone, but that could not assuage his longing, his overwhelming yearning to make them one.

It was Sophie who broke the moment. She shook her head gently, blinking rapidly to clear her vision. Then she pulled a little farther away from him and smiled radiantly. 'I can see that one of us has to keep her feet on the ground. And judging by the hazy look in your eyes, husband mine, you are presently incapable of it.'

He smiled back at her. 'I admit it, love. But…' he put his hand on her bare calf, slowly, slowly stroking down to her ankle and her arched foot '…I had much rather your pretty feet stayed just where they are. On the ground, they would soon become chilled, you know.'

She had already learned to recognise that mock-serious tone. She forced herself to ignore it. 'You said, sir, that you have important things to tell me.' His exploring fingers had begun to trace their way across and between her bare toes. They tingled in response. She took a deep breath, trying to control her wayward senses. 'If you are trying to prove my inability to resist you, Leo, you need go no further. I concede.' He grinned and moved his fingers to the arch of her foot. 'Leo!' she cried, pulling her foot away. Stroking was one thing, but tickling was too much. 'If you continue to do that, sir, my foot will not be on the ground. It will be kicking the other occupant of this bed!'

He frowned down at her, but his eyes were dancing. 'Assault your husband, would you, ma'am? Now that, I have to tell you, is a breach of your marriage vows. Probably against the law, too.'

'Any magistrate in possession of the full facts of the case—' she placed the tips of two fingers over his lips to silence him '—would agree in a moment that I had been provoked.'

'Mmm?' He took her fingers into his mouth and began to suck them.

The sensation rippled down through her belly, all the way to her toes. She tried to swallow the groan that rose in her throat, but she could tell from the sudden intensity of his gaze that she had failed. 'Provoked beyond reason.' She was trying to sound cross now. And failing there, too. She made one last attempt to cling to her sanity before his nearness overwhelmed her. 'Leo, please. Either talk to me or love me. But do not taunt me like this. One more touch and I swear I shall scream.'

He took her hand in both of his, wrapping her

tingling fingers in the strength of his own. Then he smiled down at her. 'I am bringing myself to that same point, my dearest, so I shall heed your ultimatum. It would not do, I fancy, for Lord and Lady Leo to be heard screaming by the servants in the *Gasthof* downstairs. Only think what would be their opinion of the English nobility.'

'Quite.' She could manage only that single word. Her throat felt too constricted to say more.

With a sigh, Leo lay down against the pillows and pulled her into the crook of his arm. He was not looking at her now, but his lazy fingers began to play with the long curl that curved over her shoulder and down towards her breast. It seemed he was determined to keep her on the edge.

This time she did not protest. She simply snuggled deeper into the curve of his body, waiting. She had one arm free. If he did not do something soon to break the tension in her, she would be forced to apply her fingers to his naked flesh. She could tease and tantalise as well as he.

But when he spoke at last, it was in a tone so serious that all subversive thoughts fled from her mind. 'I have a proposition to put to you, my love. There is a decision to be taken, and I think it must be yours.'

'Mine?' she breathed. What on earth could he mean?

'I am to be awarded a barony, as I said, if the Duke's recommendation is accepted by the government. It is to be in recognition of the service we rendered to the peace of Europe by foiling the plot to kidnap Bonaparte's son. I have to tell you that the Duke said, in terms, that the honour would be for us both. He knows that, without you, the plot would have succeeded.'

'And without you, too.'

'Well, that's as may be.' He stroked her cheek briefly with his free hand. 'However, a barony has to have a name. And in this case, it cannot be Aikenhead, for Baron Aikenhead is one of Dominic's lesser titles. I— No, *we* must choose another. Since my family name is not available, I have a notion to take yours, love. How would it strike you to be Lady Carstone?'

'Carstone?'

'It is the nearest English equivalent of Carstein, I believe. Would it offend you if I were to choose that? Only you and I would know the link to your German title, I am sure. But if you object, I would not for a moment—'

'The Baroness Carstone,' Sophie breathed in wonderment, allowing the sounds to roll around in her head. Sophie von Carstein. Sophie, Lady Carstone. It was as if her lost nobility were being offered to her, on a golden salver, by a knight on bended knee. And her knight, her champion, was Leo, her beloved husband, a husband who was willing to show the depth of his love by giving up his own name in favour of hers. She could not imagine a greater gift from any man to his wife.

She tried to speak, but she could not. Her heart was too full. She, who had lost everything—country, nobility, reputation—through the wickedness of her own father, was to be restored, and even elevated, by the love of the man who had married her. It was too much. Her eyes filled with tears, tears of joy and love. Her whole body trembled. She clung to him blindly.

'Sophie? Oh, my love, do not weep. I had thought only to honour you. But if you dislike it, we—'

'Dislike it?' Her voice cracked, but she swallowed

and forced herself to speak. 'Leo, it is the greatest honour you could have bestowed on me. Greater even than taking me to wife, perhaps. I do not deserve such a gift.'

He began to protest, but she silenced him, firmly, with the same two fingers on his lips. 'I do not deserve it, but I accept it, gladly, for I know it is given in love. I could not reject such a gift. Not from the man I love, and will love till the day I die.'

There was nothing more for her to say. For a long time, they simply clung together as if afraid that wicked fate might wrench them apart before their time. Then, at last, Leo began to kiss away the tearstains from her cheeks, murmuring idiotic nothings into her skin as he feathered his lips slowly down towards her mouth. Sophie's lips parted on a long sigh of satisfaction. As Lady Carstone, she was ready for a new beginning, and a new life.

* * * * *

Author's Note

The Congress of Vienna was a spectacular affair, rather like a modern-day political summit between the great powers. But whereas modern summits go on for only a few days, the Congress of Vienna went on for nine months. Most of the crowned heads of Europe were there, along with many who had lost their crowns under Napoleon and were hoping to get them back. The Austrian Emperor had expected to entertain his fellow monarchs for a couple of months at most, but the tortuous secret negotiations dragged on and on, and so he had to keep paying for the most lavish hospitality and entertainment. It almost bankrupted him.

It was a long, golden autumn, with weather just as glorious as my story describes. On the surface, everything was cordial and harmonious. The monarchs enjoyed all the celebrations together, attending balls, receptions, grand hunting parties, music and theatre; they also enjoyed the dazzling ladies who had flocked to Vienna to be part of the greatest show in Europe. But underneath, the negotiators were at their wits' end, for the Russian Emperor, supported by his poodle, the Prussian King, was determined to hold on to Poland at almost any cost. Europe was on the brink of war and remained so for weeks during the Tsar's long illness. Then, over Christmas, Britain, Austria and France agreed a secret treaty, under which all three countries would go to war to stop the Tsar's plans. Russia and Prussia backed down. That was perhaps just as well for Lord Castlereagh, the British Foreign Secretary. By committing Britain to war, he had disobeyed direct orders from London.

The festivities continued until news arrived of Napoleon's escape from Elba at the end of February 1815. From then on, every piece of news seemed to be leading inexorably to war. Within a month, the Duke of Wellington had left Vienna to take command of the allied armies that would eventually face Napoleon.

The various events I have described took place much as I have shown them, though in places I have made the timescales a little shorter than they actually were. The possible exception is the attempted kidnapping. It was widely reported across Europe at the time. It was even reported that the leader of the kidnappers was Count Montesquiou, the son of the little prince's governess, Maman Quiou-quiou. Did it happen? Modern historians tend to think it was a hoax dreamt up by the Austrian Emperor as a pretext for removing his daughter and grandson from Schönbrunn and replacing all her French household with his own people. They may well be right, but it was such a bold adventure that I couldn't resist including it in my story.

If you want to know what happens next, read the final story in *The Aikenhead Honours* trilogy, in which

Jack goes to France and finds himself caught up in Napoleon's triumphal return. Jack's story, *His Forbidden Liaison*, will be out soon.

FREE!

2 Books
and a surprise gift!

We would like to take this opportunity to thank you for reading this Mills & Boon® book by offering you the chance to take TWO more specially selected titles from the Historical series absolutely FREE! We're also making this offer to introduce you to the benefits of the Mills & Boon® Book Club™—

- ★ FREE home delivery
- ★ FREE gifts and competitions
- ★ FREE monthly Newsletter
- ★ Exclusive Mills & Boon Book Club offers
- ★ Books available before they're in the shops

Accepting these FREE books and gift places you under no obligation to buy, you may cancel at any time, even after receiving your free shipment. Simply complete your details below and return the entire page to the address below. You don't even need a stamp!

YES! Please send me 2 free Historical books and a surprise gift. I understand that unless you hear from me, I will receive 4 superb new titles every month for just £3.79 each, postage and packing free. I am under no obligation to purchase any books and may cancel my subscription at any time. The free books and gift will be mine to keep in any case.

H9ZEF

Ms/Mrs/Miss/Mr ....Initials..
BLOCK CAPITALS PLEASE
Surname ....
Address...
....
....Postcode ....

Send this whole page to:
UK: FREEPOST CN81, Croydon, CR9 3WZ